W9-AUP-133

SNEAK ATTACK

Clayton entered the park. He tasted the sweet of the cold night air and felt a stinging numbness steal into the tips of his fingers. He saw nothing but darkness ahead of him. A wraithlike silence closed in. His pistol and attached silencer made a clumsy package at his side. Then, behind him, a car raced down Cheney Street and yelped to a stop.

The driver's window lowered...a voice shouted, "*Sour!* It's gone sour! Hurry! Get in!"

But instead, Clayton ran deeper into the park. He stooped, running a zigzag. Then from the corner of his eye, he discerned movement. Yes! It was a man crouched low. Clayton withdrew his pistol, but before he even aimed, a stainless steel cartridge— a hypodermic dart—slammed into, and lodged in, the bark of the tree next to him. The distraction allowed his target to duck.

Then from behind him, he heard the clicking of metal as a rifle was being reloaded...

"A HOT NEW THRILLER WRITER"
—*Los Angeles Times*

NEVER LOOK BACK

RIDLEY PEARSON

St. Martin's
Press

ST. MARTIN'S PRESS TITLES ARE AVAILABLE AT QUANTITY DIS-
COUNTS FOR SALES PROMOTIONS, PREMIUMS OR FUND RAISING.
SPECIAL BOOKS OR BOOK EXCERPTS CAN ALSO BE CREATED TO
FIT SPECIFIC NEEDS. FOR INFORMATION WRITE TO SPECIAL SALES
MANAGER, ST. MARTIN'S PRESS, 175 FIFTH AVENUE, NEW YORK,
NEW YORK 10010.

Lyrics from *Higher Dryer* copyright © 1982 by Fletcher Brock. Used
by permission.

NEVER LOOK BACK

Printed in the United States of America

First St. Martin's Press mass market edition/September 1986

ISBN: 0-312-90528-9
Can. ISBN: 0-312-90529-7

10 9 8 7 6 5 4 3 2 1

to Franklin Heller

The author wishes to thank
Colleen Daly, Robert Pearson, Ken McCormick,
and Brian DeFiore
for their help and encouragement.

Revenge is a kind of wild justice.
—Francis Bacon

Oft expectation fails
And most oft there
Where most it promises;
And oft it hits
Where hope is coldest
And despair most fits.

—Shakespeare:
All's Well That Ends Well (II.i.)

And if you want to learn to swim
You've got to jump in the water
It's the only way you ever learn.

—Fletcher Brock

Thursday, November 20

Leonid Borikowski—the man of a hundred faces—flinched as the jet touched him down onto the North American continent for the first time.

A wig of short blond hair sat above brown eyes. Leonid Borikowski's eyes were green; his hair, black. Ten years had been added to his forty: penciled crow's feet flanked short-cut sideburns; discolored blue-black bags sagged beneath his eyes. A large orb of discolored skin stretched from below his left ear into the loose collar of a powder blue French shirt and was also cosmetic. The combined result painted a tragic story. He looked as if a car battery had exploded in his face.

No one, except for the stewardesses, had spoken to him in the last eight hours. He had flown to Montreal alone, despite the hundreds of other passengers. Just as he wished.

Behind him, and across the aisle, Karen Kwang leaned forward to afford herself a view of a man she had first noticed in Venice. The man in 5C. She was convinced he was United States Government.

His name was Minor. He worked for the CIA office in Rome. His partner, John Thompson, was glancing up the aisle at the legs of a stewardess, wondering what to do

3

about Kwang. Kwang was a reporter for Cable Watch News. She was a pain in the ass.

Kwang had made the story public. Now Minor and Thompson were trying to locate two possible assassins who could very well be in Montreal to kill the Pope. It was all a bit sketchy. But Kwang had lit a fire under her cable audience, and something had to be done quickly before every subcommittee on the Hill came crashing down on the CIA. Again.

Leonid Borikowski knew nothing of Kwang or Thompson or Minor. If anyone had told him that two American agents were aboard the flight, he might have laughed at the irony. He was an officer in Bulgaria's DS—the Durzhauna Sigurnost—an intelligence agency closely affiliated with both the KGB and Russian military intelligence, the GRU. He had once been known as an up-and-coming young actor in his native capital, Sofia. Now he was not known at all. He appeared and he disappeared. And his itinerary preceded tomorrow's headlines.

As the wheels of the jetliner spurted small rooster tails of smoke onto the tarmac, the stewardesses continued their whispers about this nightmarish man in 17D who hadn't uttered a word on the entire eight-hour flight. Their inquiries had been answered with nods and gesticulations. They believed him mute.

Borikowski had fluent command of several languages, could skillfully duplicate numerous dialects of each of these languages, yet rarely spoke in public. Orders. He attributed his survival to it.

He finished a cigarette, a non-filter, encouraged by the illuminated sign before him, picking bits of tobacco from the tip of his tongue and depositing them carefully in the ashtray, one by one.

His was the art of patience: he felt no tremendous thrill here, except at the fine detail of his acting skills. A self-pride.

His only fear was failure.

He knew the details of Crown well, having studied the operation for weeks. Anxiety over the fact that Crown was unlike any of his previous assignments hovered in the back of his mind. He pushed it away—a technique all agents were taught—and flicked the last piece of wet, brown tobacco into the ashtray.

A few minutes later the plane jerked to a stop. People jumped to their feet and Borikowski waited for them to work out their impatience as each struggled to be the first to leave.

Eventually the line began to move forward. The French of a tired child, questioning when she might see her puppy again, faded as she was carried by her mother from the plane. Borikowski stood—ducking—and then stepped into line behind Thompson, who in turn followed Karen Kwang, neither aware of the other. Thompson stood close to Borikowski's five-foot-ten and offered a good shield. Borikowski hated crowds.

He gathered his heavy gray wool overcoat from the storage compartment, and was quickly pushed forward by the heaving throng, eventually passing the last stewardess, who offered him a courteous good-bye, hoping finally to hear him speak.

Leonid Borikowski nodded.

He entered the Jetway and funneled into Customs along with the others.

If his forged papers held up under strict scrutiny, if no one recognized him, if the customs officials missed the secret section of his suitcase, then all would be well. He had been through it often enough that it did not frighten him. At times like this he realized how calloused he'd become—like a field worker's hands.

He entered Customs and quickly scanned the area, knowing there would be assigned "rovers" here: people who tried to match a face with a memorized photograph.

RIDLEY PEARSON

For Leonid Borikowski this was a place to take all precaution. Here there existed little chance of escape, should anything go wrong.

Passengers moved calmly toward the baggage claim area. A few travelers spotted friends and relatives beyond the cagelike Customs retainer and waved. Borikowski noted the balconied mirror-wall that provided additional Canadian agents the opportunity to screen arrivals. DS knew about this room, as well as other interrogation rooms on both floors. They even claimed to employ several moles in high-level positions here. Even so, Borikowski moved behind one of several textured pillars, awaiting the chaos that he expected to develop around the luggage carousel.

Karen Kwang spotted the waiting video crew from Cable Watch and smiled at a familiar face. Barely five feet tall, Karen possessed a slight frame, high cheekbones, and captivating cinnamon eyes. She wore silk exclusively, and her lips were a shiny red. Always. The crowd thickened and she could not see anyone. Only shoulders, necks, and breasts.

A beautifully dressed blond woman with scarlet cheekbones stood away from the carousel. Borikowski noticed her and immediately dubbed her a rover because she was reading only people's faces. He wondered how many of his faces she might have memorized.

Then, as if she'd heard him, she glanced in his direction. Skillfully, he bent over to rub supposedly sore feet, keeping his head low. He watched her carefully until a fat man with plaid pants stepped into her line of sight. Then he stood back up.

Luggage began to slide down the chute of the carousel and with it came added confusion. Polite shoves and outright pushes replaced common courtesy. In the roar, faint apologies mixed with quiet cursing as people struggled for their luggage. Movement would be easier now.

6

Borikowski again singled out the blond woman, and convinced himself he had not been identified. How could they recognize me under this disguise? he asked himself. It's certainly one of the best I've ever had.

No alarm showed in her face, no undue concern. Her pastel blue eyes continued to scan the crowd.

Borikowski's suitcase bounced off the black rubber bumper and came to rest, its handle facing out. He turned to intercept it.

Several yards behind him, the same young French-speaking girl he had seen being carried off the plane nervously clutched her mother's tweed dress. The father was busy collecting their luggage. She and her mother were awaiting Dancer—their pet Doberman—at the Oversized Baggage counter. Somewhat frightened by all the people and tired from the long flight, her only comfort came from the handful of tweed. Her mother assured her their pet would arrive any moment.

Seemingly divined by maternal magic, a door opened and a soft gray fiberglass cage entered the room, followed by the man carrying it, his arms extended in an awkward embrace.

He set the cage down, looked up with an exhausted face, and spilled out an endless list of reasons for his fatigue. Not allowing her a moment to interrupt, he rambled on. The mother was too polite to cut in.

The distraction allowed the daughter a moment of curiosity. Their young Doberman paced nervously inside the cage, the sedative long worn off, anxiously awaiting attention. The girl's tiny fingers deciphered the puzzle of the latch. She swung open the door to hug her friend but her strength proved no match. Dancer rushed from the cage, knocked the child to the floor, and disappeared into the crowd.

Having split his attention between his approaching suitcase and the blonde, Borikowski had no opportunity to see the Doberman as it came dashing across the polished stone floor at a breakneck speed. In a frantic motion, Dancer changed direction too quickly and lost all paws to the waxed stone, careening and tumbling into a flashy brunette resplendent in leather pants and spike heels. The brunette jumped, but fell backwards, driving a spike deeply into Borikowski's foot. Delivered so quickly and with such surprise, the pain triggered the first large mistake Leonid Borikowski had made in years: he cursed in Bulgarian.

His passport listed his citizenship as Norwegian.

The blond woman heard him and looked over. Their eyes met.

At the carousel, Karen Kwang reached out and collared Dancer in an amazing show of fortitude and timing. The Doberman whimpered and sat, cowering under the choke of the collar. A spattering of relieved travelers applauded.

Borikowski waited for his adversary's move. And she made it.

Her strides were sharp and deliberate, but her delicate face reflected utter calm as she angled toward a locked wall-phone box not forty paces away, refusing to look back. Never look back. Her job required she report any incidents, and to her, this qualified.

I will not fail, thought Leonid Borikowski. I must prevent them—*her*—from detaining me, and I must act quickly. He dropped his bag by a pillar and looked toward the large mirrored pane that overlooked the room.

With his thick jacket folded over his arm, he calculated a route that would intersect her path and set off, his right hand searching blindly for the small bead of plastic embedded in the wool, his movements silent and without effort. Blood pulsed past his ears, muting all other sounds. As he closed the distance, his fingers located the small plastic bead. With the deftness of a magician, he withdrew and cupped the four-inch hatpin. It would have to be now. One more step.

She unlocked and opened the box quickly. Her hand lifted the white wall phone from its cradle.

In synchronized motion he both caught her and ended her life, quickly driving the pin in behind her ear and spinning it. Her hand hung up the phone. Her body slackened and he helped her down into a formed plastic seat. Her stilled face looked surprised, even in death.

With little time for thought he stroked her soft hair, ad-libbing a colloquial French, comforting her and promising to be home soon. Borikowski leaned over and kissed the dead woman on the cheek. Then he smiled thinly. Most of the crowd had formed lines at the Customs counters, the carousel nearly empty of luggage.

Borikowski stood, angry at her now. As he crossed the room, he repeatedly went over the details of the past few minutes—like a bridge player reviewing the last few tricks. Without stopping, he bent over and took hold of his suitcase by the handle. He tried to convince himself that there had been no time. No other way. Realizing the news would devastate his superiors in Sofia, he reluctantly accepted a new blemish on an otherwise exemplary record. Such news might even reach Moscow.

But one cannot dwell on one's reputation. There is still the here and now—the assignment—and the need to leave this airport. *Now.*

He selected a particular Customs counter and joined its line behind a Norwegian tour group that moved quickly through.

Borikowski stepped forward.

To appear the true tourist, he declared a bottle of bourbon, knowing this was not required. The move seemed to help speed things up. He passed through without incident.

Only seconds later, as Borikowski approached the exit,

a blood-curdling scream ripped through the building. He calmly continued through the electronic doors and out into a brisk November air. He assumed that someone had discovered his victim's slack body, or perhaps had seen the thin column of blood below her ear. And that someone had screamed—because that's what everyone did.

Leonid Borikowski knew without looking.

Never look back.

8:00 P.M.
Chevy Chase, Maryland

In his right hand he held a knight beneath the lip of the table, where his opponent could not see it.

The house dated back to the American Revolution and was furnished like a summer cottage. Nothing was fancy. The assortment of furniture included wicker and willow as well as old gray wood benches and rough-log footstools that appeared to have been around since George Washington burned late-night oil, studying maps and smoking a ceramic pipe. The ceilings were low, the passageways narrow, and where Andy Clayton sat, his six-foot-four frame looked strangely misplaced, like a hand inside a dollhouse. But he wasn't misplaced. This was where Andy Clayton had lived for the past few years.

The house belonged to the United States Government.

On the mantel was a portrait of a handsome young man in his mid-thirties. The background of the photograph was blurred, but even so, the orange hue lent the feeling of a fall day in southern France, when the trees and grasses catch an auburn light and shimmer in the afternoon winds. The photo had been there since the day Andy had been moved to this house. The man smiled down from the mantel. An engaging smile. But he stood up there alone, in his silver frame, next to a used candlestick, a puddle of hard wax at its base connecting it firmly to the mantel. And for some reason, instead of auburn light, tragedy surrounded the man.

Andy looked up at the photo, as he often did between moves. Parker Lyell was not a particularly fast chess player. Parker Lyell was not particularly fast at anything, except talking. Lyell did not have Andy's large frame or rugged features; he looked more like an Irishman, with his red hair and large, flat teeth. Andy, on the other hand, looked like an ex-football player who had done billboard cigarette ads for a while. He had gray-green eyes—hazel—and brown curly hair that needed a trim.

Parker Lyell turned and faced the fire and saw Duncan's photo on the mantel and then spun back around. "I wonder?"

"Yes?"

"You ought to dust off the frame. You make him look more like your grandfather than your brother."

"He might as well be."

"Now Andy, I didn't mean—"

"They're both . . ." He paused. ". . . in a similar condition. That's all I meant."

Lyell moved a pawn from d4 to c4 and sat back in his chair.

Andy instantly used a knight to take it.

Lyell said, "What piece are you holding?"

Andy reluctantly opened his right hand. A knight.

The piece was marble, and the eye of the horse caught the orange of the fire and winked at Lyell, who moaned, "Jesus Christ! Am I that predictable?" No answer. "Another fucking pawn."

"You may wish your pawns were fucking in a few minutes. You're running low."

"Very cute. You don't mind if I withhold my laughter for that comment, do you? No, I didn't think so." He

11

studied the board. He moved a bishop, quickly. Too quickly for Parker Lyell. "Check."

It was a desperate check—a wasted move, and one that would cost him the game within the hour. Andy knew this before debating his response, and felt an odd delight at knowing his opponent was already finished—providing Andy did not make a similar mistake. And that had been done before.

Lyell said, "Who are you dating these days?"

Andy shrugged.

"Oh Christ, Andy, do you mean to say you haven't gotten over that other one yet? That must have been five years ago!"

"Seventeen months . . . but who's counting?"

"You see what I mean? Seventeen months. What are you waiting for? Shy, big guy?"

Andy flashed his friend an annoyed look.

"Okay. Sorry about that. Just trying to get a rise out of you."

Andy offered the same look again. "No pun intended?"

Lyell smiled, showing off his big teeth. "None."

Andy moved a bishop to block the check. If Lyell wanted to start trading pieces, now was as good a time as any. The move confused Lyell, who again leaned back to examine the board. He told Andy, "Marge and I are having Annie Numark over to dinner on Saturday night."

"Haven't heard that name in a long time." Annie used to be what they called a fox. Andy had no idea what they called them now, in this day and age. Black leather and *Clockwork Orange* hairdos; Barbie Dolls with razor blade necklaces. They probably referred to them affectionately as Juicy Beavers, or something equally eloquent.

"Why don't you join us? Round off the number. You ever tried having dinner with two women that went to high school together?"

"'Who' went to high school together."

"Marge and Annie."

"No, I mean it's not 'that' went to high school, it's 'who' went to high school."

"Oh, well, pardon me, Shakespeare." Lyell pursed his lips and lowered his eyebrows. "You avoided an appropriate response," he said like a schoolmarm.

"Can I think about it?"

"No."

Andy looked up, surprised. Lyell grinned and said, "Sure. I'll give you a half hour."

"Generous. What I wish you would give me is a new assignment."

"I wish I could."

"Oh, you could, all right."

"It's not up to me, you know that. Besides, you haven't finished that report."

"Correction: I've finished it four times. This is the fifth draft. The Old Man is stalling or something. Ever since Duncan he's been like a doting old maid."

"And what's that make you?"

"What the fuck does that mean?"

"Sorry."

"No. Please tell me. How am I behaving?"

"I've never lost anyone close to me, Andy. Certainly not a twin brother. I'm not qualified to answer that."

"Qualified? You're a friend. We work together—in a roundabout way. You pay me these little visits every couple of weeks and ask strange questions and misuse your pawns. I'd say you're qualified."

"Straight shot?"

"Straight shot."

"For a while it seemed you might give up. I don't mean kill yourself, I mean just kind of give up." He collected his thoughts. "You seem to be over that. But the point is: You work too much. All you do is work on that damn report. You don't go out, you don't invite people over—"

"I want to get the damn thing finished."

"And when do you think Stone will call it finished?"

Light from the fire danced on Lyell's left cheek. Andy considered the implication. "I don't believe that."

"Just an opinion. You asked."

"Another beer?"

"Sure."

Andy ducked through the doorway and into the hall, pushing away his memories of Duncan. Mari was another thing entirely. She had broken his heart and then had run back to Detroit—or so he had heard. Seventeen months ago—but who's counting? And Andy was still trying to let go.

Mari Dansforth had sashayed into The Swamp, a hotel bar on the edge of Georgetown that boasted the largest photo of Alan Alda in the world. She was a natural blonde with unnatural eyes. She sat down on a bar stool next to Andy Clayton and asked the bartender hoarsely, "Would you pour me something to remove this obnoxious heat? Forever."

"I'm not sure I can do that, ma'am."

"Then just help me forget about it, would you? Vodka on the rocks, I think." She flicked her hair over her shoulder.

The man was impervious. He mixed the drinks.

She was looking right at Andy now. His face showed nothing, like a house with no one home.

"Andy Clayton," he said, feeling obliged to say something.

"Mari Dansforth." The drink was placed in front of her and she drank half of it. "Ohhh, that's better."

"Nice name."

"Thank you."

"How do you spell Mari?"

"M-a-r-i." She sipped the vodka. He sat perfectly still. Then she asked, "What do you do, Andy?"

"I'm an account executive with Tendin Corp." This was a legitimate company that listed Andy on the payroll. Andy did not work for Tendin. He worked for the Security Intelligence Agency.

She finished her drink and cued the bartender.

"You're very lovely." The words just fell out of his mouth. He turned red. He never came on like that. He couldn't believe he had said it.

"Is that the best you've got?" she asked, confusing him by pointing to a gaudy tie he was wearing.

"I like weird ties."

She smiled at him. She was narcotic. "I like weird dresses." Hers was covered with vivid green-stemmed tulips. Each tulip was a bright primary color. The background was white and it was held onto her by spaghetti straps. She was well-tanned and the dress was tailored for her bust, though when she moved it moved away from her and revealed that she was braless.

"We used to have a bed of tulips in our backyard. The bumblebees liked them. I used to sit and watch the bumblebees come and go, all day long, their legs yellow from the pollen." He paused privately, then said, "It's a nice dress."

She rocked the ice in her drink. "We had every damn plant imaginable in our backyard. I suppose there were tulips, but to be honest, I don't remember. What happened to your backyard?"

"We sold the house."

"The tulips?"

"Gone, I suppose." He smiled thinly. "And yours?"

"Oh, it's still there, overlooking the Hudson, pretentious and Victorian. Still there for everyone to goggle at. My father likes to show off his money. That's his problem." She sipped and didn't look at him.

"Oh."

She thought of something and said quickly, "I'm not

15

bragging, mind you. I'm on my own. That's why I'm in Washington. Twenty-five years of that man can drive a person bonkers!" Her smile was pained.

"It is a nice dress," he told her again.

"And I love your tie." She pulled a soggy napkin toward herself with a long red nail and, with her eyes on the countertop, said, "You're bored with me already, aren't you?"

The comment floored him. He was fascinated, not bored. "No. Not in the least."

"I shouldn't have mentioned my father. Bad habit. Please excuse me. It puts a freeze on a conversation in a second. Tell me about yourself."

"No, please. It's not you. It's just that I'm very tired. It's been a long few weeks—these past few. I've been traveling overseas and I'm not quite caught up. . . ."

Andy had recently returned from an assignment. He had nearly caught up to a DS agent, only to lose him again. The agent's name was Leonid Borikowski.

For the last few days he'd been drinking a little too much and had been feeling far too low for his own good. So he ordered them both another, to no objection, and led her over to a private table.

They sat close to each other and that felt about as good as anything ever had.

"What do you know about failure?" he asked, breaking a long silence.

She sipped. Hesitantly she said, "I think failure's healthy."

"And . . . ?"

"We learn from our failures, don't we?"

"I'm asking you."

"Yes, well . . . I think that's true. Make enough of them and eventually you make less of them. Pretend they aren't there and you'll never stop making them."

"You believe that?"

"Yes, of course I do. I wouldn't have said it otherwise. Why? What do you think?"

"I'm not real fond of failure. And to tell you the truth, I'm not in a very good mood. I'm afraid you've caught me on an off night."

"Bad moods don't scare me away . . . Andy," she said, grabbing for the name. "We're in a bar aren't we? Bars are full of bad moods. Cheap psychiatrist—that's what a good drink is. Did you ever look at it that way?"

"Let's get out of here. I'm driving."

"Agreed."

Even by dash lights her eyes showed up like road signs. Some brown flakes had been mixed in with the green of her right eye, as if placed there to grab your attention. The MG's top was down and the wind felt good to both of them. She was not worried about her hair and he liked that.

Despite her full figure, she was not a centerfold type. Her jaw was drawn and narrow, chin pointed; her oddly shaped ears were carefully hidden beneath the blond curls. Her clothes flattered her.

They walked a path along the Potomac. She talked some more about her father's money and their problems. Her father had wanted a boy. Or so Mari thought. She wrapped an arm around Andy. They sat on a bench. Cars passed on the other side of the river. Tires whined. Music from somewhere far off.

Mari lay her head on Andy's lap and he stroked her hair. He had never felt this close to anyone so quickly. It was strangely wonderful. But he did not trust his feelings. He never trusted his gut feelings, and yet, they were never wrong. Why then? He was about to ask Mari when he noticed that she had fallen asleep.

Later, when a breeze picked up and finally cooled him off, he drove her home. To his surprise, she invited him

17

in. But he declined, and in doing so, embarrassed her. She became crisp. He did not feel up to explaining.

They kissed before he left—just once—and it felt very private, almost as if they were lovers.

And not long after that, they were.

Now, standing in his kitchen with two cold Buds in hand, Andy tried not to think about Mari. He'd done too much of that recently. He closed the refrigerator door and ducked back into the hallway.

As he entered the living room, Lyell announced, "I have examined the board and I'm not ready to concede. Is that permitted?"

"Discretion is the better part . . . and all that. But no, I don't mind. I'm only two pieces ahead. Let's keep going."

"Good." Lyell moved his queen.

"What can you tell me? What's news?"

"Is that why you asked me over here tonight, to pump me?"

"I'll let you answer that yourself."

"The big news is that two Bulgarian Aeroflot workers who have been linked to Rome and the attempted assassination of the Pope last year, are now evidently in Canada . . . Montreal, I think. Of course the big fear is that they may attempt it again, and this time on either Canadian or American soil. Everyone is up in arms about it, which of course makes my job hell."

"Who's on it?"

"Mat Minor and John Thompson I think. That's the rumor."

"Good men."

"Yes. What's been making our job tough is this Karen Kwang, with Cable Watch."

"Oh?"

"She's a dig-it-up-and-smell-it type. Very popular right now, and it was she who turned up the Bulgarians, much to our embarrassment. The Old Man asked for me to have a 'chat' with her. I'm supposed to soften her approach. Right. Quite frankly, I wish someone else had the assignment. Somebody in Public Relations or something. I'm afraid of her kind. She'll just use our talk as a springboard for another angle on the story. . . . I'll be showing her how close to the truth she is. That's very risky."

"Do you have a choice?"

"No. I'm on orders."

"I wish I'd get some different orders. Writing a six-hundred-page report on Soviet Middle East Intelligence operations is not my idea of work, at all . . . it's more like prison."

"You know what they say, Andy. If things aren't going right, then chances are you don't want them to be right."

After a long silence Andy said, "Who the hell is 'they' anyway?" He moved a bishop. "Check."

Lyell shrugged.

8:00 P.M.
Washington, D.C.

A small pink light atop the intercom on Terrance Stone's desk flashed intermittently. Working late, Stone, his secretary, Janie Luzo, and a handful of others were still in the offices of the SIA, busily trying to keep up with work that knew no hours.

Thirty-four years ago, Terrance Barnum Stone had been the president of a small New England college. But at the age of forty-seven he had been recruited by a close friend into the ranks of Military Intelligence as an advisor, and seven months thereafter, had announced his resignation from academic life.

As an advisor, he had theorized several ways to penetrate a network of agencies that the Pentagon, among others, had considered impenetrable. These same theories, when passed on to the State Department, had led to the discovery and expulsion of several diplomatic "aides" in various embassies around Washington.

Lacking a formal title, Stone had consulted for the Pentagon for three years, before, at the age of fifty, he had accepted a diplomatic appointment to the American Embassy in East Berlin, posing as a deputy ambassador. There, in the early years of the Cold War, Stone administered a small group of private citizens who helped collect reams of sensitive intelligence data. Most of the information concerned the movement of suspected foreign agents, two of whom were eventually caught in the act of espionage, compromised—doubled—and released to spy on their own agencies. These two men had supplied U.S. Military Intelligence—G-3—with the inner workings of the East German and, in some instances, Soviet intelligence communities for nearly ten years.

Stone was next assigned to prepare, for the Secretary of Defense, a comprehensive study of Army and Navy crypto-codes and their vulnerability to outside penetration. His study had led to the inception of the National Security Agency, and Stone's appointment as the Director of the Security Intelligence Agency. His agency was to oversee security activities at the NSA, and to advise on ways to prevent penetration into intelligence agencies. Following the Vietnam War, he was given a small group of former Army Intelligence officers, all in their middle thirties, to "actively recruit the assistance of foreign agents . . . and to activate an internal network of intelligence gathering in the agencies or administrations of any 'hostile factions'," a term whose definition had varied according to who held the Oval Office.

Stone pushed the button on the intercom. The light stopped blinking. Janie's voice was thinned by the small speaker. "Sir, you have a scrambled call from Solicitor General Gustav Molière, RCMP, Montreal . . . line one."

"Concerning?"

"I wasn't told."

"I see . . . Would you please give me his ABDOS on the screen, read rate thirty."

"Thirty," she said, confirming the speed at which the computer would scroll each page of Molière's ABridged DOSsier on Stone's video monitor.

Stone, who had just now been preparing to head home after another long day, sighed and waited until the first page appeared on the screen, which happened very quickly. He scanned the information, refreshing himself with Molière's condensed history: Solicitor General Gustav Molière, seventy years of age, had been educated at Cambridge, England. He had served on loan from the Canadians with British Intelligence in both World Wars, spending part of World War II in France coordinating resistance offensives. Military service included Asia, Australia, and New Zealand with promotions that read like a list of a ladder-climber's best; and now he sat on top. Just like Terry Stone.

The Old Man pushed the phone to his ear. "Hello?"

The voice on the other end, thick with a French accent, resonated with authority. "General Gustav Molière, Canadian Privy Council."

"Yes, General Molière. How can I help you?"

Hundreds of miles to the north, Gustav Molière looked down at the first page of a file marked Terrance Barnum Stone: U.S. Intelligence—Non-active. He knew of Stone, even recalled having been introduced to him a few times; but this call amounted to their first official intercourse.

"If you please, I am sending you a copy of a videotape by special courier, recorded in Montreal's Dorval airport less than two hours ago. One of our rovers—a woman—was apparently executed. Her assailant was approximately one hundred and seventy-seven centimeters tall, weight between seventy-five and eighty kilos, short

21

blond hair, skin disorder or birthmark on the left of his neck.

"Presently, our agents are working on an identity. I was hoping that perhaps your people could also look over the tapes."

Terry Stone had immediately assumed the phone call would concern the two Bulgarians and the papal visit. He reoriented himself. "With pleasure. Yes, certainly. My condolences. I know how difficult it is to lose an agent," he said truthfully.

"Yes, *merci*."

"Might I inquire as to the method of execution?"

"A needle. A hatpin perhaps. It entered behind the lobe of her right ear . . . killing her instantly."

"Your thoughts?"

"An operative . . . This was my guess, yes. Certainly none of the terrorist organizations we have been plagued with. Too subtle for them. I am certain it was an agent. This I cannot explain, but I think you are able to see when you view the tape. It was very cold-blooded, *non*? Very . . . professional. The murder went unnoticed, I am sorry to say—except, of course, by the cameras. His acting . . . he was very convincing. Very . . . professional."

"And the follow-up?"

"We are circulating the best photograph we could pull from the video. Taxis, buses, rentals. We will find him, but I would like to know who it is we are after. It is more difficult to hunt the nameless, *non*?"

"I agree completely. How may I reach you?"

Molière left Stone several numbers. They briefly discussed the two Bulgarians. Thompson and Minor were being cooperative with the Canadians. Fine.

Molière emphasized no hour was too late for Stone to call.

The tape was due to arrive in Washington shortly.

From the back seat of a musty cab, Leonid Borikowski succumbed to the visual splendor of Montreal. From the airport freeway, the sparkling lights of the city were spread before him, crawling up the sides of Mount Royal in the background, reflected in the broad St. Lawrence River in the foreground. A picturesque mix of historic Old Montreal along the waterfront, and the spectacular, soaring buildings of the new metropolis behind.

The young driver offered no conversation during the ride, uncomfortable with Borikowski's ugliness. The agent felt this and relished it, the quintessential actor savoring every morsel of deception. He rode in silence, awaiting his destination: a hotel he had named but had no intention of using.

Assuming hidden cameras had recorded the murder at Dorval, he expected cab drivers to be questioned. A remembered face to a fictitious destination would only help hide the trail and buy him precious time.

The cab jerked to a stop, throwing Borikowski forward. Marble steps and a brass banister fronted an ornate hotel entrance. A fat doorman with a bright red nose came to inquire and assist. Behind him, etched onto a brass plaque, were the words *Hotel St. Jacques*. Borikowski passed a generous fare to the driver and climbed out. As the cab pulled away he looked up and complained, "This is the wrong hotel!"

The doorman shook his head. "I will call you a cab, *m'sieu!*"

"No, don't bother. What good would it do?" Borikowski asked, slipping the man a small tip. "It's in the next block. I wish I could afford to stay here! No, I'm at Le Grand," he said, naming a lesser establishment just around the

23

corner. "I think I'll walk. It's a nice brisk night for a walk."

"*Oui, m'sieu!*" The doorman stood for a moment, thinking "brisk" was a bit of an understatement, then retreated into the warmth of the hotel foyer and the strong light, where he could determine the amount of the tip.

Three blocks to the north, Borikowski turned right, then left, then right again. The bus stop was just ahead.

His destination stood near the waterfront in Old Montreal, a run-down boardinghouse not found in any KGB or Durzhauna Sigurnost safe-file, yet one which had been carefully chosen by Borikowski's superiors.

It was safe. The desk clerk, an aged Canuck, was poor of hearing and half-blind.

Borikowski said, "Do you have the time?"

The elderly man replied casually, "*De temps en temps.*" From time to time.

"Which time?"

"The first time. Every time." The man tipped back in his chair, removed a key from the cabinet, and tossed it across the stained wooden counter. "Number twenty-nine."

Borikowski accepted the key and headed toward the stairs.

Number twenty-nine had only the remains of a nine on the door but was adjacent to twenty-seven, so Borikowski tried the key, and it opened.

Everything in the room was old and in need of replacement, including the door's hardware. Two random kicks or a shoulder-blow would open it. He threw the suitcase onto the sagging bed, grabbed an old straight-back chair, and wedged it beneath the doorknob. Dust rose from the mattress and sparkled in the room's harsh light. It would require at least five kicks now: time enough to think.

The room smelled musty. A stained and faded print

hung over the bed, depicting a harbor and mackinawed fisherman.

The loosely woven window curtain tore as he pulled it open, its brittle threads baked by a decade of sun. A rusty fire escape clung to the building, the steel deeply pitted. The window was jammed shut. He tried to open it, but it resisted and he resorted to a well-placed palm thrust, and then it obliged. Bar soap helped it to run more smoothly. Below, a narrow alley shared with the bistro across the way echoed the faint thumping of a jukebox. He shut the window and worked the fraying curtains closed.

The bed invited him: sleep. He felt as old and tired as the desk clerk, as frayed as the curtains.

Now that he had blocked the door and secured himself an alternate exit via the window, he entered the small but brightly lit bathroom. He removed the top of the commode and peered inside. A thick black plastic bag lay somewhere inside, but he could not see it. He rolled up his sleeve and groped in the water, finally withdrawing the dripping bundle and carefully setting it onto the countertop. Inside was a Soviet-made nine-millimeter automatic that broke down into pieces, giving it the underground title of the "puzzle gun." The package contained two extra clips, two small boxes of shells, a holster, and a silencer. To his delight, no water had found its way inside, as sometimes happened, and all was in order. He strapped it on, and felt better.

Opening the hidden compartment on his suitcase required two separate lock combinations and moving the latches in a prescribed order. A small door popped open on one side. The tightly packed area held several chemicals and cosmetics, two hairpieces, eyeglasses, latex noses, tooth caps, colored contact lenses, and five different sets of passports and papers.

The sink had tear-shaped turquoise stains beneath each

faucet. Borikowski was not too competent at applying cosmetics, but he was more than experienced in removing them. He used rubbing alcohol, cold cream, and thirty minutes to rid his face of his ugly birthmark and Dorval identity, changing his mind now and wishing for a hot bath instead of a nap. But no time existed for such luxuries. He focused on the sudden anxiety and pushed it away.

Forty-five painstaking minutes later he had a new wig in place—a task that should have required but ten minutes. Straight black hair now. The passport that identified a married man of forty, Dr. Franz Vogel, he pocketed, along with a pair of contact lenses.

He left the boardinghouse via a rear staircase at the end of the hall, which descended into the side alley. Using a pencil as a wedge, he propped the door open slightly, keeping it from latching closed, so that he might reenter after the front door had been locked for the night.

A light snow was falling.

Out of habit, he touched where his weapon lay beneath his coat. He then looked at his watch.

Not much time.

He reached the theater only minutes after the final curtain must have fallen, for hordes of people began pouring out the front and side entrances, chatting and critiquing, arm in arm, in search of parked cars and empty cabs.

The stage door was down an alley, and so Borikowski leaned against the brick of the opposing building, waiting for her. It wasn't long before the door opened and stagehands began leaving. He stopped the first woman to exit. As she turned to face him, he saw that she was not the right woman, but asked anyway, "Have you the time?"

She huffed, as people often do to strangers, turned her

back on him, and, picking up her pace, left the alley, spike heels clicking on the cobbles.

The next three were men.

Then a woman exited on the arm of a man, and Borikowski interrupted, asking, "Have you the time?"

"*Non, m'sieu,*" responded the soprano.

"It is five past the hour," grunted her escort. They left.

The next woman wore a red knitted cap and a clumsy overcoat that sagged from her shoulders. She moved quickly. Borikowski asked her loudly, "Have you the time?"

She stopped without facing him, then turned slowly and looked over her shoulder, as if these words had been expected. "*De temps en temps,*" she answered. From time to time.

"Which time?" he asked, taking a step closer to her.

He noticed the effect the question had. She turned completely around and stepped out of the way of two more people who were leaving now as well. She moved to the brick wall and watched until her friends had left.

Borikowski had moved quite close to her. He could see her breathing heavily.

"The first time. Every time," she replied. "I don't believe this! What on earth are you doing here?"

"I need your help. . . ."

"Yes, but the arrangements were to be made through the phone. . . ."

"I can't wait until tomorrow morning, as you perhaps thought."

"Yes . . . but . . ."

"I need you now. I've run into problems."

Another young man left through the stage door, and upon seeing the woman talking to Borikowski, asked, "Everything all right, Lydia?"

"Yes, Henry. Thank you."

"See you tomorrow then."

"Yes. See you tomorrow."

They waited until Henry had turned around the corner, and then Borikowski said, "I need your talents this evening."

She glanced at her watch. "Come with me."

She led him around the corner to the left, and together they walked a few blocks to a small pub. She opened the door and, holding it for him, told him, "The other bars would be crowded with theater types. This is better for our needs."

"Yes, fine. But you must realize I'm on a sched—"

"Shh. Buy yourself a drink. I'll take care of you in a little while."

Once inside, she did not sit with him. Instead she went to a pay phone and called someone and had a long conversation. Borikowski had ordered and paid for a beer, and he drank it alone. He then watched her make another phone call, and at the end of this one she walked right past him and left the bar. He gulped down the remainder of the beer and went outside. She was standing in the doorway of the next shop, tucked into a shadow, her arms wrapped around herself to shield her from the cold.

"Why tonight?" she inquired.

"My cover's blown. It has to be tonight."

"It will take me hours."

"I know."

"And which is it to be?"

"Vogel. Franz Vogel."

"Yes. I remember. Very well. Did you bring the passport photo?"

"Yes. I have it here." He tapped his pocket. "Can we go to your apartment?"

"Absolutely not! I just got through speaking with a

man who is waiting there for me. No, the apartment is out. We'll use the theater. I have a key."

"Is that wise?"

"It's our only choice."

"You sound angry."

She hesitated, staring into his eyes. She touched his chin and moved his face to see it in the light. She let him go and said, "I was told I might have to do this. To tell you the truth, I never thought much of it. I guess I'm a little surprised."

"That applies to the both of us. I thought I would be . . ." He changed his mind in mid-sentence. ". . . gone."

"Not likely."

"No."

She rocked her weight to her other leg. "I'm tired."

"Yes. How did it go?"

"Excuse me?"

"The performance. How did it go?"

"Oh. Well. Quite well. It's an adaptation of a fairy tale."

"I'm familiar with it. I played the role of the father once."

"In this play?"

"Yes."

"You're an actor?"

"Used to be. That is, I used to act on the stage. Now I act, but not for an audience."

"I understand."

They began walking back to the theater. He caught sight of her face for the first time when they passed a storefront with its lights up. She had a lovely complexion, and two of the most individual eyes he had ever seen. They appeared born of Italian blood, and made to be photographed; and even though he had noticed them in her dossier pictures, they were twice as beautiful in real life.

When they reached the stage door she told him, "If anyone says anything, don't answer. I'll do the talking."

He nodded.

Inside there were only a few stagehands left standing about, their voices echoing through the empty theater. They paid no attention to Borikowski, and only one person—a young woman who had tiny feet and a voice to crack glass—even bothered to offer a greeting to Lydia, and this was not a greeting at all, but a perfunctory call to business. She ignored Borikowski, as if he were a fixture on the wall, and stopped Lydia with an outthrust hand. "I keep falling out of this damn thing!" she said, pulling on the low-cut V neck of the white dress she was wearing and exposing a dark nippled breast. "Peter says he likes it to look sexy, but what with me falling out all the time I distract the audience and the second act goes to shit. See?" She bent slightly and moved from side to side and both breasts peeked out and then withdrew to behind the fabric. She remained oblivious to Borikowski's penetrating interest. "What can we do?"

"I'll tape you in before tomorrow's performance. You'll wiggle, but you won't fall out."

"Tape. That's a perfect solution. Great! I couldn't think what to use. Peter said a bra would ruin everything."

"Don't worry, Claudia. We'll take care of it."

"Great. Thanks, luv." The woman moved past them, down the hall, and turned into an unmarked room.

Lydia waved for Borikowski to follow. "She's our resident prima donna. By tomorrow she'll refuse to let me tape her. She only wanted to show off her breasts. She loves to see the reaction of strangers. She thinks every man is dying to jump on her."

"Aren't they?" Borikowski asked, tongue-in-cheek.

Lydia flashed him a disapproving look and opened a door.

The room was a mess, a disaster area of cosmetics and

wigs and bright lights. She sat him down in the center chair, so he faced the mirror, which was flanked by blinding bulbs. She asked, "Did you bring the contacts?"

"Yes." He set them on the counter amid the debris.

"The wig?"

"This is it. I'm wearing it."

She bent his ear over, caught an edge of the wig and gently pulled it off his head. Its edges were sticky and made smacking sounds as they came loose. She set it on the table. "They warned me you might need another face. But honestly, I never expected it to happen."

"I wish it had not happened. This will cost me nearly an entire day." Borikowski liked the oily smell of the room. It reminded him of his early acting career—before his services had been enlisted. And how many years ago had that been? To him it seemed an eternity.

He looked at her more closely in the bright light: her almond eyes were the color of milk chocolate, her shoulder-length hair mahogany. Her slender nose and small, oval mouth were made more prominent by elegantly high cheekbones and flat cheeks.

She discarded her coat. She wore a black shirt covered with makeup, and dungarees with tears in the knees. "Well," she said lightheartedly, "we're here now. We'll give you the best face we can." But inside she was squirming. She had been all ready to go home . . . to go to bed with Frederick, a man who had been sleeping with her for the past few nights. This delay bothered her.

She stripped his face with alcohol and then, piece by piece, began to reconstruct his looks, referring to his passport as her guide. She straightened his nose with a latex form, bent his eyebrows by plucking and re-gluing, elongated his eye sockets by applying a chemical that shrank his skin as it dried and left him with a convincing set of crow's feet at either temple. She injected his lips with a trace amount of a histamine, causing them to swell slightly.

"My lips itch," he said, not speaking well.

"It will go away. So will the swelling, somewhat; but the redness will remain."

He watched in the mirror for three hours as she applied her expertise to his face, astonished at how relatively quickly the change occurred.

At one-fifteen she stopped brushing his hair and asked, "What do you think?"

"I think you're as good as they said you were," he told her, with a perfect high-German accent lacing his words.

"Your accent is very convincing."

"Thank you. That part of the job I have under control." He stood and extended his hand to her.

They shook hands.

"I will mention how cooperative you were . . . and what a fine job you did. That's the most I can do."

She nodded, led him into the hallway, and switched off the room's lights. "I'm glad you are happy with it."

"Yes. It's a very good job."

"Thank you."

"You're welcome. Now, I only hope we don't have to meet again . . . not that I would mind, but—"

"I understand," she assured him, opening the door to the alley.

"You will remain by the phone in case?"

"Yes. I'll be home all day tomorrow as planned." She locked the stage door and pocketed the key.

"Good-bye, then."

"Good-bye."

Friday, November 21

Terry Stone's oak desk held a brass captain's clock, a family photo, and too many phones to count.

A small wet bar in the far corner was flanked on either side by the colorful spines of books. On the knotty, nut-brown walls a van Gogh seashore print hung proudly, and opposing it, an enlarged color photograph of a thirty-eight-foot ketch heading downwind, its bright blue spinnaker fully billowed. A computer terminal and a Sony television were juxtaposed on his large desk. Its oak slab, in appearance, seemed more like a landing field for small aircraft than a place for paper and pen.

Behind the unmoving Terry Stone a large and unusually thick window revealed a tightly angled corner of the impressive Air and Space Museum. The skies dumped slush on the town. The President of the United States of America was frozen in a photograph, smiling through the scratched framed glass, on the wall next to the window. The faces of many different men had been placed there over the years. And each a friend to Terry Stone.

Janie Luzo, Terry Stone's plain-looking, middle-aged secretary, gently shook the Old Man's shoulder, waking him from an unplanned nap. He had fallen asleep in his chair. Seeing his head tilted to one side and his mouth hanging open reminded Janie how aged Terry Stone was: bony face, thin white hair, postured shoulders, aqua-blue eyes. Stone's chin pointed sharply and his large ears matched his ability to listen well. That was what Janie attributed Terry Stone's success to: he was the grand master of listening.

"Humm? What is it?" Stone groaned.

"The NSA called, sir. They've received a package from Canada. Your eyes only. I thought . . ."

"Yes. Thank you."

"I called Marvin, sir. Your car will be ready in ten minutes."

"Thank you. I'll freshen up and be right there. Oh, and would you pour me a traveler?" he asked his secretary.

"Decaf?" Her small eyes showed fatigue.

"No, I'm afraid I'll need the real thing tonight." He focused on the clock and saw they were well into the early hours of another day: 12:30 A.M. "Boy, I really dozed off, didn't I?"

"It's good for you, sir. You should be home in bed. They shouldn't ask you to stay up all night like this. It's unhealthy."

Stone thought, Only Janie and Marvin can talk to me this way. Then he said, somewhat insincerely, "Duty, Janie. It's all in the name of duty." He winked.

Minutes later, clad in winter coat, a steaming cup of coffee in hand, he was walking through the hallway of his "hidden" offices. He felt good about sending Janie home, but felt sorry for the janitor up ahead meticulously mopping the floor. The man was bent over the bucket, his posture wrecked by years of it. The area reeked of ammonia and detergent.

The custodian saw the Old Man approaching and immediately moved his bucket. Stone was cautiously attentive of his full cup of coffee. The janitor bowed and that embarrassed Stone. After crossing the slick floor, Stone returned the bow. The custodian grinned toothlessly, unable to hide his pleasure. Stone mumbled something about team efforts and thanked the man for his individual contribution. It made the man's day, week, year. He couldn't wait to tell the wife.

Traffic was light. Stone and Marvin Krebs passed the time in "weather-talk," as Stone called it. Mindless chatter.

Marvin had been with the Old Man for over thirty years, and he knew more about Stone's private life than just about anyone—the two heart attacks of a few years before, his hospitalization for exhaustion, and the day Stone's wife had died—her death triggered by the loss of their son.

While Marvin waited in the reception area of the giant National Security Agency, Stone was being escorted down a wing of the building by a gray-eyed woman with an incredible waistline, pug nose, and freckles. Her dull, broom-straw hair hung short. Stone could not remember her name.

As they reached a guarded doorway, the woman asked, "How's the coffee?" referring to the fresh cup in his hand.

He sipped it. "Oh yes, quite nice. You made this?"

"Yes."

"Not bad for a computer expert," he added, winking. He dug deeply for a polite smile, feeling his total exhaustion, and handed her the cup, explaining, "Allow me to get out my card."

"My pleasure. And in case you've forgotten . . . my name's Toni."

Stone nodded, as if he had not forgotten. He inserted a gold plastic card into a gunmetal gray box mounted by the door and rested his hand on top. A light passed beneath it, taking a palm print. The door swished open. He gently took his coffee from her, remembered his card, and entered.

An optical device allowed only one entry at a time, so the door closed behind him.

Inside reposed the world's largest intelligence agency computer. Extravagant security guarded the room, including uniformed Marines. The guards had always bothered Stone. Still did. He thought, Any person, and most certainly experts, should be allowed to work in peace.

Considering the hour, the room appeared frightfully busy. Stone shivered. He did not know if the chill was from the powerful air conditioning or because of the imposing power this room commanded. It was part of the New World, the New System, and he wasn't sure if he approved.

A moment later the security door admitted Toni. She pulled a cardigan sweater reserved for visitors off a nearby peg and offered it to Stone. He accepted.

She led him to the far corner, where a video recorder was hooked up to a television and also to the computer—screen glowing. Stone instructed her to break open the sealed package and load the cassette.

They watched.

He studied the man on the screen thoughtfully. Pensively. The first time Toni began to speak, he cut her off by requesting another viewing.

Toni obliged, but this time, surrounding Borikowski with a computer-generated box of light, she stayed with his motions. In the next replay the small box of light was now enlarged and filled the full screen, showing Borikowski in close-up. The quality of the picture astonished Stone. What will be next? he wondered. For some reason, he hoped he would never find out.

They watched it four times, the last time at a slightly slower speed. Stone fiddled with his hands nervously, eyes glued to the screen, missing nothing, trying his best to duplicate the thoughts of the man pictured in front of him. The dog. The woman. His apparent calm. The interception. The kill . . .

The tape finished, but Stone continued to stare at the screen. Toni waited patiently.

"What do your machines say?" he inquired dryly.

"No positive ID so far."

He smiled a secret smile.

"I have a list . . ." she offered hesitantly, made nervous by his expression.

"No, dear. No list. You've done fine."

Stone requested and received a private room with a phone. He dialed a number carefully, waited to hear the man's voice, and spoke the code. When the initial exchange finished, Stone added his message. He received an acknowledgment and hung up.

Andy Clayton would be waiting at a highway turnout along the Potomac.

Since Stone was already with Marvin, he decided to use the limo. He could not help but be reminded of his last visit to Chevy Chase several months earlier. Andy Clayton had acted distant and cold, and Stone had been very worried about the man. After an initial conversation, which had tended toward argument, Andy had said, "I don't understand why I'm still inactive. I'm like a prisoner here."

"Now, Andy," Stone had begun. "It's just not like that."

"I'm useless here!" Andy had actually yelled at Stone—and for the first time ever. "Listen, I may have lost touch for a while. But that was months ago! I was *upset!* Fair is fair—"

"This has nothing to do with fair, Andy," Stone had snapped in interruption. "Fair has nothing to do with anything. This simply *is.*"

Now, months later, with Andy Clayton's situation not

much different, Stone watched the snow hit the windshield. Miserable weather.

The drive took Andy twenty minutes.

Following procedure, he waited alongside the limousine. Marvelous Marvin—as Andy called him—pulled himself out of the car and closed his door. They shook hands firmly. Before opening the back door, Marvin warned, "He's tired, Andy. Take it easy on the man."

Andy nodded, hunched his big shoulders, and ducked inside. Plexiglass divided the interior, isolating the driver. The back seat, where Stone and Andy sat, was dark and quiet.

"Nasty weather," Stone offered as an opener.

"Yes, sir."

"I've got something that I think you might be interested in."

"In what way, sir?"

"That has yet to be defined," Stone said truthfully. He thought, You're the only agent within a five-hour flight from here who could possibly help to identify the man. If I'm wrong, you're back to Chevy Chase and your report. If I'm right . . .

2:43 A.M.
Montreal, Canada

Leonid Borikowski climbed the scuffed and rusted staircase to the door that he had jammed open with a pencil a few hours before, his mind still working out the details of his new schedule. He would have to catch a train tonight, something he didn't look forward to. Mounties would be everywhere.

The door opened on complaining hinges; a pale bulb shadowed the hallway. A thin slat of ivory light lay across the hall, emanating from the partially open door to room thirty-one: the room adjacent to his.

Alerted, he approached cautiously, his fingers immediately touching the handle of his gun for reassurance. He walked past, ready. A voice called out, its range female, "Hello there. Bone-jooer."

He wanted to pass by but he stopped and looked. She was not what he had expected. This was not her neighborhood. Not even close. She looked haughty and well bred. She might have been pretty once. Added years had stolen the charm, like cobwebs clinging to the eaves. A liquor bottle, more empty than full, sat beside a glass that held but one last sip.

She spoke with a faintly British accent. She was soused. "The booze is probably better than the company, but you are welcome to both. Won't you please come in?" And then she added remorsefully, "Please?"

With his hand still resting on the butt of his weapon, he nodded, and continued to his room.

She tried again. "Please."

He entered his room, switched on the light, and closed the door. The room was cold. The sound of cars stopping in the street caught his attention. He parted the fragile curtains and again they ripped.

Two small cars idled as four uniformed Mounties climbed out of each, one group of which approached another boardinghouse situated across the narrow street. Due to the hour, the boardinghouse's front door was locked, so they pounded on the door and announced themselves with intimidating authority. "This is the police. You must open this door at once!" Lights appeared behind previously darkened windows. Finally the Mounties were admitted and ushered inside by an overweight man in a robe and stocking cap. From this vantage point, across the street and up one story, Borikowski could see down into the office, as the light came on. The manager

41

took his seat behind a large desk. The Mounties remained standing. The manager answered some questions, his mouth moving without sound, his hands rubbing fatigue from his eyes. Then they handed him a photo and he shook his head no. But it became obvious that the Mounties intended to search the building, for the three left the office and did not reappear on the street. Instead, one by one, lights began to fill the opposing windows.

Two patrolmen from the other group suddenly appeared below in the alley. They peered through the windows of the bistro, and inspected a Peugeot that was parked in the alleyway.

Borikowski knew the routine well enough, though he was surprised at how quickly they had narrowed down the area. He hurried into the bathroom and used toilet paper to dry the sink, then flushed the paper. He touched both towels and took the only damp one into the room and placed it carefully under the mattress, where no one would look for it. Now, if the old Canuck had trouble turning them away, the Mounties would find no evidence of use.

He knew he had been gloveless while changing faces, so he wiped down the bathroom fixtures and surfaces, taking no chances.

But then, following a pounding on the door to the boardinghouse, he faintly heard the old Canuck arguing in a frantic French; and much too suddenly the two Mounties in the alley had noticed, and were heading toward, the rear staircase.

A rare panic took him. He could not remember if he had knocked the pencil from the hallway door. Suitcase in hand, he switched off the light and left the room, locking it. His panic increased: the door to the back fire escape *was* still propped open and he could hear footsteps coming up. Not only that, but now he could plainly hear a conversation going on in the lobby.

Was he cornered?

He quickly considered the alternatives: he could remain in this boardinghouse, relying on the face and papers of the mythical Dr. Franz Vogel, but that might mean questions and even possible detention—a situation he could ill afford; or he could attempt to remove the two policemen coming up the back stairs—kill them if need be—but their deaths, any trouble, would only confirm his presence in Montreal, which in turn would make an exit from the city even more difficult than it already promised to be. He would not further hinder this assignment. It was in enough trouble already.

Then it occurred to him.

She still sat exactly as before, glass in hand, eyes sad and distant. He stepped inside, intentionally leaving the door unlocked, and waited for her reaction. She was in a stupor. He placed his suitcase on a chair and opened it. Then he switched off the light.

As he approached her she turned to him and smiled, her eyes cloudy. A streetlamp's light, filtered by the woven curtains, covered her in a gentle shading. She stood and dramatically helped her robe off her shoulders and onto the floor, leaving her in a busty nightgown.

Borikowski heard the footsteps stop and the hallway door squeak as it was opened. He was prepared to use the fire escape if she protested or resisted, but she did not. He walked over to her and took her relaxed head between his hands. She was feverishly warm. The rich smell of alcohol surrounded her.

His right fist caught her on the edge of her jaw with enough force to put away a middleweight. Her head snapped backward and he caught her mid-fall. Immediately, he carried her over to the bed, removed her nightgown, and placed her between the sheets. From the condition of her skin, he guessed she was in her late forties or early fifties.

He undressed quickly, placing the gun under the pillow, and then climbed above her, ready to perform. The actor.

When he heard the Mounties but one room away he began rocking the bed, his skin rubbing against hers. It had been quite some time since he had slept with a woman; and even unconscious, she was exciting him. His erection was immediate.

A knock on the door and an introduction: "Royal Canadian Mounted Police. Please open the door." He had the bed shaking like a locomotive now, certain that the sound would carry into the hallway.

As the Mounties opened the door for themselves, Borikowski saw his own profile—like that of a shadow boxer—spread across the wall, the rhythmic thrusts beneath the sheets very convincing. Above his outline, he saw the silhouettes of two uniforms. After a long moment, the door closed and the footsteps moved on. He forced three very loud grunts and then slowed the rocking to a stop. He rolled over and lay beside her, annoyed by his erection and his desire to have her.

The bed, the comfort, was too inviting. Knowing no trains would run at this late hour, he set the alarm on his watch to wake him, locked the door, and lay down beside her. Sleep came instantly.

Ninety minutes later, she still slept heavily. He dressed quickly and quietly.

When he entered the dark alley, suitcase in hand, he noticed the Peugeot coupe was still parked beside the bistro, its left front fender mangled. He went back up the stairs quietly and into the hotel, where he located a coat hanger. Within minutes he had the car running.

After a short drive, Montreal's Central Station loomed beside him, its architecture strongly European in a city that confused its influences. He drove past and parked three blocks away. He tried to relax. In a few hours the terminal would come alive, crowded with the influx of day workers. In the confusion of rush hour, disguised as Franz Vogel, he would board a train bound for Detroit: the Passageway.

3:00 A.M.
Washington, D.C.

Lights advanced behind a line of stenciled numbers. The elevator doors grumbled open. Andy Clayton and Terry Stone passed through two security checks and were finally inside the Old Man's office. Stone sat behind his desk; Andy sagged into one of the red-leather chairs.

"I received a call from Molière, RCMP," Stone explained. "He asked us for an identity run on a videotape recorded at Dorval only hours ago. A rover was killed."

"Molière . . . Molière . . . why does that ring a bell?"

"Privy Council, Solicitor General of the Security Service . . ."

"Older man, Foreign Legion type . . ."

"The same. According to a well-placed mole in the Soviet's Canadian operation, Opal, they have achieved a high level of penetration in the Security Service. This worries us. The rumor is they may be after Molière. If we lose Molière, the walls may come tumbling down. He's very important to us."

Andy nodded, but still asked, "Why all the concern? Why me?" He felt increasingly nervous sitting across from Stone's pallid face.

"I need you for confirmation. You're qualified and close at hand—" Stone's inflection implied he was in mid-sentence, but he stopped.

45

Andy's brows came together over the bridge of his lumpy nose. He wanted to say, "Qualified?"

They viewed the tape together. As ordered, Toni waited at the National Security Agency some miles away, the computers of both facilities connected by a trunk line. She was there to help if necessary—and it was. Andy's attention settled on the segment where the unknown agent withdrew the hatpin from the collar of his coat. Computer enhancement allowed a close-up of just the man's fingers. Andy turned to Stone and announced, "I have a positive ID."

Stone thanked Toni via his speaker phone and hung up. He left Borikowski's enlarged hand frozen on the screen.

The two men settled back into the warm wood and leather of Stone's office. The captain's clock ticked, intruding.

"You're certain it's him?" Stone inquired, having mentioned no name.

"He hasn't any use of his right index finger. Fires a gun using his middle finger. That much I know from experience. It's definitely *Dragonfly*."

"Coffee?" Stone asked, wanting some himself.

"Please."

Stone rose and walked over to the coffee maker. "What do you think, Andy?" he asked, delivering the coffee.

"It's him. No question. We haven't had a chance to double him in quite some time . . . we both know that. From what you say about the Security Service, I would have guessed he was here to try for General Molière. But it's more likely he's in Canada to advise one of the terrorist groups, which means he won't be here long. They used him as an advisor in Beirut . . . among other things." He paused. "I'd like the assignment, sir."

"That's one of my concerns. . . ."

Andy waited.

Stone's silver head rocked from side to side. "I'd like to try and double him. Of all my agents, you're the most familiar with him. That leaves me little choice." Stone paused deliberately. He wanted to underline his next comment. "Listen, I want you to remain objective."

"Yes," replied Andy.

Neither man smiled, but Andy was dancing inside.

Leonid Borikowski. Another chance.

5:54 A.M.
Washington, D.C./Montreal, Canada

A dusting of snow, whipped up by swirling winds, obscured the corner of the Air and Space Museum from Terry Stone's office window. Snow meant trouble for Washington no matter how little the accumulation. Stone heard a click on the phone line and pushed the receiver closer to his ear.

In his greenhouse, which overlooked picturesque Old Montreal and the St. Lawrence, clad in a smoking jacket and wool-lined slippers as he moved among his gardenias, Gustav Molière sipped lightly on mineral water while tending to a dreadful case of spider mites. His manservant Pierre, amazed to see the General so alive at such an uncivilized hour, held the phone with an extended arm as if it were diseased. Pierre detested telephones.

"Terry Stone here, General. The line is scrambled."

"Ah yes! I hope it is the good news, M'sieu Stone."

"I wish it were. We have a positive identification."

"*Oui!* Please to continue."

"Interpol code: *Dragonfly*."

A stray static buzz filled the line, silence on both ends.

In the greenhouse, Pierre had now taken over for the General and was waiting for approval to remove a yellowed leaf and withered bud. Molière nodded to Pierre

47

and replied into the phone, "I should have known they might send *Dragonfly*."

Stone fiddled with a pencil. "Then you are familiar with the agent?"

"But of course. He's a consummate actor who has penetrated any number of intelligence facilities. He's believed to have killed several agents as well as acted as a consultant for a number of terrorist organizations—which means nothing but the trouble for us, I am afraid."

"General, if I may . . . Due to our mutual concern over the possibility of direct threat to our respective security . . . I would, with your permission, be pleased to offer the assistance of an intelligence officer familiar with *Dragonfly*. We could have him up there shortly, if need be." He hoped he'd phrased it right. He hoped Molière would take the offer.

"Absolutely. We would be most grateful," Molière said, tossing the glowing cigarette from the doorway, watching it fall end over end into the slush.

Relieved, Stone dragged his flat-nailed fingers through thin hair. "Very well, he'll leave immediately. Contact's tag is George Baker. I wish us both luck."

"Thank you, M'sieu Stone. And I shall mention your generous cooperation to our prime minister. Good day."

As Stone hung up the phone, he gazed blankly at the curtain of falling snow, his head spinning from lack of sleep. He poured more coffee for himself and freshened Andy's, aware that even with a coffee maker he could not make a good-tasting cup. He buzzed Janie.

When Andy entered the room he looked as tired as Stone. As he sat, he felt a nervousness in his ostensibly calm boss. His fingers polished the chair's brass tacks. The smell of coffee helped him notice his cup had been refilled, too. You shouldn't be waiting on me, he thought, pitying the Old Man this late hour.

Stone stared into the black coffee and saw his own face looking back at him.

Andy raised his cup of coffee and said, "To Duncan."

"Yes. To Duncan." Stone's heart sank, and he wanted to explain why, but did not. "And to having a double in the DS."

They toasted.

After a time Stone said, "I want you to check in with me whenever possible. This will be your operation, Andy. I want you to know that. No more mistakes from involving too many others. We learned that lesson with Borikowski the last time. But I feel I should warn you that there's a chance this is nothing more than a ruse to lure you out into the open."

"I know."

"They would like to double you, too. Remember that." Stone made the coffee travel in a perfectly symmetrical funnel in the center of the cup. Plenty of practice.

"Yes."

"And I also have a mole in Montreal who could really help here. He will only meet in person—no phones—and he only contacts us here. But I will put the word out that we need help, and I'm certain he'll come through. I'll relieve his usual contact and leave that up to you. But if it is all to work, you must check in."

"I understand."

Stone took a minute to unlock a drawer and rummage through a file. He wrote something down and handed it to Andy. "There's a phone booth at that address. If you receive the code word, then go to this phone booth. It will ring on the hour. Let it ring four times, and then answer it. Don't say a thing. Just hang up. Exactly two minutes later a car marked as a private taxi will stop next to the booth. Get in. Tell the driver you want to go to New Holland."

"My contact's in the cab?"

"Yes. He'll be driving."

"Got it." Andy handed the paper back to Stone, and the Old Man inserted it into a small shredder mounted in his trash can and shredded it into dust.

"All right. Let's make our code word: JACKPOT. That will mean he wants a meeting."

"Fine. JACKPOT it is."

"Well, that's about it," Stone said. "The rest will be handled in Processing, downstairs. Documents, a weapon, and the rest." Stone stood slowly, arm extended.

They shook hands.

"Remember, Andy. We only want verification. We'll want to coordinate a trap with the Canadians—that's the way these things are done, eh? Identify and locate, understood? Turning him is another matter."

Andy nodded, though he knew his chances of ever finding Leonid Borikowski were slim. He reached into his coat pocket, withdrew a black billfold, and handed it, smiling, to Terry Stone. It was Stone's wallet. One of Andy's streetwise talents was pocket picking—he was very good at it. This particular ritual had been an ongoing joke between the two men for years, but with Andy away for so long, the Old Man had forgotten.

Stone shook his head, accepting his wallet with a rueful grin of remembrance spreading over his face. "You really shouldn't do that."

8:04 A.M.
Montreal, Canada

Congested by Central Station's arriving commuters, Montreal's Belmont Street churned with a colorful mixture of umbrellas and overcoats. The illuminated cross atop Mount Royal was being taken from the sky by the clouded sun.

50

After threatening water had receded from the city in 1643, Paul de Chomedey, Sieur de Maisonneuve, climbed Mount Royal with a wooden cross as an act of thanksgiving. Now, three centuries later, an electric cross gleamed over the city—consecrating the mountain.

Borikowski still sat in an uncomfortable position behind the wheel of the Peugeot. For the past few hours he had studied even the most distant sounds, worrying it might be his pursuers. Leonid Borikowski worried often. He would have welcomed sleep, but dared not even doze. His head felt thick and dull, and he was extremely cold. He wished he was back in Bulgaria.

He entered the throng of commuters walking toward the station, and bought a newspaper from a rosy-cheeked vendor with tattered half-finger brown gloves and a green wool jacket with big buttons. The front page showed fuzzy photographs of the two Bulgarians and an article on their possible threat to the Pope. There was nothing of his victim.

The crowd of people thickened at the doors to the station. He suspected two were agents: the man banging his hands together, and another in a thick overcoat, both outside in the cold. You don't know me, you fools, he chortled. I don't know you. We're even. You're looking for the wrong man. I am Franz Vogel now, not that ugly wretch who stabbed your agent. No. He is well behind us. I am a doctor, a rich doctor, who walks with a lilt to his step, has a heavy German accent when speaking one of his four languages, and is feeling a little tired.

Lifting on his toes, he saw uniformed police throughout the station; they were singling out all males and obviously requesting identification, which was creating bottlenecks at every gate. The others roamed the terminal scanning the crowd, stacks of photographs in hand. But none showed this face.

Knowing the all-important role luck played in the success of any operation, and not liking the odds he saw, Borikowski intentionally dropped his paper, knelt to pick it up, turned and walked away.

With few alternatives, Leonid Borikowski—*Dragonfly*—accepted the contingency plans he had once argued against. He detested the thought of working *with* others. He had wanted to do this alone! He took hold of his anger, pushed it into a reserved corner of his mind, and closed the door. His anxiety passed.

Scuffling shoes, mindless chatter, clicking of metal-tipped umbrellas on the sidewalk: swarms of pedestrians headed for work. Borikowski entered a breakfast café beneath a pale green awning frayed by the wind. The door shut, shaking rows of small bells. Coffee aromas and a thick cloud of cigarette smoke. A capacity crowd surrounded tables littered with egg-yellow plates and coffee cups. He approached an aged phone booth that supported a listing, three-legged cigarette machine, its dull enamel chipped and scarred, pulled the bifold door closed, and dialed.

Lydia answered. *"Bonjour?"*

"I've lost my watch. I wonder if you have the time?" He knew by her hesitation that hearing the code again had surprised her.

"From time to time."

"Which time?"

"The first time. Every time."

"The rental's broken down." Primary plan aborted.

"Very well. Location?" What backup plan are we using?

He appreciated her professionalism, knowing from her dossier that she was young but well qualified. He thought, The Durzhauna Sigurnost, the KGB, never helps any agent to look good. To do so only threatens their own job security. They make themselves look good, and because of this they obtain all the gasoline they need, the nicest cars, and a dacha on a lake. But this woman's dossier is clean. Even complimentary.

He said, "Three blocks, near the Beta Shop." Contingency Plan Three, Basilica of Mary. "One more thing," he added, telling her to meet him in one hour.

"Yes?" She posed it as a question, but was in fact acknowledging the message.

"Never mind." Message terminated.

She hung up. Borikowski caught himself thinking she had a beautiful voice.

The coffee was far superior to airplane coffee; the food, much needed. He sat at the counter, pleased the café was busy enough to keep the plump waitress from bothering him. He needed a few moments of peace.

He relived the scene at the airport, feeling the spike heel digging into his ankle, hearing himself swear. . . . Embarrassment colored his cheeks.

And now who was involved? Interpol? The Americans? The Security Service? Were they all involved now? A few hundred trained professionals after one fugitive?

Stupid mistake.

8:30 A.M.
Washington, D.C.

"Goddamnit all!" In his office, a bleary-eyed Terry Stone faced the television. He switched it off and looked at the person in the chair across from him. "Kwang must be stopped. She'll spoil the whole thing!"

Chris Daniels, a gaunt young man in his early twenties, predictably dressed conservatively, today in a dark suit, white shirt, and patriotic tie. His SIA identification tag was clipped to the breast pocket. At the age of fifteen, he had graduated summa cum laude from the University of

Michigan, at sixteen had received a master's in communication, and at seventeen, when his employment application to the CIA had been detoured to the Security Intelligence Agency due to age requirements, had been handpicked by Terry Stone to serve as an assistant.

One of his first contributions to the SIA was inventing an agent code that utilized newspapers' crossword puzzles. The simple cryptograph allowed agents in the field to be notified of events without phone conversations or clandestine meetings—simply by deciphering the morning paper's crossword puzzle. The Crossword Code had been so successful that Daniels had been promoted almost immediately. And then again. And again.

Now Daniels was Stone's Intelligence and Communication Administrator—his right-hand man—and had just recently obtained one of the highest security ratings in government.

His thick lips opened to emit a peculiar falsetto, as if he had never outgrown adolescence. He began, "Borikowski didn't follow established routes. For weeks now, Interpol has been hinting at a new corridor that they claim has opened up between Murmansk and Vardo. There has been an increasing number of Soviet mini-subs spotted in that area by our Eye-10 satellites. At first it was believed they were on reconnaissance missions, like the one that went aground in Sweden; but traffic at known corridors has slowed down. He could have gone from Petrozavodsk to Murmansk by boat where a series of lakes connect by marshland. An airboat, perhaps. He would have then boarded there and shipped on to Vardo. In any event, we missed him." After a moment Daniels stated, "Sir, Captain Clayton has made two previous attempts to abduct him."

"Yes."

"But *Dragonfly* killed his twin brother—"

"—Yes—"

"—Duncan Frederick Clayton: code *Hummingbird*."

"Yes. Listen, I'll have Numan follow up on this mini-sub theory. Central and the Bureau, respectively, are watching both sides of the Canadian border and keeping tabs on all commercial transportation. We've used the snow as an excuse to cancel the president's schedule. At least *he's* safe. The State Department is leaking that we've blown Borikowski. If that makes it up the chain of command in time, they may call him back. . . . Is there anything I'm overlooking?"

"The press?" Daniels asked.

"Yes. We must keep a lid on it, eh? I would like to brief Lyell on all of this," he said, referring to Andy's chess partner of the night before. "I want the press shut down. Especially this Kwang woman . . ."

"Lyell has already arranged a meeting. She's agreed to stop in Washington on her way to Memphis."

"Fine."

"If I may, sir?" Daniels asked, pushing his glasses up the bridge of his nose.

"Please."

"Using Clayton seems a risk."

"You're unfamiliar with both men, aren't you? Borikowski, you see, is the classic KGB or DS operative: he follows orders and orders alone. Which is not to say he's incapable of improvisation. Quite the contrary, he's clever and an excellent actor. But he sticks to a schedule, Chris—a preconceived plan—and in this way, he's the exact opposite of Andy. Have you briefed yourself with Clayton's records?" Stone asked, quizzing Daniels, as was his custom.

"Yes, of course: Georgetown University, like all the Clayton men; Army Intelligence in Vietnam, G-3; father died in a commercial plane crash; his mother's in a security ward in a hospital in McLean. His most recent assignment was MES—Middle East Security operations—a post he held for several years. Following Duncan Clayton's abduction two years ago—and subsequent death—he was given leave. He's tried for Borikowski twice: Bucharest and Prague, I believe. Following Prague he was assigned the task of writing a detailed report on MES."

"Correct . . ."

"In 1975, he was able to remain underground in Kiev for sixty-two days without being captured." Daniels sounded impressed.

"Code name?" Stone asked, still quizzing.

"Following Kiev: *Chameleon*. Now: *Baker2*."

"Correct. Know how he did it?"

"Not exactly."

"Curious?"

"Absolutely."

"Picked pockets. MI trained them that way. Change identities; obtain local currency. He finally stole a tourist's passport with a close-enough photo—and that got him out. He's our best at remaining underground."

"And that's why you chose him?"

"Essentially, yes." Stone sipped his lukewarm decaf. "The leaks we've been having prohibit a group effort. Borikowski's too good at spotting agents. Andy has a nose for *Dragonfly*. Our last attempt to take him was compromised by leaks. Not this time. Andy will check in here. This way, we gather the data but leave the chase to Andy. I think he's a driven-enough man to pull this off. He loved his brother—twins you know—and well, there's more to it than that. Put simply, he's the best surveillance man I have. And he also happens to have captured more enemy agents than any other SIA agent. I simply picked the best man I had available.

"You know, as well as I, that if we turned this assignment over to the CIA," Stone continued, "there'd be a bunch of guys in trench coats on street corners with walkie-talkies: sad but true. Not only that, but within forty-eight hours the entire country would know about it. We can't risk that with Borikowski."

"Yes. I see what you mean."

"Besides, we have a deeply planted mole in Montreal. Don't forget that. Borikowski will be following a plan, rigidly. Andy will be following instincts. It will be interesting to see how it turns out. If our mole can find out the plan, Andy should have him."

"He may kill him."

"Indeed," Stone allowed, knitting his brow and looking away from the young man. "It is a possibility—something I've considered. But he knows I want a double in the DS." Stone seemed to be convincing himself. "Either way, Borikowski must be stopped. He's never handled a light assignment. And, as you well know, we have reason to believe he orchestrated the Beirut embassy massacre. We certainly can't afford that again."

"Or the Pope."

"Or the Pope," Stone agreed.

"You're fond of Clayton, aren't you, sir?"

"Fond? Hardly the word," Stone said, avoiding the truth. "In the past, he's given us all nine yards, Chris. He wants this man badly. I owed him the assignment . . . if there is such a thing."

"And what about Bookends?"

"How do you . . . ? Oh, yes. I keep forgetting about your new rating." He paused in thought. "Andy was never told much about Bookends. Only generalities. That was my decision." No one, other than myself, knows everything about Bookends, he thought. Not even you, Chris. "At the time, I thought it prudent to remove him from action for a while, so we told him that we wanted an in-depth report on the MES operations. We've made him go through five drafts. It's taken him seventeen months."

"I see. But *they* may be after *him.* It could be a trick:

using Borikowski's presence to lure Captain Clayton out again. The bait, if you will. After all . . . didn't Bookends call for both brothers to be abducted?"

"Yes. True, they may still be after him." Stone waited quite some time and added, "But they've tried before, haven't they? And they haven't gotten him yet." He looked intently at Daniels. "Nothing comes for free, Chris. It's all a gamble." He toyed with his glasses. "All a gamble."

10:00 A.M.
Vaughnsville, Ohio

His hair was the color of polished sterling silver. His fillings were gold and showed when he laughed. Dr. Eric Stuhlberg, dressed more like a surgeon than a research scientist, edged his way around the large counter that stood in the center of the laboratory and sat down in front of the electron microscope. Next to him a plump woman with domed cheeks and sparkling eyes sat at a stool taking notes. Dr. Mellissa Sherman looked tired.

The laboratory, a combination of glass and white tile, had no windows to the outside. Buffed stainless steel and bright lights predominated, reflecting the room's sterile atmosphere. Stuhlberg's thick German accent, muffled by the paper mask, sounded hollow in the room. "Well, that's it. The 1134 is what I recommend we show him. What do you think?" he asked Sherman.

"The 1134 or the 1137. Yes. And we should have the XN–125 available to show him the saline effects, don't you think?"

"Excellent." Stuhlberg pushed his stool away from the microscope and rubbed his eyes. "Would you mind wrapping up for me?"

"Not at all," Mellissa Sherman said genuinely, and began the work. The recombinant bacteria was held in small glass petri dishes. She wore thin plastic gloves, as did Stuhlberg.

He asked, "Isn't it remarkable that something so small may soon solve one of mankind's largest problems?"

"It's exciting, is what it is." She looked into Stuhlberg's gray eyes and wondered what it was like inside that mind. "And you created it, Doctor. You should be very proud."

He smiled, his fillings glistening. "I wouldn't go that far, dear. All I did—we did—was to alter it. *He* created it." Stuhlberg grinned reverently. "*He* created everything. *He* guided us as we struggled along here." Another assistant turned to listen. "There was a time in my life, Mellissa . . . when I was about your age . . . and I saw where the world was headed . . . that madman and his Third Reich. I fought those people. I fought with my heart, mind, and body. They had killed my two aunts, an uncle, my brother-in-law, and my father—God rest his soul. I vowed that someday, rather than fight, I would try to make a positive contribution to society. . . ." He was unstoppable now. The remaining assistant turned to listen. Stuhlberg never rambled like this—had never mentioned his past. Curiosity hushed the room. "And I don't mean teaching or writing books. Academia was fine for a while, but as I grew older I desperately wanted to honor that vow I had made so long ago. I wanted this. . . ." He looked around the lab and now noticed he was the center of attention, which clearly embarrassed him. "Oh my," he exclaimed, "it would seem I've made a spectacle of myself."

Mellissa Sherman said, "We're all very proud, Doctor— proud to be working with you . . . to be part of it—"

"Hear, hear," agreed one of the assistants as he applauded Stuhlberg. The two others joined in the applause and Dr. Eric Stuhlberg looked to each of his three assistants, his smile wide and profound, thinking, I couldn't have done it without all of you. He then hung his head, and Mellissa Sherman kissed his silver hair.

Dr. Eric Stuhlberg was weeping.

10:00 A.M.
Montreal, Canada

A small jet flew from Andrews Field to Mirabel airport in Montreal, and arrived at ten o'clock on an overcast Friday morning. From there Andy was driven into the city by a small man who wore a black chauffeur's uniform and who seemed indefatigably satisfied with life. He struck Andy as the sort of man who would have made a good preacher, for his mouth moved incessantly and his words were filled with great expectation. The car's radio played an instrumental version of "Everything's Coming Up Roses," and this made the passenger smile.

From an underground garage, Andy rode an elevator to the sixth floor. He was greeted by a man wearing an aide's aiguillette and shiny brown boots. After a polite welcome, he was led down several hallways, past two security checks, to General Gustav Molière's office.

It was a small museum: a collection of nineteenth-century firearms adorned the west wall, and on the east wall hung a stuffed Canada goose next to a mounted eighteen-pound steelhead trout. The room's colors were masculine, and it smelled like sweet oil. A desk lamp with a jade-green glass shade cast a warm light across Molière's face, which was creased with folds of skin and featured a large nose flanked by big round eyes. The General rose to greet his guest. Andy introduced himself as George Baker. They shook hands and then both sat down.

After a few minutes of polite conversation, Molière handed Andy a maroon folder from his cluttered desk and settled back into the thickly cushioned throne. "You may read through this, *non?* But if you would prefer, I think, I can save for you the time."

Molière was of another era—both noble and full of a sense of history—his presence captivating. "After the incident at Dorval last night, we did the usual checking of ground transportation, et cetera, but with little luck. We know our subject traveled by taxi into midtown, to a Hotel St. Jacques, but from there he was on foot. He planted a false lead with the doorman.

"This led to an investigation of the bus lines. One driver remembered him vaguely, but couldn't be certain. We then searched Old Montreal—the end of the route, and a likely place for a person to try and hide—but I am afraid, made no contact. However, to my delight— though I must admit my subordinates view this skeptically—around three this morning, a Peugeot was reportedly stolen from an area only four blocks from where the bus line ends . . . and now has been discovered, only minutes ago, three blocks from the Central Station: our downtown rail station. So, you see, we may be closer than we think."

"He's on the run. That's good. He'll need backup. Anything from your undercover people?"

"We are full with the reports. Due to the papal visit our energies for the last two months have been aimed at avoiding any possible terrorist threat to the Pope. In that regard, we have, of course, collected a voluminous amount of undercover-reported activities. On the international view, I would say," he explained, shuffling through some folders and finally examining the papers in one of them, "the only pertinent information would be the alleged arrival of two Bulgarian Aeroflot employees whom I am certain you have heard about." Andy nodded and Molière took a moment to light another cigarette, sip some water, and continue. "Other than *Dragonfly* last night, well here, you take a look." Molière leaned for-

61

ward, grunting quietly, and handed Andy another thin maroon folder marked in a French code that Andy did not understand. Fifteen entries of known international criminals and suspected agents lined the page, none of whom had any legal right to be in Canada. Most were marked with detention periods and dates of extradition; five were marked as *Present Whereabouts Unknown*, an asterisk and reference number alongside each. One of these read, "Nicholas Testler aka Kubler aka Brine." Andy read it twice and swallowed his urge to question Molière about the man. The report indicated Testler had been back and forth between Detroit and Montreal a number of times, but had yet to be apprehended. Although an odd son of a bitch, Testler had provided Andy with helpful information on more than one occasion. Testler had an uncanny knack of knowing everything about everyone. Andy feared that mentioning the man might draw attention to him, and thus lessen Andy's chances of finding and using him. So he said nothing.

"So, we wait," Andy stated, leaning forward and handing Molière a photographic enlargement. "Maybe this will help. You could circulate it among your border stations. We are doing the same at ours."

"*Qu'est-ce que c'est?* Excuse me, wh—"

Interrupting the translation, Andy said, "*C'est son bag. Il y à une tache au coin,*" with perfect inflection. It is his suitcase. It has a mark in the corner.

Molière smiled. He studied the photograph—an enlargement of a computer enhancement.

At first glance it looked no different than any other Samsonite; but two inked-in arrows pointed out the difference: a deep scratch bisected the upper corner of the bag, most likely the result of hasty baggage handlers. The rut created a perfect triangle with the bag's top corner. It was as distinct as a fingerprint, as individual as a signature. And it marked Leonid Borikowski's suitcase.

Andy went first to the train station and then to where the Peugeot was parked. Two detectives still worked inside the small car. They were tearing it apart. When Andy first touched the car he could *feel* Borikowski; he *knew* the agent had been in the car.

But he also felt strangely misplaced here, as if living someone else's life, and wondered if the assignment was indeed well placed in his hands. He wondered about his own intentions and motivations, and questioned the validity of them, not knowing if he was here to please Terry Stone, himself, or his brother.

Back at the hotel Andy tried to contain his impatience by playing chess against the computerized chessboard he traveled with. But he couldn't help thinking of Duncan, and of Duncan's killer. In his contemplation, he had decided that, yes, he hated Leonid Borikowski. And he *owed* him—if lives and deaths can be counted on balance sheets like so much small change. He owed him—or so he had let himself believe for nearly two years.

But who's counting?

He dressed for a run.

11:28 A.M.
Autoroute 40, Canada

The winter storm hovered above the Montreal sky. Falling snow hid the spires of the Basilica of Mary, Queen of the World. A young couple strolled by. An icicle hung from a streetlamp. An Audi sedan pulled out of heavy traffic and came to a stop in a no-parking zone in front of the basilica, skis and poles in the roof rack. Behind the slapping wipers loomed an oval face, blurred by the running water of the snow melting against the glass. The headlights, dim in the afternoon light, blinked once.

Borikowski appeared from nowhere.

He glanced into the car through both side windows. The back seat was empty, as was the passenger seat in front. He opened the door and tossed in his suitcase, which she helped onto the back seat. A moment later he fastened his seat belt and looked over at her.

She wore a lawn green jacket flecked with white wool, open against a loose cranberry blouse revealing an enticing bit of smooth-skin cleavage. Her pants were mauve cashmere. The fabric reminded Borikowski of the woman he had murdered at Dorval.

His voice was ragged from the cold, his facial muscles taut. "Autoroute 40, south."

"Our good-bye didn't last long."

"No," he returned. I don't like you already, he thought. I don't like working with other people and I especially don't like pretty young women who cause my imagination to run wild. I wish you'd go away.

She drove the Audi through an intersection and turned right into lighter traffic.

Lydia Czufin, for all her apparent calm, felt dizzy with excitement. She had been preparing for this assignment for a long time, yet had never expected the legendary Durzhauna Sigurnost agent to require her assistance. She had thought their meeting last night had been the end to it. But there he sat, less than two feet away.

She fought back a grin of delight.

She knew Montreal well. She merged the Audi into the traffic on the Decarie Expressway, entered a tangled cloverleaf, and accelerated onto Autoroute 40, listening to the soft stroke of the wipers and wondering what he might say next.

She deposited a paper sack onto his lap.

He peered inside without a word and removed a box of a special plaster-saturated gauze. "We'll need a motel room," he said in Vogel's high German. "Stop as soon as possible."

"There are a dozen motels—"

"*No Russian!*" he snapped. "I am Dr. Franz Vogel, you are my wife. We are German! We speak German, French, and English! No Russian!"

Stunned by his outburst, Lydia struggled to maintain her composure. Her strength was self-control, and she used it conscientiously now to avoid an ugly encounter. She started again in perfect high German. "There are a dozen motels over the next fifteen kilometers, but if I may offer an opinion, I think we should wait until Brockville or one of the other outlying towns. The Mounties and Security Service have a stronghold on this area of Montreal—informants everywhere. By the time we reach Brockville—you see, it comes under the authority of the Provincial Police—it should be safer."

"Very well," Borikowski said, unhappy with the delay, but acquiescing.

They drove for ninety minutes with little conversation, only occasional glances. Inspections. Leonid Borikowski was not without reputation, even a degree of fame— something nearly unheard of in Soviet Bloc intelligence.

Now realizing she had become a part of it, she expected the operation to help her career, maybe even lead to another promotion. So her attention fixed on doing everything right—the first time. She longed to shop the nicer Moscow stores reserved for officers of higher rank, to move into an apartment that had a full kitchen and no rats. This is special, she thought, not allowing her eyes to travel back onto him. A rare opportunity. I must take full advantage. But he is hard-edged and even more strict than I had expected. Treat him delicately, woman, she instructed herself. He liked you last night. Remember how important his first impression is.

Lydia Czufin had always been made aware of her astounding beauty by her father and mother, both of whom were dedicated Party members. Her father had been an army officer—a policeman—in Moscow, her mother a clerical secretary in the Kremlin. She was 100 percent Russian.

And yet, as much as she had tried, she could not deny her appreciation of cities like Montreal and Paris, where a woman was free to shop any store, where there were no rations on food.

Her father died tragically in a Soviet prison, a convicted murderer. Lydia had been old enough to understand that her father's temper had destroyed him. Jealousy. The same temper that had forced her to avoid boys, despite the arguments of her mother, to live away from life. And then, following his death, her mother had pulled the only strings left available to her and managed to place her daughter in the KGB, an organization that would allow travel, allow her daughter to see the people and places of the world, to leave the city that held memories of confinement and a father who tried too hard to be someone he wasn't.

Her first foreign assignment was Paris, where she had posed as a model. Six months ago, at the age of twenty-three, she had returned home to her mother with questions about men. She had confessed she had slept with one while on duty in Paris. What she did not mention was that there had been another. And another. Some chemical change had taken place, which she did not fully understand. Yes, something had changed dramatically. Down there. It was all she thought of anymore: down there. A constant desire had taken her, a physical desire, and she imagined that this was how drug addicts felt.

Always wanting more.

The two women had had a long talk together.

Now, she remembered again the last bit of advice her

mother had given her before she had left for Canada: "Lyditchka, most men want only one thing from a woman—especially a pretty woman—and they are willing to promise anything to get to it. Anything. Remember, promises are nothing but words." Then she had looked even more deeply into her daughter's eyes and had demanded, "If you give to them what they want, Lyditchka, make certain they keep their promises."

But her mother had been concerned with long-lasting love; and Lydia was not concerned with this at all, no, only with physical pleasure. Ohhh . . . the pleasure of *it*. Recently, what she called her "itch" had become greater. But that was fine. She had since learned of ways to please herself, and these felt almost as good. Sometimes better.

She and Borikowski drove through the storm clouds and into winter sunshine where the green-blue water of the St. Lawrence River was broken by the wakes of a few tugs and their barges. The two were impersonating the Vogels—a married couple on vacation in this rich and beautiful country—and for a short stretch of time it actually felt that way.

But then she slowed the Audi down, a turn signal blinking.

Brockville.

The small motel was a glorified row of cinder block cubicles, identical but for the number on the door. Mrs. Vogel registered with the pale and balding man in the office, explaining casually—as was her forte—that her husband needed a nap, that they would not be staying the night but were happy to pay for a full day. The manager, stimulated by her unusual beauty, fantasized what her partner actually had in mind. Others had used these rooms for an hour or two: lovers who were unfaithful, travelers bored with the highway but not with each other, teenagers experimenting with newfound sensations. The balding man had his own sickness, and witnessed these encounters from unseen vantage points behind certain walls and curtains. He had watched them undress each other, fondle each other, sweat in each other's arms. A sickness he lived with. And he could scarcely wait to devour this beautiful woman's body. A sheen broke out across his brow, and his groin throbbed with anticipation.

As she pulled the Audi around to a parking space, Lydia asked, "Will we be driving all night?"

"I'm not sure yet."

"If you do not mind, I would like to change clothes. I am too warm. I will not take long."

"I don't mind. Why should I mind?" Borikowski questioned in a perturbed voice. She's controlling you already, he warned himself. Be careful.

"Thank you. Room seven."

The room was a modest attempt at comfortable accommodations. A sole queen-size bed dominated the small space. Two quaint prints of the St. Lawrence hung on the wall. A television set, the name rubbed off by insistent fingers, sat atop a veneered chest of drawers.

The door to the bathroom was between the bed and a row of curtained windows on the far wall. The room smelled of pine disinfectant. He placed his suitcase on the floor, drew the drapes shut, and removed the box of gauze.

Lydia brought him a towel and an ice bucket partially filled with warm water.

Borikowski had removed his pants. He soaped and shaved his right leg. He read the instructions on the box of plaster.

"If I may?" she said, interrupting his concentration.

"Yes. What is it?"

"You seemed to take particular notice of the radio news when they ran the brief story on the woman killed at Dorval last night, and yet you hardly seemed concerned at all by the story on the two Bulgarians they are chasing."

He had no idea he had been so obvious. "Very well. The woman . . . she was a rover. I killed her.

"As for the two Bulgarians." He laughed. "It would be my guess they are my cover. You understand? After Rome, the Pope will not be dealt with again. In my opinion that shooting was a warning. If they had wanted him dead, that's exactly how he would be. The two others . . . I believe . . . were merely created to draw attention from my entry."

"Yes. So sorry for asking."

He grunted, annoyed.

She turned, entered the tiny bathroom, and pulled the door closed behind her.

The balding manager had already taken his position, one rheumy eye peering through a special slit he had created for this purpose in each and every curtain. He had gone out the back door of the office and slipped between a leafless hedgerow and the yellow painted cinder block of the building. The narrow space provided him with privacy.

He watched Lydia close the door to the bathroom, place her small suitcase on the covered toilet, and open it. Casually, she undressed. The manager began rubbing himself.

His only disappointment came from her athletic thighs, so unlike the rest of her delicate body. Every gem has its flaw, he allowed, his breaths deepening, the rubbing continuing. She was dressed in panties and bra, and was searching through her bag for clothes.

The man's heart raced. His hand increased its pace. God, how he wanted her naked. Yes. Yes. Yes. Go to the man in the room, he willed. But she did not.

Instead, she rubbed under both arms with a damp face cloth, dried with a towel and rolled on some deodorant, which came packaged in a plastic cylinder edged with purple flowers. She began to dress, this time in a skirt, dark stockings, and cotton blouse. She packed her dirty clothes into a plastic bag and into the suitcase.

The little man was not pleased.

He inched over to the windows of the bedroom, searching for his incision in the curtains, finally located it, and spied in on Borikowski, who was sitting on the edge of the bed nearly through the quick task of donning a cast.

Then the door to the bathroom swung open, seemingly hitting the manager in the face, which threw him off balance and dropped him into the snow.

He stood back up, angry now because the woman was fully dressed and conversing with the man on the bed, who barely took notice of her. Fool!

An object moved on the bed. The manager's heart pumped heavily. Dark metal. Sinister. What was it?

Borikowski moved and the object slid a few inches. Then it came clearly into focus: the knurled handle; the thin black barrel; the trigger. *A gun! Terrorists!* Jeeesus, Mary, and Joseph! *Criminals!*

The man ran quickly back to his office, his balance tenuous on the slick ground, nerves tense.

The media had turned Canadian terrorism into front page news for the last year. There had been bombings and cold-blooded murders of innocent people. The little man thought, It has to be stopped before it becomes commonplace. Like Paris.

His hands shook tremulously as he grabbed for his office door and hurried across the worn rug to the phone. He bumped the wastepaper basket and scattered its contents. His eyes searched a three-by-five card taped to the glass of the desk top: RCMP! Of all the people! *He* had never expected to be calling *them*. He had always feared the reverse situation: them arresting him.

Borikowski knew the cast, though dry to the touch, would require another half hour or so to set fully. But due to his new schedule, he did not have any extra time. Resting an arm around Lydia's firm shoulders, he hopped out to the car. She helped him into the passenger's seat, walked back to the trunk, and returned with a pair of crutches. She had followed Plan Three to the letter.

He had expected no less.

By this time the manager was busy explaining the situation—with certain omissions—to the Royal Canadian Mounted Police, surprised by their apparent lack of concern. Then he heard the Audi's engine and shouted too loudly, "They're leaving now!"

"The car, *m'sieu*. Please, calm down. We need a good description of their car."

With little time, the frenzied man rushed to the nearest window. Then he ran back to the phone. "It's a foreign car, European I think, dark, with a ski rack and skis on the roof."

"What make? What license number?" the policeman questioned, knowing that at this time of year the description fit several thousand cars.

"I couldn't see! Jeeesus, Mary, and Joseph! They're gone! Heading south on 40. He had a gun! By the Mother of God, it was the biggest pistol I've ever seen!"

It was, in fact, one of the smallest automatics made.

The Audi gained speed and pulled into the light traffic of the autoroute. Borikowski took a few quiet minutes to go over the "script," as he called it: He was the victim of irony, an orthopedist who had had a skiing accident, his wife now driving him to America to sightsee for the duration of their vacation. The slopes were no fun with a broken leg. He carefully reconstructed Franz Vogel's past, in case he needed a detail quickly.

Lydia seemed nervous. He was not impressed by her. She moved her shoulders and legs often, and reminded Borikowski of a snake. Steamy and sexy. Uncontrolled and uncontrollable, as if she was ready to take her clothes off. He knew this was absurd. But of course it wasn't. It was exactly right.

She served a useful purpose—for the time being—and that was enough. Their joint cover and "script" would work well. If all went as planned, then at Detroit he would be allowed to be on his own again—according to the rules of this operation. He looked forward to that.

Fifteen minutes passed quietly. Lydia worried and fidgeted. She was horny; and for the first time in a long time, she was mad at herself for it. She wondered if he liked her choice of clothes, for he had said nothing. She wondered if she was too stiff and formal, for he had not indulged in conversation. She wondered why he seemed so distant. She decided he was a loner. She had never liked loners. Too independent. She liked men who wanted her; and he did not seem interested at all.

She continued to fantasize about a promotion, continued to coach herself through her anxieties. She recalled more of her mother's advice—advice that had helped Lydia to be transferred to Europe, and eventually Paris. Her mother had admitted regretfully, "To gain a position of power, of importance, one must be constantly alert and prepared to make any sacrifice necessary. That which seems so distasteful today may bring prosperity tomorrow, Lyditchka. Remember this." And on that night, Lydia had watched secretly as her mother had paid three quarters of her life's savings to a disgustingly brash KGB officer who had dozens of necessary connections. Two weeks had passed, and Lydia's mother had not slept well and had not eaten well, fearing she had made a horrible mistake, for there was little to stop the man from simply walking away with the bribe. But, to their mutual relief, Lydia received notice, shortly thereafter, that she had been accepted into the GRU and had been transferred to cosmetology school in Leningrad, and would be given a Paris assignment following her schooling.

Her mother had been right. As always.

She thought, And if she had it all to do over again, I know she would. It's the way of the world.

She squirmed in her seat and looked over at Borikowski, who was running his finger along the raised seam of the glove compartment.

Borikowski somehow knew she was about to speak, and he welcomed it. His attention had fixed to the whirring of the wheels, and he was becoming sleepy.

She said, "The cast bothers me. It's my duty to protect you, and with that cast—"

"Don't worry, please. Our superiors know what they are doing. What agent in his right mind would don a cast? You understand?"

"Yes, but if we should have to run, or—"

"There is no need for concern. It only interferes with clear thought. Understand?" he admonished, depressed by her sophomoric attitude. "The cast is perfect. Brilliant. Who would think of it?"

"And my clothes?" she asked, instantly regretting having mentioned them.

"Listen," he said sternly, wondering seriously now if she was an asset or a liability, "they're fine. Everything is fine. Let me do our worrying. Relax and enjoy the view. It's nice, is it not?"

She had no argument there. The afternoon sun had once again found its way between the constant clouds and was pouring down light. Next to the highway a bottle's broken glass sparkled. "Yes, it is lovely. I am sorry for my questions. I have never been a wife," she joked lightly, "and it's not as easy as I once thought."

In the opposing lanes a police car passed. Both of them saw it. "It's slowing down," Lydia announced. Her eyes followed it in the mirror.

"Are you carrying a weapon?" Borikowski inquired hastily.

"Not that they'll find. It's hidden over here in the door panel. It ejects quietly and quickly. But I don't think we should jump to conclusions. We'll have plenty of time to use our weapons no matter what they try. At the moment, it's—"

"What caliber?" he interrupted.

"Nine millimeter."

"Semi-automatic?"

"Yes."

"Tell me if they cross the highway. I must know exactly when." He reached inside his coat, took hold of his weapon, and then rolled down the window. His movements were quick and intense, like a person ready to put out a fire.

The police car crossed the median, skidding through the snow. Its lights began flashing. "Now!" she spat out. "They're crossing now." She watched as Boriskowski tossed the weapon. It traveled ten feet and disappeared into the snow. She was incredulous—it was as if he had practiced this routine a hundred times. He stripped off his jacket and removed the canvas holster. He looked perplexed, and suddenly the rehearsed section was over; he appeared trapped in stage fright. He just stared at the holster. Then his spell broke and he glanced over his shoulder at the approaching vehicle. He seemed tempted to toss the holster out the window too, but did not. "Shit! I need to dispose of this!"

"Give it to me. Take the wheel."

The police car's siren kicked on, two hundred yards back.

In the confined and limited space of the car, their motions seemed frantic. He took the wheel. She grabbed the holster from him, folded it twice, lifted her skirt, pulled down her underwear, and pushed the folded canvas between her legs. She pulled the skirt down and took the wheel, refusing to look at him.

Leonid Borikowski was dumbfounded. And impressed. It was a perfect idea. "I thought in the door panel," he explained.

"No room," she said.

As the police car closed the distance, its siren sounded like the wail of a tortured cat.

Borikowski put back on his coat. He took a deep breath and released it.

The police car was fifty yards back.

"Why are we doing this?" she suddenly questioned.

"I think I know what happened. Use the weapon if you have to. But only if you have to."

She snapped her head toward him.

"Be natural. Pull over. Go on! Pull over."

Slices of the bright lights caught Borikowski across his eyes. His head throbbed. He hated bright lights. Both vehicles pulled over and stopped. The cat groan purred and was then silent.

Borikowski also hated cats.

The Mountie's door shut. Uniform shining and pressed, gold stripe down the pant leg, he marched over to the driver's window—visible in the rearview mirror from his crotch to the double-stitched, pleated shirt pockets. He stood in back of the door post, his right hand casually covering his holstered gun. He bent over, cautious and ready. His breath caught the cold of her window and marred the visibility.

Lydia rolled the window down, her face obviously not what the officer had expected. He pursed his lips.

Borikowski's French had just the right amount of German in it, a combination difficult for even him, and one that required absolute attention. "What seems to be the trouble, officer?"

The man's tough face came clearly into view for the first time. A labyrinth of blood vessels mapped his nose and cheeks. A history of fights with fists and pipes and

75

sticks had chiseled his nose. He was clean-shaven and bony. Simple-faced and boyish. Untrusting. "Hands on the dash, if you please. Thank you."

They looked strange like this. She spoke first, appropriately intimidated but sexy and charming. "Was I going too fast?"

"*Non, mad'm.* May I see your driver's license and registration please?"

"My hands?"

He nodded to her.

She located the documents and handed them politely through the window, an actress practiced and confident. She was ready to shoot the man.

The Mountie said, "If you please."

She returned her hands to the dash.

"Thank you."

The Mountie inspected her papers. "Passports please. Slowly. You first," he told Borikowski.

Borikowski had to protest. No male would just sit there. "What is this all about?"

The Mountie didn't answer. After a moment he had both passports in his hands, then he said, "Just checking, sir. Vacation?"

Borikowski continued his feigned anger. "You check every car on the highway, do you?"

She ignored Borikowski. Her voice was chatty—powder room chatter, and was laced with a thick East European accent. Not by design. It was the only way she could speak. This was why all *her* passports listed her homeland as West Germany. "Skiing your Laurentians—I have the most difficult time pronouncing that—some of the best snow we've seen in years, superior even to Gstaad. We were both going a bit too fast I suppose, although you know, we've skied much faster than that. Franz, you see, hit a mogul terribly hard and his binding released." She reached over and took Borikowski's hand off the dash and held it in hers. The maternal wife. "Poor thing. His right binding stayed tight . . . kept his balance for a moment . . . I heard it break. What do you call it, dear?" She looked inquisitively at Borikowski, who thought she was taking things a little too far. Astonished, he found himself appreciating her. She *was* good.

"Compound."

The officer nodded. He had seen them. "A fresh cast?"

Lydia, her hands free now, reached to trigger the release of the hidden gun, but Borikowski leaned across her, preventing the move.

She liked the contact.

The Mountie took a step backwards. "The dash please!"

They obliged.

Borikowski grinned and explained, "That damn rain earlier in the day, officer. I was caught in the slush in Montreal. I'm afraid it destroyed the first cast. It became much too wet. Took it off myself. We stopped in . . . Brockville?" He looked inquiringly at her, his body still pressing against hers. She was very soft, he suddenly realized. Very soft. And warm.

"Yes, dear . . . Brockville."

"Brockville. I put this one on myself. Pretty damn good job, if I do say. I've put a few thousand of these on other people, but never on myself. That was a task. I'm a doctor of orthopedics." He smiled sarcastically.

The officer nodded. The hand covering his gun unobtrusively popped off the safety strap. His thick lips moved slowly. "Would you happen to be carrying a gun, sir?"

"Of course not! You have laws against that. I must say, I wish I was, with all the trouble you Canadians are having." He paused and said, "I know what's happened: those motel rooms are wired with cameras. Someone was watching us. Am I right?"

"We'll search the car, if you don't mind," the Mountie declared, looking at them suspiciously.

"Of course I mind," Borikowski told him.

A glint of hazy sunlight sparkled from the edge of the Mountie's badge.

Lydia thought, You knew before they even pulled us over. That's why you threw the gun. Now I know how you've survived.

After a signal the backup officer joined them on Borikowski's side of the car.

They were instructed to get out of the car, one at a time, Lydia first.

The Mountie patted her down and, without being lascivious, spared her no contact. He turned her sideways and brushed over her chest and back simultaneously. His hand hit the lump at her crotch and without any hesitation she blushed and said, "My time of month."

The Mountie stood, nodding, but refused to look at her.

Borikowski thought, Nice touch.

The search took ten minutes. When they opened Borikowski's suitcase he said, "I still assume we were being watched. . . ." He had to steal their attention from the bag. He could not afford for them to inspect the bag closely. And if they began to . . . "You'll find a hair dryer in there. It's black. I used it to dry the cast. That's your weapon."

She thought, Nice touch.

The red-nosed Mountie studied the hair dryer. It did look remarkably like a pistol, and from a distance . . .

Borikowski sensed they were safe now. It was over.

A minute later they were back in the car. The Mountie said, "Everything seems to be in order, *mad'm, m'sieu.* I am sorry for any inconvenience."

"I don't appreciate my privacy being violated. If you have people at motels—snoops—I certainly hope you'll make them better informed. And what of my wife? How do I know whoever it was didn't watch my wife undress? What about that? I should sue. . . ."

"Be polite to the officer, Franz," she said, appropriately annoyed at her husband. "You're jumping to conclusions."

"If you're done drilling us, we'll be on our way," Borikowski told the officer.

The policeman returned the passports and looked Borikowski in the eye. "Sorry to have delayed you. Drive safely."

They drove off.

When they were well away she asked him, "How did you know?"

"I didn't. All I knew was that without that gun, we were as legal as the next couple."

"What about bullets?"

"Someplace they could never find them."

"We were lucky."

"Yes, and I hate the word."

She smiled. They were closer now. She told him, "Take the wheel. This thing's uncomfortable."

And he did.

12:37 P.M.
Washington, D.C.

Alone in a small and private conference room in the glossy new DeLaney Hotel in downtown Washington, D.C., Parker Lyell and Karen Kwang shook hands.

As she sat down he had a moment to study her beauty, and thought, I'll be damned. She *is* a classic.

He prepared himself for a kind of verbal gamesmanship comparable to hunting buffalo while hidden beneath a buffalo hide. He knew he would remember this conversation for a long, long time. Like it or not. It was always so when he admired his interviewee.

Lyell put his faith in body language and habits of speech, and as a result, knew some things about Ms. Kwang before either opened their mouths. She was a very closed person, ladling on charm or vinegar depending on who you were and what she needed. She was untrusting yet compassionate, self-conscious but bold. When she sat, her legs were crossed tightly; she chose to keep the pencil between her fingers at all times, and—he thought—she'll wave it around. Her eyes were little black vials of venom.

Although she lived in a sea of them, Karen Kwang was not enamored of occidentals. She assumed that most saw her first as a Chinese-American; second as a woman; third as a person; and last as a journalist. That didn't please her.

Lyell decided that Karen Kwang had the most sensual mouth he had ever seen in person. Bar none.

"Welcome to Washington, Ms. Kwang. I trust your flight was comfortable?"

"Yes. Thank you."

He had no intention of saying, "You are even more lovely than you appear on television." But it tumbled out of his mouth, ungracefully, and then shaded his cheeks scarlet.

"Thank you," she said, unmoved by his flattery, and very accustomed to these openings. You want to be on my good side? she wondered. Then get to the point.

"To get started, Miss Kwang—"

"You don't like what I'm saying about all this spy business, yes, I know, but let me tell you something, Mr. Lyell. If you expect to try and sweet-talk me out of this, you can pick your old-fashioned butt up and haul it out of here. This story happens to be hot, Mr. Lyell. And, I might add, this story is accurate! Anything else you may wish to say might be better said through counsel. Now, I don't know about government men, but this Chinese bitch is in a big hurry, and she doesn't particularly care for her itinerary to be interrupted for an Old Glory pep talk. Clear?" She removed her tape recorder from her purse. "Choose your words carefully, sir." She depressed the two buttons and the red light sparkled. "Because you, Mr. Lyell, will be on this evening's news."

"Now really, Miss Kwang, there's no need—"

"Anything else, Mr. Lyell?"

He reached for the tape recorder, but she snatched it away. "Damn it, Miss Kwang," Lyell exploded, "there are people's *lives* at stake here; there is national security; and you and this network are *compromising* our effectiveness."

"First Amen—"

"—dment, yes, yes, yes. The familiar war cry of the oppressed correspondent, and I have no intention, *we* have no intention, of limiting anyone's Constitutional rights. I come here as a liaison between your government and you, not telling you to stop . . . I'm *asking*, don't you see that? I need your *help!*" He was red in the face now and much too surprised by his own outlandish behavior to look at her, or say any more. He hoped she would just storm out and leave him be, but to his surprise, she did not.

She preached: "The People—with a capital *P*—have a right to know what's going on, Mr. Lyell. And until they put barbed wire all along coasts and close every airport and form a government press agency—which, believe me, sometimes looks not too far away—some of *us* are going to keep trying to maintain an objective inside view of *you*. Period. Exclamation point! Sold by the column inch or edited onto magnetic tape, that's what *we do*, and until you shut down the presses and pull the plug, we're going to keep on doing it! You think we're the only ones running with this story? You think we're hitting with low blows? Not true! Not true! This story was picked up by the wire services"—she drummed her long, hard nails against the table—"and ran in a few hundred newspapers. Talk to them. I'll tell you what you can tell your bosses . . . you can tell them that if they don't want espionage in the news, then they should either do less of it, or do it better." That said, she stood abruptly and shoved out her hand, grabbed for his, gave one brief shake to it, and offered sarcastically, "Good day," along with a ten-cent smile in million-dollar lips. She fled quickly, pulling the door closed behind.

"Fuck off!" Lyell barked, knowing no one could hear. On his pad were two words written in thick block printing: NO WAY.

1:06 P.M.
Montreal, Canada

Andy jogged down the sidewalk, dodging people who did not move out of his way. He finally saw the park he had been searching for, crossed with the light, and kicked out. Within minutes he felt the first tingling sensation of his pores opening and he smiled, happy to be out, happy to be away from Chevy Chase, happy for the first time in ages.

He had tired of writing. And rewriting. And rewriting. It had been a terrible life—the last seventeen months.

He thought, Next time they try that, I'll quit altogether. They'll give me a new name, a new home, and a new life. And although I fear even the thought of retirement—of a new identity and new friends, and worse yet, saying a silent farewell to all those I have known and allowing them to believe I'm dead—I know now it is far better than the nonexistent life I have just left.

His concentration was not on his running but instead

on the computerized chessboard back in his room. He had left it to make up its mind—for this particular model took as much as thirty minutes to make a move in the advanced mode—in what could be the final moments of the game. Although he would have preferred a match with Parker Lyell, the machine would keep his senses sharp and make him all the more difficult to beat upon his return. So now, he considered the four or five moves available to the electronic board, and tried to establish his own response given the different possibilities. . . .

Molière, concerned with other possibilities, had sent over a video recorder and tape by special messenger only an hour ago. Andy had sat in his luxurious hotel suite and had viewed a five-minute tape of Karen Kwang's "Hot Spot" several times.

Try as he might to keep his mind on the imagined chess scenario, Andy kept seeing Kwang standing on a bridge that overlooked the city and kept hearing her report, and became disturbed at the idea of a single reporter compromising an assignment. The woman needed silencing, and as far as he was concerned, the sooner the better.

"Federal agent" indeed! She could have at least called me an "intelligence expert." Baah! She must be stopped before she gets in the way.

He rounded a turn and saw the lighted cross above the city, and lengthened his strides.

Anticipation is cruel, he thought, as cruel as fulfillment sometimes is. He hummed the words to a popular rock song, singing the melody silently inside his head:

> *And if you wanna learn to swim*
> *You've got to jump in the water.*
> *It's the only way you ever learn.*

Then he thought, But what if the water's too deep? What if you drown? That's a hell of way to learn a lesson!

He finished the nine miles, still singing the song, and returned to the hotel.

2:45 P.M.

As Andy was coming out of the shower the phone rang. He answered it, "Here."

The voice of Terry Stone said, "Renegotiate." The line went dead.

Andy dressed and found a pay phone in the lobby and made the necessary call, complete with an introductory code. The room phones patched through a switchboard, and thus were considered unsafe. A pay phone was much more difficult to tap. He reached a United States 800 number and was put on hold. Then he dialed another six-digit number—while still on hold—and the line crackled. Andy heard the familiar buzz in the background. Stone's voice said, "Scrambled. Maintain 'soft code.' Anything to report?"

"We don't have much." Andy felt his damp back. He had not had time to towel off. People mingled in the lobby of the hotel.

"We do now. The top dam broke." The Executive Code has been broken. "A flower has been intercepted. Our friends have your cargo." A woman is involved. KGB Canada—Rhinestone—knows about the scratch on the suitcase.

"Impossible. I delivered the cargo only this morning."

"We're bailing." There is a leak somewhere. We are trying to seal it. Then Stone repeated, "A flower, eh?"

"I don't believe that—"

"Hear me out."

"Yes."

"He's aborted and gone to a contingency—"

"—Yes—"

84

"—Which may include a flower. The flower may be delivered, eh?"

Stone was implying that a woman was traveling with Borikowski—flowers—and that she might be checking in on a regular basis to a headquarters—delivered.

Andy was unsure why Stone insisted on being so cryptic. Scrambled calls were usually extremely safe. There was something or someone Stone did not trust.

"Your end?" Stone asked.

"Not much to report. I may pay a visit this afternoon to someone who may have seen our friend. Transportation is being arranged."

"We used tracing paper to draw a *W*." Andy knew the *W* meant WEST, and assumed the oblique reference to tracing paper had something to do with phone traces.

To Andy, WEST meant Detroit, a city known in intelligence circles as the Passageway.

And Detroit meant Mari Dansforth.

"Soft is not easy," Andy said, implying he wasn't absolutely certain of the message.

"A *W*."

"Yes, I got that."

"I see. Good. By the way . . . I hit the jackpot. Do you copy?"

"Jackpot."

"Yes."

The line went dead.

Jackpot: The mole wanted a meeting.

But he was not concerned with moles, or broken codes. Andy was thinking about Detroit. About Mari. Why did just the mention of her name bother him? Why had it ended the way it had ended, full of pain and distrust?

Now he saw Mari's face in his mind's eye, her funny little ears, her speckled eye. He could feel her heartbeat against his chest. He could taste her. . . .

Why didn't I give her a chance to explain? Even

85

though *she* hurt *me*, I should have been more kind. I threw her to the dogs. I was wrong. She was wrong. And I blamed her without hearing the reason. Wrong. Wrong. Wrong. But perhaps that's why I still have the hook set in my lip; why I'm still dragged along by the monofilament of memory and the reel of desire.

Damn you, Mari. I think I still love you.

3:00 P.M.

Andy followed Stone's orders to the letter, and at exactly three o'clock the pay phone began ringing. He counted off the four rings, picked it up and hung up. At half-past the hour, a private taxi pulled up next to the booth and a chilled Andy Clayton climbed in. The driver wore a blue knit cap. Andy talked to the back of a head.

"New Holland, please."

The cabbie nodded and the car sped off into light traffic and slush, spraying several parked cars and one very annoyed pedestrian.

Andy, accustomed to dealing with informants—moles —sat back and waited until the man felt like talking. To Andy, moles were a strange breed of human, who for some reason found the high risk of playing a traitor a fun game. A few had personal reasons for their double dealing, a justification that usually came in the excuse of a dead friend or relative, and, of course, on this level Andy could empathize.

His heart still hurt for Duncan.

Each of us has our own contrived reasons for being here, thought Andy. Each a story to hold onto, an anchor to give us roots upon unstable ground, a created importance that is no more real than anything else. And we live in this world of make-believe, of self-importance, where each and every act is given significance and a special, tiny space in our brain so that we may retrieve it someday and study it, as if this too held some real importance.

The driver spoke English, slowly and in a low voice. His head remained immobile and his shoulders only moved when he turned the wheel, and then the whole car would move too, and both men would lean to one side; and when the car straightened out, they straightened out. "The woman at Dorval last night was killed by *Dragonfly*. You know of this agent?"

"Yes."

"He is traveling with a woman. Her name, I don't know. Yet. I do have a description. She is young and quite beautiful. She is in possession of many passports and all the right papers and she will be quite difficult to trace. Still, her beauty sets her apart from others. She has almond eyes. Beautiful eyes. Chocolate. Shaped like Sophia Loren's. You can't miss her. If you can find her."

"Anything else?" Andy asked, somewhat amazed Borikowski would travel with a partner.

"Yes. Let me speak."

"Go ahead."

"He is on orders. If his cover is blown, if he encounters a problem like the one last night, he is to use this woman. She is a cosmetologist. She's responsible for altering his identities and will travel as his partner for as long as he deems necessary. Understand? The DS is well aware that in your files he is listed as a 'solo.' She is there to help hide him. You won't be looking for two of them, for a couple. At least, that is what they think."

"Interesting."

"Shut up and let me talk. I don't have much time."

Now Andy was angry.

"He will leave her in Detroit, if all goes smoothly. He will be on his own again—"

"Detroit? You're certain it's Detroit?"

"Absolutely. Now listen! You won't find him, if he does

this. He has at least five separate identities that he can travel under, and you know how good an actor he is—if you know anything at all. I think I may be able to obtain a few of his fictitious names, but it will take some time. Meanwhile, you must find a way to blow his cover, or at least, make him believe his cover is blown. This will force him to stay with this woman. He is on orders to do so. This much I know! She is your only hope of finding him. You understand?"

"Yes." And Andy knew this man was right. Alone, Borikowski would be next to impossible to locate. Unknowingly, by trying to hide him, the DS had set their own trap with a pretty woman—an almond-eyed woman.

"She has dark hair. But of course, they could always change her looks. I don't know all that much. I'm working on it. She has brown eyes, like I said. Medium height. But listen, they have ears in Washington. Many. I would advise you not to tell anyone about her just yet. They are bound to overhear it—especially at Central—and that would blow her, and they'd go to another contingency, and I have no idea what this might mean." He turned onto a busy street and stopped at a light and said nothing, as if someone might read his lips through the glass. Andy sat back and waited for the light to change. The gray clouds overhead swirled and twisted and wrestled with the cold air. The driver's hair was dark brown and trimmed short. A car pulled alongside with the radio up loud. The driver of this car was rocking his head to the apparent beat of the music, silently keeping time and mouthing the words as the pulse of the bass guitar could be felt inside the cab. Then the light changed and the taxi moved on. "So, you see, it is better if you give me some time and you stick to trying to blow *Dragonfly*'s cover. I don't know his operation yet. I may be able to get something. I can't tell how much others know, and unless they know, there is no way I can know. We will have to wait.

What I have heard is that he is headed west. I don't *know* that. Only words. It could be wrong. But this woman. I'm quite sure that is right. Give me time. I'll be back in contact as soon as I learn anything. Now get out, and pay me something. Tell me to keep the change. But don't look at my face. You look at me, and you'll never meet me again."

It was then that Andy noticed that the rearview mirror was angled down to show the front seat, not the man's face, and he realized he knew only the back of this man's head.

The taxi jerked to a stop and Andy climbed back out and followed the man's instructions.

When the cab pulled away, it splashed his pants with brown muck. To play the part, he hollered at the cab, only to realize he was not playing a part at all. "Go to hell, asshole!"

4:13 P.M.

"Scrambled," Stone finally said.

Andy was back at the same pay phone in the lobby of the hotel. "Are we 'soft'?"

"No, we're fine."

Andy relaxed. He didn't like speaking in code. Still he kept an eye on the lobby and other pay phones nearby. "We must blow his cover as a solo. He's on orders to keep her along if we do. I have a description of her, but request to keep it to myself. The word is that you are full of leaks down there."

"Mail the description to me in an overnight letter. I'll lock it up and won't open it unless I have to."

"I understand. No problem."

Stone then asked, "Any ideas?"

"If he's blown to the press, he'll keep her along."

"Yes, we'll give it a try."

"Say hello to Karen for me," Andy said.

"Ah, yes! A wonderful thought."

The line went dead.

6:05 P.M.
Detroit, Michigan

The Buick pulled up behind a long line of cars, with Borikowski behind the wheel. The traffic was bottle-necked by the Customs checkpoints, and many drivers seemed unduly annoyed with the delay. On the dashboard, Borikowski had both passports; and Lydia, next to him, leaned against the door, head slumped as if asleep.

Borikowski could finally see that the delay was being caused by trunks being opened and luggage being checked. But when Lydia had called in to Rhinestone, four hours ago, she had been warned that the border patrols might be looking for Borikowski's scratched bag. Thus alerted, Borikowski had dropped the Audi off at a garage in Dunport, leaving it for "repairs." Lydia had rented a shiny new Buick, and at a highway rest stop had given Borikowski a new face. His papers now identified him as Peter Trover of Westinghouse Corporation, Detroit. The cut in his suitcase had been repaired using an epoxy purchased at a Sears in Dunport. The color had been changed by red spray paint. Lydia had done a perfect job with the paint, and Borikowski had no concern that the suitcase might identify him. He mentally reviewed Peter Trover's history, so that he might not slip up, and felt confident in his preparations.

Nearly ten minutes later, two officials waited as Borikowski rolled down his window. He supplied them with the documents, making no attempt at idle conversation.

He handed over a key and waited for the trunk to be searched, as his eyes kept careful watch between two police cars that were parked on the United States side, and his rearview mirror, which showed only the open trunk. The spare key was in the palm of his hand.

He was unsure what he might do if there were additional problems, but Lydia's revolver was taped to the seat beneath him, and between it and the key in hand, he felt well prepared.

As it turned out, moments later, he and Lydia were waved through with a polite smile from a gaunt, uniformed man.

When they were well away from the checkpoint, Borikowski turned to Lydia and said, "We have a couple of hours to kill. Where would you like to eat?"

"Someplace Italian. I love Italian food."

7:05 P.M.
Washington, D.C.

The office smelled like coffee. Stone looked across the cup's rim at Parker Lyell's red hair, which nearly matched the color of the leather chair. Lyell's hands were folded across the notebook on his lap; his watch crystal caught the overhead ceiling light, glinting. Stone said, "She won't help us?"

"No, sir. I would recommend we don't approach her that way. She's convinced she's on a hot story. If we try and woo her over, she'll laugh in our faces and probably tell her audience what we're up to, and that would tip our hand."

"Have you thought about using the White House press secretary's office?" Stone asked.

"Yes, but as you pointed out, it won't do us any good if only one or two newspapers go with the story. We have to

91

have them *all*. And Kwang is the front runner on this. She's the main source. It could backfire on us. . . ."

"We're in a bit of a pickle, eh?"

Lyell shook his head. Although the top sheet had been removed from his notepad, there still remained the impression left by the words, "No Way." He said, off the top of his head, "If you want a lady like Karen Kwang, you're going to have to trick her."

Stone looked up. "Yes. Trick her, eh?"

Lyell sat forward in his chair and looked intently at Stone. "We could try. She might fall for it. Of course she'll need two sources. We couldn't be certain who she'd turn to for the second source. . . . We would need someone to confirm."

Stone pulled a piece of paper from a tidy stack. He put on reading glasses and said, "There's this Robert Goglan. She had breakfast with him this morning in Montreal. He's with the Security Service."

"You're having her followed?" Lyell gasped.

"Pardon my bluntness, but what I do and don't do is my business. Mine alone."

Lyell sat up straight. "My apologies, sir."

Stone continued. "When *anyone* is suddenly privy to classified information, it's my responsibility to—"

"I understand completely."

Stone removed the glasses. "As I was saying, this Goglan is someone she might turn to for confirmation. He's Molière's vice-deputy in the Security Service."

"What if her first source were to indicate that only one or two American Intelligence officers knew about this, but in the Security Service—"

"It was common knowlege."

"Exactly."

"Yes. I like that. Then we could lean her toward Goglan. Besides, that's close to the truth. There would be very few who could verify this for her. Most would say they know nothing; because they don't."

"But will Goglan go along?"

Stone toyed with the stem of his glasses. "What the hell would you do, if your job was on the line?"

7:12 P.M.

Minutes later, Lyell was gone and Daniels sat in his place. The chair was still warm, and that seemed to make Chris Daniels nervous.

"I've chosen you to do a very important job for me."

Daniels blinked once and pushed his glasses up his nose.

Stone continued. "As an operative."

"An operative!?"

"Yes."

"But do you think I'm—"

"Yes. I do. I want the person to be nervous and frightened, and I think you will be. Anyone else would be acting. Besides, there's no one else I trust to do the job just exactly as I want it done."

"I'm honored."

"It's not dangerous."

Daniels exhaled and some color returned to his face, and Stone knew he had said the right words.

"It's tricky, Chris. It has to be done just right."

"I understand. May I inquire as to the nature of this 'job'?"

8:20 P.M.
Memphis, Tennessee

She was dragging a razor carefully down her tawny legs, her Asian eyes in full concentration. She completed a stroke and peered through the bath water at her thigh,

93

then at her unnaturally thick wedge of pubic hair, which she considered a sign of sexual prowess. She kicked her leg in the water to clean it, soaped up a spot on her thigh, and worked delicately with the razor again, afraid of nicking herself. She forgot about her new story for the first time in days and thought only of the invitation she had received to a nine-thirty dinner this evening with Stony Bergstrom, owner of a competing network, aware of his reputation as a ladies' man and wondering if he would dare make a pass—and finally, how she should react. Secretly, inside, she hoped he would.

It's all falling neatly into place for me, she thought. The awards, the hot news, the luck, even the rag newspapers with all their salacious innuendoes about my promiscuity. Now this story, pieces fitting nicely, no denials, large shares—and even an invitation to dine with Stony Bergstrom! Here I am shaving my legs in what is essentially fifty gallons of jasmine tea with floating rose petals, and thinking about how one seduces a man twice one's age. Oh how I'd like a major network anchor job, another three hundred grand a year, and six weeks' vacation.

She soaped up the other leg and began shaving, wishing she hadn't left the rum and orange juice by the sink and therefore out of reach. She knew how rum sweetened her breath and made her kisses divine. She had been told a hundred times.

That's when the phone rang.

She stood up, her breasts, stomach, and legs pink from the heat of the water, and scurried across the dark blue bathroom tile, watching her small "boobs"—as she called them—in the full-length mirror as they bounced slightly with her steps. She scooped the drink off the counter, and dripped her way into her bedroom, a large open space with a thin mattress on the floor and a mirror on both the far wall and the ceiling. A low lamp sat alongside the futon, and next to it several books and a princess phone. On the far wall, next to the mirror, hung a lovely Japanese scroll that depicted, in multicolored stitching, a waterfall and a single woman sitting on a rock, holding a parasol.

"Hello?"

The voice was unusually high for a male—a young man. And it seemed almost as if an electronic device of some sort was being used to make it so.

In fact, a device *was* being used. But it only added some fuzz. It had nothing to do with the falsetto quality.

"Ms. Kwang?"

"Speaking." She looked across to the mirror, lifted her legs straight out in front of her, and, holding them off the ground, patted her tight stomach with her right hand. Water dripped off her heel. She pulled a pillow under her bottom to catch all the wet in an effort to keep the futon dry.

"I have something for you, Ms. Kwang. It concerns your most recent 'Hot Spot.' I love you, Ms. Kwang. I think you're the most beautiful woman in the world." Daniels turned red on the other end, but he was reading the words that Terry Stone had written down and he was doing a fine job of it. "This is what you've been looking for."

"Who is this?"

"You can't be serious. I work in a division of the American Intelligence community. That is all you need to know. This is reliable information, as I'm certain you will see when you receive it."

"Listen, buddy. Who the hell gave you this number? Is this some sort of joke?"

"You arrived home this evening at 6:29 after purchasing bath soap at a drug store three blocks from where you live."

Karen Kwang couldn't get any words out. She was horrified. That was exactly right.

The voice said, "You still think this is a joke?"

"I'm being followed?"

"I would be extremely careful if I were you, Ms. Kwang. We tried to warn you. You are playing in the major leagues. Not like that women's softball team you play on."

"Oh my God! Who is this? What the fuck's going on here?"

"I have sent you a package. In this package is a claim ticket to the Longworth Hotel's coat room. Go to the hotel, Ms. Kwang. There is a silk jacket there for you. You like silk, don't you, Ms. Kwang? Sewn into the coat is the information you are looking for."

Karen saw herself in the mirror. She was tucked into a ball, one arm grasping her knees against her chest, and all across her skin were goosebumps. She was terrified.

Stone, listening in on an extension, nodded for Daniels to continue.

"Very few Americans can confirm this information, Ms. Kwang. You are welcome to try whomever you like. The Security Service is another story. I gleaned this information from them. Do you understand?"

"W—w—what?" She wasn't seeing clearly now. She took hold of the drink and chugged the remainder and then took three deeps breaths. "What are you saying?"

"I love you, Ms. Kwang. If you like this, I can do it again sometime."

Chris Daniels hung up.

Terry Stone smiled.

Karen Kwang had gulped her drink too quickly. She felt sick. Then the buzzer rang, and the apartment house's doorman told her a package had arrived.

She mixed herself another drink. Stiff. She drank it even more quickly.

"You really think that'll work?"

"You were brilliant."

Daniels blushed.

"Any woman who looks as nice as she does will allow her own vanity to be reason enough for anything. Trust me. I know what I'm doing."

"And you're sure it's all set?"

"Yes. I received confirmation ten minutes ago. They sent the photos and the information electronically, and they're all in place. Don't worry, Chris. We fooled her. She'll take it hook, line, and sinker."

"I'm not so sure I was convincing."

"Oh, yes. You were convincing. I'd bet she's already on her way."

And she was.

8:44 P.M.
Washington, D.C.

Chris Daniels had left to send someone else out for chicken-in-a-bucket. Both he and Stone were famished.

The intercom's pink light flashed at Stone, indicating another call. He punched a finger-worn button, wishing his anonymous offices were more modern.

Janie's voice sounded so pleasant that Stone never even suspected he had kept her from a dinner date. "Dr. Bonner, line four."

Stone punched line four, remembering to hold the receiver an inch from his ear. Clyde Bonner had a habit of yelling into phones.

"Hello, Clyde," he said in a somber tone. "I certainly hope you're not pestering me about the budget, already. I appreciate your breaking the Executive Code; but you know my hands are tied on this one. We won't know about the budget for another week or so."

"I know that, Terry. Not really. Though the reason I'm

calling may give you some more ammo to help us win said same."

"Go on."

"I have a de-coded intercept. Message reads: 'RE-LAY—TARGET CONFIRMED,' unquote. Thought you should know about th—"

"Origin?"

"Amtrak station, downtown Boston."

"Destination?"

"CROWS NEST."

Stone unlocked his bottom desk drawer with two keys and slid it open, thumbing through the file headings and selecting one. He kicked the drawer shut with shiny, though well-worn, shoes and locked it. He read from the file, pivoted in his large chair, phone wire following, and typed an alpha-numeric code into his terminal keyboard.

He began to read. "You said relay?"

"Yeah."

"Nothing yet?"

"No. When they relay it, I'll let you know."

"Boston?" Stone asked.

"How about that?"

"I was hoping for something from Detroit."

"Nothing yet—to or from—that I've seen."

"I want to know where that message is relayed to, Clyde."

"Not to fret, Terry."

"I'll be waiting. Thank you, Clyde."

8:51 P.M.
Detroit, Michigan

At ten of nine a phone company van pulled to a stop in back of the Detroit Sheraton. The driver, a round-faced man in his thirties, got out, walked around to the side door, and slid it open. The leather tool belt lay in a coiled heap on the floor beneath a series of bolted steel shelves and adjacent to the slowly heaving chest of the man who was actually on Michigan Bell's payroll. This round-faced man was not. He, however, controlled the situation now: he had the leather belt; he had the cap on his head with the stenciled logo across its front; he had the tool chest. Complaints about the hotel's phone system had been carefully seeded to assure a repairman would be called in—the rest was up to this man. He pushed the button outside the service entrance and was admitted without question, ushered to a service elevator, and directed to the door of the room marked DO NOT ENTER, an area that housed communications and support equipment for the four-hundred-plus rooms and suites.

It was too easy, far too easy.

The impostor silently nodded his thanks and entered the spacious area, quickly descending stairs that led to the communications subfloor. He passed racks of sophisticated electronics. The last few rows contained the phone pairs for each room. There seemed to be thousands of them.

The man expertly switched the incoming pairs of room 314 with those of room 414, glanced at his watch, and sat down onto the cold floor, fingers nervously tapping on his knee. His full attention was riveted to the Motorola pager clipped to his breast pocket. His job half over, he waited for the pager to signal him. The minutes suddenly felt like hours.

9:01 P.M.
Washington, D.C.

The brass captain's clock ticked insistently, impervious to Terry Stone's impatience. "I want every detail of every VIP itinerary you can lay your hands on. No! Of course I know the Pope is heading to Boston, but I'm talking about the others—the ones we aren't thinking about! Check the Pentagon, the State Department. We're overlooking someone, and I want to know *who*," he barked. He stared at the two other receivers lying on top of his green blotter, forgetting which belonged to whom—disgusted with old age. The buzzer and light on his intercom went on and off sporadically. He tripped the button.

Janie's thinned voice announced, "*Baker2*, line three, scrambled."

Stone hung up the two receivers, believing this the more important. "Scrambled."

"Here." Andy stood in a side hallway at one of many pay phones that lined the walls.

"Detroit?"

"Yes."

"We have you booked on a commercial flight for Boston at twenty-three hundred tonight. I think his target is in Boston. Repeat, Boston. Confirmation in a few more minutes. We'll place I-force on alert. I'll contact you as soon as I've heard."

"Room six-twenty-one."

"I'll give you to Janie. She'll take the details," Stone said, punching a button and leaving instructions with his secretary.

He leaned back in the black, overstuffed chair and closed his tired eyes, wondering if, in fact, Clyde Bonner and the NSA's computers would be able to locate the destination of a phone call that was to be made at exactly 9:05 P.M. EST.

He assumed Leonid Borikowski would be on the other end of that call.

And at the moment, Leonid Borikowski was all that mattered.

The clerk behind the registration desk spoke politely to the man paying in cash. He handed Borikowski the key to 414 and motioned for a bellman. Borikowski declined assistance. "It's only the one bag. I'm fine. Could you please check to see if any mail was forwarded for me?"

There was a thick envelope addressed to Mr. Peter Trover. The clerk handed it to Borikowski, who thanked the man and then entered an empty elevator. Inside the envelope were several folded pages of single-spaced typing. Taped inside of this was a copy of a key to room 313. There was no message in the letter; it rambled on about a sales problem at Westinghouse.

The elevator stopped at the third floor.

Less than a minute later, Borikowski swung open the door to 314, entered, and closed it behind himself, simultaneously checking his watch.

In one minute and seven seconds, he hoped to hear Rhinestone's confirmation.

Janie's voice, heard over Terry Stone's intercom, had only begun the name, "Clyd—" when he switched her off and grabbed for the receiver to his private NSA hot-line. "Go!"

Clyde Bonner spat out his words professionally fast. "A triple relay: first to Del Ray Beach, Florida; second from Florida to Flint, Michigan; last was from Flint, Michigan to Detroit, Michigan. Final destination: the Detroit Sheraton. The caller asked for room four-fourteen—repeat,

101

four-one-four. Connection was secured and tranmission took place. Same message, 'TARGET CONFIRMED.'"

Stone said, "Got it!" and hung up. He hit a button, a light flashed, and he pushed another button on top of a speaker phone in the middle of his desk. "Janie, it's Detroit. Notify Parker Lyell immediately. I want him in Detroit."

"Affirmative," she replied.

He hoisted a receiver to his ear. "Go."

"Here," Andy responded.

"Room four-fourteen, Detroit Sheraton. Repeat, four-one-four."

Silence.

Andy Clayton had already hung up.

9:06 P.M.
Detroit, Michigan

In the sub-basement the pager sounded on the leather belt of the impostor. Two beeps escaped before he shut it off. The man grabbed his screwdriver, knowing he had little time to complete his work.

9:32 P.M.

Andy Clayton and Agent Hugh Long were standing side by side, facing the hotel. Long had been a boxer in the Navy and looked it. Andy wrapped both hands around the styrofoam coffee cup to warm them. As both men spoke, blue mist fled from their lips.

Andy asked, "Well?"

"They sealed it up."

"And?"

"Rooms four-one-four and three-one-four were both

registered to the same man, a Mr. Peter Trover." Long shook his head. "Both empty."

"A switch?"

"We checked the pairs. Everything is in order, but a maintenance man remembers letting a phone repairman in right around nine o'clock. Probably switched the incoming pairs."

"Probably."

"Do you want them to search it?"

"Are you kidding?"

"Hell no. We've done it on occasion."

"No," Andy said, disappointed. "We don't know who he is, or what he looks like. Forget it, Hugh. It's useless." Then, reconsidering, Andy asked, "How many guests?"

"Seven hundred and sixty-three."

"No," Andy affirmed.

Long shrugged. "Just a thought."

"What did they say at the desk?"

The two men crossed the street and continued walking. "The tie salesman convention has most of the rooms on nine, ten, and eleven. A writer's conference has the second floor. One hundred and five guests registered in the last ninety minutes . . . all writers."

"We would have arranged it the same way. Well, thanks for trying." Andy stopped walking and looked back at the huge hotel, which occupied most of the city block.

Long asked, "What if we'd found him?"

Andy looked curiously at the man. "We didn't," he said, thinking, I had it pictured. Borikowski holding a telephone, and me in the doorway of the hotel room, smiling—about to blow his head off.

10:55 P.M.

Leonid Borikowski answered the knock on 503 with a ten-dollar tip ready in his right hand. The waiter pushed the cart into the room, the white linen tablecloth brushing Borikowski's suit as it passed. A bottle of Ultra Brut was submerged in crushed ice and wrapped with a napkin of matching linen; and a copy of the check lay beneath the base of the cut-glass vase, which held six long-stemmed red roses and greenery. He signed the check and handed the waiter the ten. Borikowski shut the door after the waiter and went about opening the bottle.

Looking at his reflection in the champagne bucket, he was thankful to be alive and in good health and able to enjoy such extravagance.

Although he was taking chances by staying the night in a fancy hotel, by ordering champagne and maintaining a high profile, he was enjoying it immensely. He could not remember ever having done anything like this. Ever. And that, he supposed, was why his superiors had devised such a plan. Just when your opponent thinks he knows you well, change. Yes. Change.

Muffled by the closed bathroom door, he heard Lydia showering and he pictured her naked. He felt the twinges of an erection and chastised his adolescence.

He knew the type. She wanted a promotion, better clothes. He warned himself not to touch her, not to allow her to seduce him, if that was what she had in mind. It would only cause trouble. Still, he kept imagining her lathering herself with soap, thinking how nice it would be to feel even a moment's tenderness.

A few minutes later, the bathroom door opened and her long, lean, freshly scrubbed body stood glowing in the doorway. A steamy mist escaped from behind her. She had borrowed a white button-down shirt from him and was wearing it like an open robe. Beneath it she wore a thin white slip that revealed an ample amount of bosom. She had the firm, round breasts of a young woman. Her shoulders were very square, her posture perfect, her hair damp and somehow sensual. She was smiling, and her chest moved in and out, up and down, in great waves. Her eyes seemed half-asleep.

"Well? What do you think? Do I look like a bride to be?" she asked, knowing the answer, spinning on her toes like a model at the end of the ramp.

Borikowski was not going to address that question. He pressed with both thumbs and launched the cork. It hit the ceiling, then ricocheted off a lamp, rebounded off the edge of a chair, and looped in spiraling arcs until it died in the center of the red carpet. A breath of white mist escaped from the mouth of the bottle.

He poured.

She inspected the flowers, touching each casually with the red-painted nails of her long fingers. They drank. His eyes ran down her in such a way that she felt as if he had touched her most personal spots. She blushed and thought she might giggle.

It was just as she had hoped.

Borikowski caught himself staring and looked away, feeling his loins stirring.

He suggested they sit down.

"You are beautiful. Honestly. Drink up. Champagne must be consumed before a half hour passes."

"I didn't know that."

"Yes. That's what I've read. To tell you the truth I don't get the chance that often to find out. DS agents are not as privileged as KGB agen—"

"Not true. You should see my apartment. It is tiny. Bugs! Even rats! It's terrible."

"Are you spying on me?" he asked pointedly.

She had not expected such a question. "No. And I'm not KGB, I'm GRU."

"That's not what I was—"

"It's the truth!" she said, indignant.

"You're reporting."

"Why would they have me do that? That's ridiculous," she said, lying. "Who cares if you believe me?" She took a large swallow of champagne and he refilled both their glasses.

"But you're GRU; I'm DS. You're Russian; I'm Bulgarian. You *always* spy on the other agencies."

"Yes. I see what you mean," she offered, allowing him some ground. "Of course I will write a long report and someone in the Kremlin will no doubt read it and it will mention your code name. So yes, I see what you mean. So sorry."

He laughed and had to wipe off his lips. "So, I am right!"

"Yes." She returned his smile. "Oh! Wait just one minute! Lieutenant Sczlovlog asked me to bring you something," she said, standing quickly and allowing the slip to ride up her leg.

He watched her small derriere shift muscularly back and forth as she headed to the bathroom, hearing the unmistakable sound of slip against skin.

She returned in seconds, and handed him a bottle of the finest Russian vodka.

"My favorite."

She collected two hotel glasses and returned with them, allowing him to pour for her first. They toasted and drank the full two ounces he had poured for each of them. They drank another small amount and washed it down with champagne.

She reached over and kissed him.

He had somehow expected this, and they both smiled.

"My turn for the shower," he said awkwardly. "I feel as if I've been dipped in a vat of oil." He motioned toward the champagne. "Please, help yourself." Then he asked, "What about my face?"

"Go ahead and shower." She smiled. "Try and keep your face out of the water, if you can. It does not matter.

I will have to touch it up for you anyway. Do what you like."

He left the bathroom door ajar to keep the conversation going. He removed the wig, eyebrows, and thin strips of tucking tape. "I'm curious about you."

"And I about you," she replied honestly.

"Why did you quit the dancing?"

"I've told you. There never was any dancing. Only a dream of a dancer. There is some difference between the two."

He nodded, but of course she didn't see it.

"When I realized dancing was not possible for me . . . because of my father's wishes . . . I studied foreign language. I joined the theater group in makeup. I painted dancer's faces. Then my mother managed to place me in the GRU. She saved me."

"I'll be out in a minute," he told her, forgetting to close the door.

He stepped into the spray of hot water and felt nearly two days wash from his skin. Then he heard her pull the bathroom door shut, leaving him to his steam. Try as he did, he could not stop thinking about her body.

The vodka slowly melted though him and he experienced his first true moment of rest as he stood washing shampoo from his stubby scalp. This operation is going well now, he told himself, as he turned the water hotter still. I have a jump on the Americans and the advantage of surprise. Lydia did very well with the police, and I will recommend her—for whatever good it may do . . .

The shower door opened. Lydia had removed his shirt, leaving her in just the glossy slip. A smile played on her face, something between a smirk and the all-knowing smile of Buddha.

In the mirror he saw the long line of her back as she slid the slip up and over her head. His erection was immediate; he stood staring at her.

Her stomach was very flat, her young breasts firm and their dark nipples taut. She had extremely thin arms and a narrow waist, and sturdy, athletic legs. Her feet were long but slight, with delicate toes. Between her legs there was no pubic hair, just absolutely smooth-shaven skin. And for this reason she appeared both the temptress and the little girl.

Her eyes were hypnotic.

She stepped into the water with him, and he reached out for her. But she dropped slowly to her knees, kissing his chest, and below.

Her lips were soft and her knowledge great, and Borikowski had to take hold of the shower's spigot to keep from falling.

She led him down onto the bathroom floor so that he lay on top of her; they kissed passionately. She moved beneath him and helped him to enter her.

Borikowski arched his back and looked into her eyes. He returned her smile and whispered, "We're insane." She nodded, and then her eyes closed tightly, drops of water on her face like tears of joy.

They both smiled for a long time. And then she screamed.

11:05 P.M.
Columbus Grove, Ohio

Dr. Eric Stuhlberg was wearing his yarmulke when she let herself in through the front door. He was kneeling before the yahrzeit candle, saying kaddish. She could see him through the thin slit left between the sliding doors, his blue hair typically spun atop his head like cotton candy, his shoulders slightly drooped. No windows were open, it was so cold outside, but even so the candle's flame danced yellow atop the wax stick, and she wondered why it moved. Because this house is full of drafts, she thought to herself, chilled by seeing him so religious, knowing the ceremony was to honor her parents: his brother and his brother's wife, who were no longer. No doubt he was unhappy she had not joined him. She knew she should have; she felt bad about being late and now looking in on the privacy of his moment. She took off her coat and hung it by the door on a tall wrought-iron stand that hosted thin, bent, metal leaves.

He came out a few minutes later. He grew shorter every day, or so it seemed to her. "I heard you come in," he told her, looking into her eyes. It was obvious he had been crying. "You sit. In there." He pointed. "I will join you."

"I'm sor—"

"Hush. Don't try. Please. May they rest in peace. Sit. I'll join you." He took hold of the thick wooden banister and it creaked as he pulled on it for support, climbing the stairs as if it might be his last effort in life. He looked so old and frail, she thought, her eyes following his arduous climb. His feet were slippered, and he had on white socks.

When he joined her, he poured them both a glass of dark purple wine and they took small sips. She looked at the hundreds of lines in his face and wondered if they were from age, worry, or weather. Perhaps all three. Lord knows he'd seen his share of the world, of hate, of oppression, of genius, and was still alive to talk about it.

But he wasn't talking.

He was staring at the coffee table with his milky blue eyes and, for all she knew, was counting the lines in the wood to determine the tabletop's age. He was like that. Long trances. She supposed he was a genuis. Everyone who knew him called him a genius—the country's leading expert in DNA cell fusion. She called him "Uncle."

"Uncle, it's just that it makes me so sad."

"They were your parents. You owe them respect. You children . . . so quickly you think you grow independent. You pretend you are not Jewish."

"I'm not Jewish."

His eyes penetrated the dim light in the sitting room, cutting the air with a discontent as apparent as the gold ring upon his finger. "You are Jewish. You will always be Jewish. It is in your blood. Because you do not go to the temple means nothing. You cannot use that as an excuse. You should be ashamed."

"No God would let them die like that. I don't care what anyone says. Either there's no God, or he's lost his ability to . . . to think straight."

He rocked his head from side to side. "We will sing together now. And please, do not ever speak this way in front of me again. I have failed my brother. Yes. Do not shake your head, Ellen. He would curse me a thousand times if he had heard you say that. You must learn to respect the past, my dear. Not run from it. That is what my brother, your father, would have wanted. Instead you take your mother's name and cast away your father's religion. May you someday be forgiven."

"I love you, Uncle."

"I know."

"I mean it."

"I know you do. And I love you, child. You are my blood. You are my . . . We should sing. Enough of this. Let us sing."

"But it's late. I'm tired."

"Tomorrow night you're at that theater. Tonight you are here. We sing." Eric Stuhlberg closed his eyes and began to hum an ancient melody. Ellen Bauer joined him.

11:05 P.M.
Detroit, Michigan

In his hotel room, Andy answered the phone. "Here."

Stone's voice said, "Item one: I think we've blown his

cover. Item two: A message has been delivered here, for you. I don't like that. It reads, and I quote: 'We meet tonight at Perry Park, eleven-thirty. Nicky.' Unquote. Be extremely careful. It may have been seeded."

Terry Stone hung up.

Andy knew that Stone distrusted and disliked the former intelligence man, Nicholas Testler, mostly—Andy had decided—because the man had gone off on his own, disassociating himself from organized intelligence activities: "a stray," as such agents were often referred to. But to Andy, Testler was merely a man to keep a careful eye on while one gained sensitive information. Testler's information had always been accurate and timely. This, no one could argue.

Granted, Testler was something of an enigma. As an ideologue he favored democracies, and to Andy's knowledge, had never relayed misinformation to the West's intelligence community. His past involved the British, Canadians, Americans, and Koreans. Code names *Pidge*, *Widgeon*, *Black Dove* had all been his at one point. He had been assigned to the Soviet desk of the Canadian Security Service for nearly a decade, gaining a number of international intelligence contacts, before resigning and setting up business as an independant "consultant."

So now he worked for money instead of stars and stripes. A Terry Stone would never understand this; but to Andy, retirement made sense. Testler, like so many other agents, probably had a sizable nest egg stashed somewhere, and dabbled in espionage only rarely, perhaps to feel the excitement again, or to stack the deck against the "enemy"—whoever that was—or to pick up a thousand dollars' spending change, or to impress the ladies.

One point in Testler's favor was that the SIA needed help. Even the Old Man knew that.

The cab pulled to a stop two blocks from Perry Park. Andy pushed all these thoughts from his mind and focused on only this moment—right here, right now— excitement stealing him away like a narcotic, filling him with a dangerous sense of urgency.

It was moments like these that Andy lived for.

That Testler knew Andy was in Detroit meant the SIA leak had turned into a flood. It increased the risk factor. It increased Andy's enjoyment.

He entered Perry Park from Cheney Street because Warren Avenue was filled with noisy traffic. He tasted the sweet of the cold night air and felt a stinging numbness steal into the tips of his fingers. A brisk wind magnified the punishment. He pushed away the continual drone of cars, hearing only two distinct sounds: first, his own shoes clapping against the sidewalk; and second, nearby, a house door closing—the knocker gently thumping the wood.

He saw nothing but darkness ahead of him. A wraithlike silence closed in. He stepped forward slowly and at full attention. His pistol and attached silencer made a clumsy package at his side. Then, behind him, a car raced down Cheney Street and yelped to a stop.

Andy spun around. . . .

He ducked low and edged to his right until obscured by a small tree and hidden in its shadow.

The driver's window lowered, but the face within the car remained a silhouette. A voice shouted, "*Sour!* It's gone sour!" and Andy recognized it as Testler's. "Hurry! Get in!"

Andy looked around. "Shit!" he said, realizing his vulnerability.

"Hurry!" Testler encouraged again.

But instead, Andy ran deeper into the park. The only

light came from a few footlamps that followed the snaking sidewalk through the park.

He stooped, running a zigzag, and now heard everything: airplanes far overhead; cars close by; a ship's lonely hoot on Lake St. Clair. Faster, he ran through the park. Testler's car had rounded the block, and Andy watched it speed away.

Then, from the corner of his eye, he discerned movement. Yes! It was a man crouched low, over by the jungle gym. Andy withdrew his pistol, but before he even aimed, a stainless steel cartridge—a hypodermic dart—slammed into, and lodged in, the bark of the tree next to him. The distraction allowed his target to duck behind a cement hippopotamus and disappear.

Then, from behind him, he heard the clicking of metal as a rifle was being reloaded.

Up ahead a middle-aged couple appeared at the edge of the park, walking two leashed German shepherds—Andy assumed that the door he had heard close belonged to these two. The couple saw him coming, for they both stopped short and the dogs strained against their leashes.

"Hold!" barked the husband, confused.

"Attack!" shouted his wife, suddenly afraid and anxious to see the dogs work. She dropped her leash and one German shepherd bounded toward Andy, who yelled, "No! Federal agent!"

"Hold!" the husband reaffirmed, and the dog skidded to a stop.

Then Andy cut sharply to his left, and as he did, the next dart missed him and embedded in the woman's chest. She fell to the path without so much as a word, and her husband was unable to break her fall.

"Attack!" the husband shouted, jerking his arm in a line toward the darkness and away from Andy, who continued to run toward the park's edge.

Both dogs raced into the darkness.

The man who had hid behind the hippopotamus stood and fled.

As Andy jumped the park's low stone wall, he heard one of the dogs whine, followed by a painful human scream; and as he glanced over his shoulder he saw the husband holding his wife's head off the ground as she lay in the slush-covered grass.

Then a loud gunshot report slapped the air—and another—and the barking ceased.

Saturday, November 22

12:01 A.M.
Detroit, Michigan

The city had headed to bed. Thirty minutes ago the streets had been chaotic; now they were spotted with an occasional taxi cruising in search of a fare. Three such cabs had pulled alongside of Andy, but he had shook his head and continued to walk. His nerves had settled down only a few minutes ago. Until then he had been reliving the incident repeatedly.

His first suspicions had fallen on Testler. It had been proven time and time again that every agent had his or her price. For some it was money; others, travel; still others, the promise of enduring notoriety.

Of course, Testler could argue that he had tried to rescue Andy, but that could also be seen as nothing more than a ruse to establish Testler's innocence, in hopes that if the attack failed—as it had—then the same bait might be used again. And perhaps the second time, the fish would be caught.

The alternative scenario involved either a phone tap—unlikely given the precautions taken—or surveillance. For Andy, this meant avoiding the hotel. To him, drug darts were almost more frightening than bullets because they were used rarely, and only when the opposition intended to try to turn or double an agent. Of all his fears, captivity and torture were the most grave.

The only other situation he could construct to account for the two men at the park was that Testler had been either bugged or followed. But he refused to believe that either the KGB, GRU, or most certainly, the Bulgarian DS, was capable of such long-range planning and foresight.

Then his refusal to believe changed to doubt; his doubt fizzled away, and he didn't know what to think.

So he went back to thinking about Mari . . . and whether he should or shouldn't.

An all-night gas station had a pay phone and a directory with its pages still intact. She was listed in the city's white pages under M. J. Dansforth. He dialed her apartment, but no one answered. So he decided to walk to the address and make his decision then and there. . . .

He walked beneath the overpass, a cobweb of highways to his right and left, Wayne State University trapped between. By all calculations, he was in his sixth mile and had not far to go. The highway noise was deafening and proved that not everyone was asleep. He passed signs for the Edsel Ford Freeway and the Chrysler Freeway and the John Lodge Freeway and the Detroit Industrial Freeway, all within the same two blocks. The motor city was living up to its name.

Then, for some reason, he started thinking about that night again.

She was posed on the other side of the chessboard at his house, wrapped in his seersucker robe, her leg bent and cast over the arm of the chair.

"You're beautiful," he told her.

She lowered her eyes. "You said that last night when we were making love. It was very nice."

She moved a chess piece, but Andy didn't see. She had triggered some vivid images.

God, could she make love.

"Your move," he explained gently, not wanting to rush her.

She laughed. "I already moved." She pointed to a pawn. "Here, from here."

Andy slid a bishop across the board and knew her next move would take a while.

He watched her study the board, watched her ankle rocking back and forth, watched the muscles of her leg flex. A deep black voice sang from the room's speakers, "This must be love!"

He excused himself and disappeared into the kitchen. When he returned, a red ribbon protruded from his pocket. He stoked the fire. She looked up from the chessboard and, upon seeing the gift, exclaimed, "Andy!"

"From Andy to Mari. All my love." He handed her the package.

"'Can't buy me love,' Drew," she said, using his nickname and quoting the Beatles.

"I've been a distant stranger lately." He paused, because her ankle stopped rocking and broke his thought.

"Guilty." She attempted a forgiving smile, but failed.

He then admitted reservedly, "Duncan, again. I apologize."

"Accepted." And now her smile sparkled. She thought, You see. I'm learning. She told him, "I'm going to open this in bed. Enough of this game. Hurry up." She pulled herself up out of the chair, the falling robe robbing Andy of a glimpse of her leg, and left.

"Andy?" she inquired from the bedroom.

As a lover, Mari was neither innocent nor ignorant. She was experienced, mature, and passionate. Just her tone of voice excited him.

He ducked through the doorway into the bedroom. She was snug in bed, moonlight etching the blankets through the delicate drapes. She managed to get the top

119

off the tiny box, and then lifted the cotton out. "Andy . . ." she gasped, seeing the ring.

"This one's for fun . . . but maybe one of these days—"

"Shhh, no promises, Andy. Remember?" She reached for his hand. "Only hopes." She took his hand and buried it in kisses. "Gifts or no gifts, I do love you."

Andy smelled the cognac on her breath and wondered how much she had had to drink. He could never quite tell.

She lay propped against a pillow, toying with the ring, which was now on her finger. She said, "A diamond and two small emeralds. That's good luck, you know."

"I didn't know."

"Yes, well, it is. It's a very nice present."

"You're the one, Mari. For me, you're it."

She teased, "What is this? A game of tag?"

"Could be," he replied, crawling onto the bed.

She softly touched his forehead. "There. I tagged you. You're *it* now. Why don't you climb in here and tag me back?"

He took off his clothes, slipped between the covers, and pulled against her warm body. He touched her where she liked to be touched, and kissed her where she liked to be kissed, and before long she began to purr happiness.

Mari liked to be kissed.

Then she moved beneath him like a gentle wave; and for a few wonderful minutes he knew the true meaning of bliss.

Later she said, "You know, Andy. I've told you about Vassar and my aff—"

"Weakness for foreign tongues . . . no pun intended."

"You're cruel," she moaned, about his reference to the Dean of Languages and a love affair that had nearly cost her her certificate of graduation. "And I've told you about my fascination with power—"

"With Washington."

"Same thing. And my father and I . . . and all of that."

"And that he saved your sheepskin by making a generous contribution."

"That was money."

"That was power. It was also an act of love. You overlook those things with him, Mari. That's not healthy."

"You're lecturing."

"You're right."

"All this time together, and I still don't know a damn thing about one of the most important people in your life. Now's your chance. Tell me about him."

He lay back, discontented. "Listen, sometime I'll fill in the details. I loved the man, Mari. He's dead. That's enough."

"Not for me."

He thought for a moment. Lines creased his forehead. "Okay." He resigned himself. "You ever have someone swear you to secrecy as a kid?"

"My brother Ryan did once. He had bought a switchblade in the city and made me promise not to tell."

"Good enough. You must keep this to yourself. It's illegal for me to talk about it."

"Illegal. That tends toward the dramatic, Andy."

She obviously wanted to keep this light. But for Andy the weight was apparent, even in the expression on his face. His voice was low. "Duncan and I each did two tours in Vietnam. In '72 we were recruited to Army Intelligence. Shortly thereafter we were recruited by the Federal Government."

She chuckled nervously, a forced laugh that he paid no attention to. "You're with the FBI?"

"Sort of."

"The CIA?"

"Sort of." After waiting for her to say something, he said, "You're angry."

She looked at him curiously.

"I couldn't tell you," he said defensively.

"I'm not mad at you." She blinked. "Surprised, is more like it."

"We worked together for years."

"Spies?"

"Sort of."

"Jesus Christ, Andy. You're a spy?"

He smiled at her. "I can't tell you exact details. . . . I became seriously ill while on an assignment in . . ." He caught himself. "Anyway . . . I had a rendezvous all set up. We were trying to capture a top Bul—a top agent. Since I was sick, Duncan took the assignment for me.

"He left at eight o'clock on a balmy September evening when the Mediterranean looked like a piece of molten turquoise. I remember he made some joke as he stood by the door. Something about me arranging it all. . . ." A lump of clay the size of a tennis ball lodged in Andy's throat. He gave himself a moment to digest it before continuing. "I remember sensing the operation had soured— as we call it. I told him that, and he scoffed at me: 'Enough of your profound intuition. That's called a fever.' He smiled and left."

Mari began to cry, and hated herself for it. "And he never came back?" she asked.

"It should have been me, Mari."

"That's not right to say."

"Still, it should have been me."

She sobbed quietly for a few minutes and then collected herself and adjourned to the bathroom. Annoyed that she had allowed herself to come unglued, she turned and said spitefully, "You can't live in the past, Drew. That's what you always say to me. Jesus Christ! I don't believe this!"

"I don't believe this." She was standing above him. He was shivering on a street bench facing her apartment building, which was large and intimidating in the pale night sky.

122

She was wearing tight blue jeans, small spiked heels, and a tweed English riding jacket. Her blouse was white cotton, and since the jacket was only buttoned in the middle, he assumed she was cold.

"Hello."

"Hello, yourself," she returned, pulling her arms around herself to fight off the cold and her swelling anxiety. "You look horrible."

"Thank you. You look wonderful."

"I didn't mean . . ."

"I know."

"Well, what are you doing?" she asked nervously.

"Waiting here for you."

"Why didn't you wait inside, in the lobby?"

"To be honest . . . I wanted to see if you came home alone or not. I wanted to think."

She nodded, all knowing. "I'm alone." She paused. "Have you thought?"

"I've thought."

"So. Let's go inside. I'll fix you some tea."

He stood slowly, his bones creaking, and she reached out and hugged him strongly. He wrapped his arms around her and squeezed, and wondered how all this time between them could suddenly disappear. He heard her sniffle.

Neither wanted to let the other go, but the embrace was over quickly. Stepping back, Mari said, "I've never forgiven you for not calling. I left so many messages . . ."

"I know . . ."

He and Mari had been dining in a small Italian restaurant in Georgetown, watching the parade of summer people through the window. The two of them, at a small table covered with a red-checked tablecloth and glowing mock-kerosene lamp, had sat beneath a hanging Boston fern, neither talking, a good bottle of Chianti nearly empty.

Mari was beginning to slur her words. Again.

It had been another long, hot day in the city and she was tired and on edge. Andy had fiddled with his butter knife, tapping time to a melody only he could hear.

"Are we spending too much time together?" he had asked sincerely.

Mari, snapping out of her dull trance, had taken a moment to answer. "Oh . . . no. I don't think so." Then she had looked at him strangely. "Why do you ask that?"

"We seem to have run out of things to say to each other. You look kind of bothered. Or is it bored?"

"Me? No. Not at all. I was just . . . thinking . . . that's all." Then, she said truthfully, "It's one of the things I like about you and me, Andy . . . silence isn't anxious." She had wiggled her finger at him, as if lecturing. "So talk."

Why do I take things so seriously? he had wondered. Why, when Mari's gift is spontaneous comedy? Is it because of Duncan? Or am I just using him?

She had said, "I'm supposed to be afraid of scaring you off . . . and I guess I am. I don't want to lose you."

"I see we're getting down to the fine print," he had complained, leading her into it, yet wishing to avoid it.

"You're damn right we are," she had blurted. "I'm in *love* with you, mister! You may not like the idea, but that's the way it is! What are your dreams?"

Then she was crying. Others in the restaurant were staring.

"I don't have dreams, Mari. I still have nightmares. I think you're tired."

"Damn you! That doesn't count as an answer. That doesn't come close."

A stubby little man with a white apron wrapped around his waist had delivered two steaming plates heaped with fresh pasta, and had cleared away the empty bowls. He had looked at the two of them sheepishly, attempting to excuse his presence.

"Mari, you're a prize. You know that's how I feel. But commitment is another thing."

"Oh, we're not committed, is that it?"

"You know what I mean."

"I can't believe you, Andy!"

"Mari, you don't have to make this into a—"

"Big deal?"

He had closed his eyes, thinking, Oh shit, here it comes.

"This is not a **big** deal?" She finished her Chianti in three swallows and spat at him with her eyes.

"Mari. You've had too much to drink."

Then she had stood up, forcing the chair back all at once, and had wavered upon outstretched arms while leaning over the table toward him, her face made grotesque by the lamp's yellow light and harsh shadows. "Bastard!" she had hissed. "That's a cheap shot, mister. You just lost your screw for tonight. That's all you keep me around for anyway."

"Mari!" he had interrupted. "It's however you want to make it."

"I don't want to 'make it,'" she had snickered, thinking herself clever. "No thanks, professor. Good night."

Andy had sighed.

To his surprise, she had walked out without so much as a glance, and had melted into the teeming masses. He had picked her up at work, so he knew where she was headed. She would take a cab back to her office building and drive the three blocks home. He knew her well enough not to worry about her driving the three blocks; and though he had been tempted to try to catch up with her, he had left her alone.

Instead, Andy had dragged his fingers across the packets of sugar, absorbed in the sputtering sound.

Then he had turned over the check.

Stupid idiot! he agonized. Don't fuck this one up.

He had driven to the Potomac's Oxford Club Boathouse. If he had been by the ocean, he would have stood in the waves. If he had been alone in the woods, he might have shouted. Instead, he had inserted his copy of the club key into the door, and had let himself in.

On the other side of town, Mari's evening had taken its own course. She had made the short drive safely, but then had left her keys in her purse. She had left her purse in the car. And she had locked the car. It was a Volvo wagon—dark blue—and she had been in no condition to challenge its locks.

So she had rung Mike Gannett's apartment.

Mike Gannett had challenged the Volvo and had retrieved her purse and keys.

Mike Gannett had been invited in for a thank-you drink.

Mike Gannett had made a pass. And Mari had been only too willing.

That was when Andy had taken his first pull on the twin oars and felt the scull shoot forward, watching the dock of the boathouse lift and fall, lift and fall, the low wake lapping at its floats. Stroke, stroke, stroke: he assumed a cadence of heartbeats, counting five and pulling. Five and pulling. The cadence quickened, until he pulled for a final time and tucked away the oars like a bird tucking away its wings at landing.

The needle slid along the mirror, and the moon rose in the sky.

He had showered and toweled off and changed back into his clothes.

He had driven back to apologize, or to try to.

He had used the key she had given him.

He had switched on the bedroom light.

And there they were.

1:00 A.M.

Her apartment was on the seventeenth floor. Its living room was spacious, the walls covered with colorful modern art. It was comfortable: thick shag rug, floor-to-ceiling windows overlooking a piece of the city as well as Lake St. Clair, powder blue couch, and a mahogany coffee table with mahogany legs.

Her blond hair hung in thick curls. She closed the door and took his coat. Her speckled eye glistened in the light of a prismed chandelier.

Hanging up his coat in a narrow closet, she offered tentatively, "The booze is over there, if you want one. Please make mine a Perrier and twist. You'll be happy to know that after you left me I managed to just about kill myself with my drinking."

He suddenly had nothing to say. He wondered where to begin. Too much in the way. Moods. Misunderstandings. Their past. He walked over to the wrought-iron, glass-topped bar cart and located two bottles of Perrier and two highball glasses.

"But no longer," she continued, heading to the couch and sitting down. "I'm back with the living. Look out." The couch was behind him. Standing with his back to her bothered him greatly. As they opened, both bottles hissed at him like a snake. The kitchen was a small efficiency, extremely clean. In the freezer he found ice. The cubes cracked loudly when he poured the sparkling water over them.

"I'm sorry I never called you." He walked around the couch and handed her the glass. Only then did he sense her nervousness.

"So am I. I'm sorry about the whole mess," she explained softly and sincerely.

"Me, too," he returned redundantly. He wondered, Is that all? Is that all we're going to talk about—*it*? Do we just pick up and start again? "I'm confused," he complained, feeling the familiar golf ball lodge in his throat and suddenly feeling uneasy and sorry for himself. "What the hell, Mari?"

"Sit down."

She noted he chose to sit in a chair facing her, rather than next to her on the couch. He brought the chair closer and sat down, resting his glass on a coaster atop the coffee table.

She lifted her glass to her lips and sipped, peering over the rim at him, her one speckled eye catching the light.

"Who was he?" he asked out of the blue.

She knew whom he was referring to.

"Talk about one of life's big mistakes. I never blamed you for how you reacted, only for not returning my calls. What a stupid thing to do—to let happen. I just allowed the whole damn thing to happen." Now she whispered, her voice strained. "I'm sooooo sorry. I can't tell you . . ."

His temptation was to comfort her, to take her into his arms. But he resisted the urge.

After a while she said, "I threw away my one great joy in life. You were the most wonderful thing that had ever happened to me."

"And you, me," he admitted.

"Really?"

"Oh, yes. Absolutely."

128

She stood and found a Kleenex in the kitchen, and he heard her blow her nose. When she returned, her mascara was streaked. She touched his jaw affectionately before sitting down. She told him, "I waited for your call. Several days. Then I started drinking really heavily."

"I'm sorry I didn't call."

"Are you really?" she asked incredulously. "I think I got what I deserved."

"I could have been more understanding, though. I took it personally."

"I can't imagine why," she said sarcastically, blowing some hair from her eyes with a huff.

"It was several weeks before I saw it for what it was."

"And what was that?" she asked curiously.

"In my opinion, it was all a result of my refusal to make a commitment. I imagine what was going through your head was: 'If I'm not committed, then I can screw anyone I choose to.'"

"What was going through my head was Chianti."

He ignored the comment and continued. "Would I have ever known about it, if I hadn't walked in unannounced? I doubt it. No. Hopefully, you would have woken up the next day, kicked that guy out, and kept it as one of those secrets better left untold. It was my fault for barging in on you."

"It's funny how the same incident can have two totally different perspectives."

"Such is the nature of life. Is it not?"

She smiled. "Yes. Maybe even the substance of life. I need another hug." She stood up, and there was no refusing her.

Tentative at first, their embrace lasted for a long time and grew more affectionate.

He pressed her head against his chest; his heart beat quickly. She reached around him, locked her hands, and squeezed.

"I've missed you terribly." A few of her tears ran onto his sweater and rested there. "I don't suppose we'll ever be able to start over, will we, Drew?" she asked, disappointed.

He thought about this and said, "No. We'll never start over," and then added, "but maybe we can continue from where we left off."

And she squeezed him strongly.

There was no attempt on his part to remove her clothes or to touch her skin, or to make advances, and had it been anyone but Andy Clayton, this might have worried her. But she knew this man. If intimacy was ever to happen again, it would take some time.

They released each other slowly. He went back to his chair. She went into the kitchen.

As she explored the refrigerator she talked him into a good stiff drink. While she warmed up some leftover soup, he excused himself to the privacy of her bedroom phone and, due to the late hour, sent an overnight letter to Terry Stone at the SIA. In soft code he outlined his near-abduction in the park, but requested that Stone—or someone—attempt to arrange another meeting with Testler. He closed with Mari's address and apartment number, but left no name.

While he ate three helpings of soup, they sat together on the couch and stared out the windows at the city. The bottoms of the clouds were lit by the glow of the city and looked more like the inside of a gigantic circus tent.

Andy finally said, "Tell me about the booze."

"It was terrible."

He waited patiently. She collected her thoughts for a moment and explained, "I stopped eating. I didn't even notice. I'd been drinking my meals. Mornings were the worst . . . always my chance to stop. . . . I was hospitalized five times. Thrown out of two for smuggling in a bottle." She tried to smile. "I was wild. Too wild. My father even

130

visited me! Imagine that. I bet some doctor asked him to do that," she added as an afterthought and laughed privately. "The doctor who treated me was a recovered alcoholic. He put me in touch with an organization . . . and I started over.

"I learned how to get by a minute at a time. I found my own sense of . . . of . . . faith." She winced, expecting a negative reaction.

"Religion?" he wondered aloud.

"Loosely termed."

"That's nice."

"You honestly think so? Or are you being sarcastic?"

"Honestly."

"I thought you might laugh."

"No. Whatever it is, it suits you. You seem content. Stable."

"Boring?"

"Only time will tell." He flashed her a little smile, and for no apparent reason, she suddenly felt isolated and removed from him.

She said, "There's an expression I've picked up that I think you'd understand. Would you like to hear it?"

"Probably not."

"It goes: 'God grant me the serenity to accept those things I cannot change; the courage to change those things I can; and the wisdom to know the difference.'" She paused.

"Are you trying to make a point, Mari?"

"Am I?"

"About Duncan?"

"Yes, I am, Drew."

"Let's not forget I'm on assignment."

"It's his killer, isn't it?" she asked.

"I can't say," he interjected sincerely. "I'd like to, but I simply can't."

She nodded, and he saw in her a strength he had never

131

seen. She wasn't going to ask again. She told him, "You could use a little wisdom."

"No doubt about that."

"Do you actually think you can do anything? It's not possible, Drew. It's behind you." She stared into his eyes, but he was off on a train of thought with a long hill to climb.

He finally said, "I go back and forth. For a long time I wanted to kill him."

"And now?"

"Now, I'm not sure."

"That's an improvement."

He glared at her.

"I'm serious," she said.

"I've killed before. . . . I was working surveillance, hunting VC who had infiltrated Saigon. I convinced myself it was self-defense. To this day, I have not forgiven myself those deaths. Others gave me reasons. I was told they were doubles, or terrorists, or they were running drugs to our troops . . . things like that. But once, I stabbed a man who simply walked around the wrong corner at the wrong time. I don't know if I killed him . . ." He paused. "But I tried to; and I left him there; and he had nothing to do with anything."

"Oh my God!"

"It was war, right? That's what everybody kept saying. War. It was Asia. Worse things came before and worse things were to follow . . . but I was there. . . ."

She remained silent.

He said, "I've killed five men in my life. Five that I know of . . . and I remember each as clearly as I remember anything. It's not a pleasant thing, no matter what the justification. 'There but for the grace of God, go I,' and all that. It was wrong. And it doesn't get any easier. At least for me it never did. It gets harder. You take an extra second before squeezing the trigger or plunging the knife . . ."

"Drew!"

He was lost. ". . . a second longer each time. And then you realize that someday soon that extra second is going to cost you."

"Drew. You have to take yourself off this assignment."

"In that second of time," he continued, "they'll kill you, instead of the other way around. And then it's all over."

She couldn't look at him. He wasn't with her.

"So, you see? I'm not all that anxious to kill him. I'm not saying I won't, because I . . . hate him." He looked directly at her, but she saw only the loops in the fabric of the rug. "I had trouble with that. With hate. I had never fully acknowledged its existence in my life. I was the kind of person who held 'an extreme dislike' for another. Never hate.

"Not anymore," he continued. "I've learned to hate him, and it feels much more honest." She finally looked up at him, as he continued. "But one thought did occur to me: What if *he* has a brother? What if I become *his* target?

"I've been writing this damn report on the Middle East, and I can't help but see the parallel between the senseless killing there . . . and how I feel. Young men killing other young men because their fathers killed each other. What possible good comes of that? Still, it's been going on for two thousand years, and it will continue another two thousand. . . ."

"Listen to what you're telling me, Drew. There's no point to it."

"To his death, perhaps not. But Borikowski has been connected to the American Embassy bombing in Beirut. Fifty-four lives, Mari. Thirty-seven of them were intelligence officers! My brethren! Now he's on our ground—unfamiliar ground to him. But where is he? Is he here in Detroit? Is he planning another bombing . . . an assassination? Today? Tomorrow?" He looked at her wildly. "Do we just let him go? Let him do whatever it is they sent him here for? Is that what we're supposed to do?"

She ran her hands through her hair.

He said, "On one level, Mari, we're at war. We'll always be." He paused and sat up straight. "I'm on orders to find him. Who knows what that may involve? I'll tell you one thing: hate is an oppressive bedfellow. And I hate the man."

She seemed drained and ten years older. Their talk had crushed her. "Speaking of beds . . . I'm exhausted." She looked curiously at him. "Where would you like to sleep?"

8:00 A.M.
Williamstown, Ohio

The white truck pulled up in front of his house as it always did, exactly at eight o'clock.

Mellissa Sherman sat next to him on the ride into the country. She was plump and pale and younger than she looked. And brilliant.

"Good morning, Doctor."

"Morning."

"How was it?"

"Last night?"

"Yes."

"Terrible. It's that child. She's her father's blood. She does what she wants. She thinks she knows everything. It was terrible."

"I'm so sorry."

"Yes. And so am I. I have failed him. With all the excitement at the lab . . . I should have given her more of my time."

"It was she who moved out, don't forget."

134

"She told me she was going to move back in, quote, 'when you need me, Uncle.' I told her I need her now."

"What did she say to that?"

"She laughed. She said, 'I mean when you *really* need me.'"

"And?"

"And then I laughed—chuckled is more honest. She amused me. She still amuses me."

"That's healthy."

"I suppose."

Mellissa Sherman's eyes sparkled when she spoke to him; she had so much respect for the man. She had never dreamed she would be this close to him, had never dreamed they might work together. And now it had been nearly two years.

She said, "The visit is on."

He perked up immediately. "Are you certain?"

"Yes. It's set for Sunday."

"That's tomorrow."

"Tomorrow morning. You'll pick him up on the way in."

"Splendid! You know, I thought that the confusion of a few weeks ago would ruin everything. I thought the FBI might prevent him from coming." He thought a moment and she did not interrupt. "It's probably because of my age. They probably think I'm going to die."

"Nonsense."

"I'll tell you one thing: I won't die before I see this project through. I've never felt so confident and so . . . so . . . proud of any work, like I do with this."

"It shows. You look younger every day."

"I doubt that, Mellissa, though you're kind to say so." He smiled. "No. I doubt that. It's just that so much of my life has been study, theory, you know. And now a contribution. Something tangible and real, not numbers or

135

words. It lives and it does what we want it to. It's exciting. You see! Even an old man can still get excited."

Mellissa Sherman smiled back at him.

She was excited too.

11:00 A.M.
Detroit, Michigan

Andy awakened at eleven o'clock on Saturday morning on the couch in Mari's living room. He found her note in the kitchen explaining, with much regret, that a previous *commitment* with a youth drug program would hold her until after three, and that she hoped he would be there upon her return. Next to her signature was drawn the smiling face of a cat. He phoned Hugh Long, who put him in touch with Parker Lyell. Lyell had flown in early morning: still no word on a second meeting with Testler. Lyell did, however, arrange for Andy's suitcase to be transferred from the Ramada to the back seat of a taxi; and to Andy's delight, the bag arrived an hour later. Not willing to risk being spotted on the streets, he put in his miles by running in place for ninety minutes, and then killed the early afternoon in the first five chapters of a paperback.

4:41 P.M.
Arlington, Ohio

Borikowski guided the Buick along route 68 south toward Williamstown. Lydia, asleep in the passenger seat with her head against the window of the locked door and her hands folded in her lap, woke as he nudged her. Her almond eyes slowly crept open, fixing on Borikowski. She reached over, touched his arm tenderly, and mumbled a hello.

"We'll be there any minute now," he explained. "Wake up if you can."

Lydia sat up, withdrew a hairbrush from her purse, and brushed her hair, using a small mirror attached to the back of the visor for reference. "It's strange, Leonid," she said. "Since you called me, since we met at the Basilica of Mary, I haven't known what the next minute will bring. You're the only one who knows where we're going or what we're doing. . . ."

"For this, I am sorry."

She laughed vigorously. "Sorry? I was going to thank you. Each moment is only what it is. Tomorrow means little . . . an hour from now means little . . . because for me there's only the moment. It's a refreshing change from holding oneself to a demanding schedule. I should live this way more often."

"But . . ." He somehow knew her next word.

"But, all of a sudden . . . I can't explain . . . it's not important."

"Tell me, please."

"I shouldn't . . ."

He hesitated, but he could not avoid telling her. "I'm interested. I want to know what you're thinking." He paused. "Tell me. What were you going to say?"

She explained sheepishly, "It's nothing."

Silence.

He searched a pocket, lit a cigarette—something she had not seen him do. Then he said somewhat apologetically, "We are to separate today." Inside, he felt guilt for having had sex with her.

"Oh . . ." Her dark brown eyes darted back and forth. "I see." She pushed her black hair from her eyes and continued to brush, though out of nervousness, not necessity. Her hair looked lovely. "We should have made love again." She forced a smile.

He asked sarcastically, "Did we make love, or did we have sex?"

She glared at him.

He felt miserable for having made the remark, and blamed it on nerves and anxieties. Still, he reasoned, she had acted like an animal—certainly the most stimulating sexual partner he had ever experienced, bar none. It was almost as if . . . almost as if . . . she couldn't control it! That was it. It was wild abandon.

She told him, "There is little I can say to you, Leonid. I wish this didn't have to end right now. I enjoy your company. I enjoyed last night." She leaned across the seat, intentionally placing a hand on his thigh, and kissed him quickly on the cheek. "You're a wonderful lover." She hoped this might change his mind.

"We're to separate. That is that. Orders," he explained caustically.

He steered the vehicle into a self-serve gas station, parked by the pumps, and began filling the tank. As he stood by the car, hand squeezing the cold metal bar, he glanced over to a coin-operated newspaper dispenser, which was chained to a steel post by the station's door. Although a fine wire mesh partially obscured the front page, there was no mistaking the headline:

BULGARIAN AGENT SOUGHT IN INTERNATIONAL
MANHUNT!

He released the handle, stopping the gas, and ducked behind the Buick, so that the station attendant could not see him clearly. He returned to the front seat. His face was an angry red.

Lydia, still trying to think of a way to convince him to keep her on the assignment, was just then adding some pale red lipstick to her lips.

"Finish filling the tank," he demanded, slamming his

door. He groped for his wallet, fished it from his back pocket, and handed her a twenty. "Pay the man, and buy one of those newspapers." He cocked his head. "In the stand over there."

"What is it? What's wrong?"

"Do as I say! Hurry!"

Lydia felt perspiration break out under her arms. What is it? she wondered. He's scared to death!

In a few minutes, she returned with the newspaper, frowning as she scanned the article. She opened the passenger door, her face the color of ash.

"*No!* You drive!" he commanded, and snatched the paper from her.

> UPI—Memphis— The United States intelligence agencies are searching for Leonid Borikowski—the so-called man of a hundred faces—in connection with the alleged murder of a Canadian agent Thursday night at Dorval International Airport, this according to CWN correspondent, Karen Kwang.
>
> Borikowski, a Durzhauna Sigurnost field operative, is a known assassin and advisor to terrorist organizations such as the Italian Red Brigade and the Middle East's Z, and is said to have close ties with international assassin Carlos.
>
> Borikowski is believed to be in the Great Lakes region, and traveling alone. He is reportedly an expert in disguise and language. Kwang revealed three photos, allegedly all of Borikowski. All photos show different men. Border patrols between the United States and Canada have been increased, and State Police in sixteen northern states have been put on alert.
>
> The public is advised the man is armed and . . .

"Bitch!"

"I can't believe it!" But Lydia was secretly pleased. Perfect! She knew what this meant.

"Bitch!" he shouted again.

"What do we do?"

He looked over at her. The car was still parked in the station. Incredulous, he hollered, "Drive! Get me out of here, you idiot! They're staring at us! Drive!"

She looked over her shoulder, her face red, and saw the attendant staring through the dirty glass of the window. She steered the car out of the station.

"Slow down! Don't draw attention to us." Then he added, still reading, "It's terrible! How could this woman know this? I'm ruined. This operation's been foul from the beginning. Why is it our superiors can never organize a workable operation? Fools!" Then, quickly correcting himself, "Forget I said that. I did not mean it that way." He knew that such words repeated could bring him undue complications at home.

"How does it affect—"

"Shhh!" He continued reading.

He read the article through twice.

"Okay," he finally said, "we think this out. First, I must travel alone for the next thirty-six hours. These are my orders. However, I may need another face—something I had hoped to avoid—later on. We will, therefore, arrange a possible rendezvous, as I was instructed to do in the event my cover was blown."

"But with your cover blown, aren't you taking a risk?"

"You're damn right I am! But my orders are clear. Damn! Stupid American press! Stupid operation. I'm a walking target now . . . a walking target!" He read the paper yet again.

Then he said, "We need to kill a few hours. Get back on the highway and find a rest area. We have to make new plans. . . ."

11:07 P.M.
Columbus Grove, Ohio

Ellen Bauer rounded the corner, looking up at the moon as it struggled to be seen through spotty gray-black clouds. Winking.

Are you laughing at me, Mr. Moon? Are you? Laughing at my accent like everyone in school? Damn you. Damn them all!

She walked down her long gravel driveway, which her uncle referred to as an "alley"—words that annoyed her. It led to a small brown-shingled one-car garage, which her landlords had remodeled and now rented. Cute. Quaint.

Her uncle didn't approve because of the resulting isolation. He didn't want his niece living tucked away off the beaten path, forty yards from the nearest house—a house that was now vacant, although she had avoided telling him that. Her landlords had won a sweepstakes, and were off in Florida. Or was it Mexico? Somewhere.

Unlocking the door to her little apartment, she opened it and entered. She switched on the light and reached to push the door shut, but her hand hit fabric. Spinning on her heels, her arms flailed instinctively, attempting to defend herself. Her mouth fell open to scream but no sound came out. Her knees rattled. There was more than just the one man—a man whose face was as bland and pale and lifeless as a cheap Halloween mask—for another gloved hand slapped around her head with such force that it split her lip, filling her with so much fear that her head swam in a fuzzy haze, passing quickly into utter darkness.

Lydia and Borikowski had spent three hours parked in the car in a highway rest stop. They bought dinner from the drive-in window of a McDonald's. Then she dropped him off at the Dunkin Donuts at 11:30, exactly as planned. Her nine-millimeter semi-automatic lay inside its holster, under his left arm. Some locals were watching a high school football game on the television.

On the way in he passed a coin-operated newsstand and considered putting a quarter into the machine, removing all the copies, and dumping them into a trash can not five feet away. But he resisted. A mistake now could cost him dearly.

Moments after ordering a jelly-filled and a cup of black coffee, another man entered and sat on the pink stool to Borikowski's right. His face was as bland and pale as a cheap Halloween mask. He ordered a jelly-filled and a cup of black coffee and set some car keys on the counter. These keys fit the rented Dodge parked just outside. The eight dollars the man set down clearly in Borikowski's view had another meaning entirely: a total of eight special agents had made it onto the continent, eight of Spetsnaz's Kolyma squad.

Borikowski slipped his hand over the keys and whisked them away with the deftness of a magician, tucking them into his coat pocket.

The jelly-filled wasn't too bad, although certainly beneath comparison to a fresh French pastry.

Four Polaroids depicting a nude and bound woman had been left for Borikowski in the glove compartment of the Dodge. He slipped them into his sports coat pocket, along with the ammunition clip they had left him as well. The clip held seven very expensive, miniaturized drug-dart bullets.

142

It was time to follow the memorized map in his head—time to locate the Pine Ridge Motel, pick up a room key, and wait out the night in a much-needed sleep.

His patience was beginning to fray. The actor was nervous. Curtain call in a matter of hours.

11:32 P.M.
Detroit, Michigan

A bouquet of flowers had been delivered to the front desk.

It was from Parker Lyell.

The envelope was sealed. The note inside was taped shut on three sides, insuring it had not been tampered with.

It read:

1) You are rated HOT.
2) JACKPOT.
3) NT yes. Pit Stop, twelve midnight.
   Contact Dominique.
   PW = Taylor's handle
             PL

HOT meant that Andy's security could not be assured, and so he was either to return to Washington or continue undercover, but under no circumstances was he to phone the SIA until Lyell provided him with a new rating. Instead Lyell would be his contact. Dialogue was now restricted to handwritten messages such as these, and/or Chris Daniels' Crossword Codes, which, if used, would appear in the morning papers for several days to come.

This did not alarm Andy. It was standard operating procedure to rate an agent HOT following an abduction attempt. Andy laughed inside at the fact that the new rating had taken nearly a day to be put into effect. It proved that in some ways the SIA was no different than other government offices. He assumed Stone would have experts sweep the SIA offices and phone lines for listening devices and would try and make certain the SIA was not the site of compromised information. Within twenty-four hours Andy's rating would change to WARM, and then soft codes would be reinstated and communications reestablished.

JACKPOT meant that the Montreal informant wanted another meeting, and Andy thought it strange this would not be handled by another agent. Why me? he wondered. Why do I have to go all the way back there? Someone fouled up the arrangements. What a pain in the ass.

The most urgent information was the news of Testler. Contact made. Twelve midnight. Andy flipped through the Yellow Pages and found the Pit Stop listed under nightclubs. He wrote down the address and turned to a page in the front of the directory that showed a map of the city and located the street. Taylor had been Duncan's middle name. Duncan's handle, or code name, had been *Hummingbird*, and Testler wanted to use that for the password.

It was going to be a busy night. The romance, which had not yet begun, was over. He finally asked her loudly, "Do you still keep a wad tucked away?"

"How much is a wad these days?" she asked, peering around the corner and into the living room.

"Two thousand."

"That is a wad!" She forced cheer onto her face and left the ice cream melting on the kitchen table. "Come on. I'll show you lesson one in outsmarting the common criminal." Her hand begged him to take hold, waving in the air at the end of a rigid arm. They headed toward her bedroom, as she explained, "I've been robbed four times in this apartment. They've never found the cash. They end up with appliances and an occasional piece of jewelry."

"Four times?" Amazed.

"Yes. But they never look inside my dresses." She swung open a bifold louvered door and revealed a perfectly ordered and well-organized display of the latest fashions. She reached across him to take hold of a canary yellow evening gown. It was white-cuffed and, Andy thought, very smart. She unfastened a safety pin and withdrew a small speared stack of twenties and hundreds from within the dress.

A purple skirt yielded five hundred dollars. An evening gown, three hundred.

Andy had never fully understood her fascination with cash. She never had less than a thousand dollars available at any given time, and always had it stashed in trick hiding places: everything from tennis ball cans to fake toothpaste tubes. She called it "escape money," but it was more than a reserve fund. It was a toy. He supposed the attitude was due in part, if not in full, to the security of a generous trust fund, and that the trust made this sum look like so much spare change.

She was counting.

"You do this, even with the Irishm—?"

"Billy came *after* the robberies. Haven't had one since." She thumbed the last bill. "Seventeen hundred and fifty dollars." She waved the stack.

"You've gone insane!"

She smiled wisely. "No. I've gone sober. There's a big difference." She held the stack high in the air. "I'll make you a deal."

"No deals," he replied.

"No cash," she told him bluntly, pulling a string that turned off an overhead light, and closing the bifold doors.

"What's the deal?"

145

"I'll give you this, if you'll return here after the meeting. I keep your suitcase as collateral."

"That's blackmail."

"Business."

"I can't make a guarantee, Mari. If there's a flight available later tonight, I'll have to take it."

"I didn't ask you for a guarantee." She leaned slightly against the bifold doors and they moved. Her arms, and the money, were held behind her in a warm and intentional pose. "I asked to keep your suitcase."

He wanted to make love with her. Right now. Standing up.

"I'll try," he said. "I promise to try."

She stuck out her hand. "Deal." And she offered him the money.

11:50 P.M.

The door to the Pit Stop was painted a black-and-white checkerboard, like the winner's flag, and was down an alley. Chunks of wood burned in a trash can, but no one stood by it. Andy walked up to the fire, and that was when a voice said "Bonjour."

Andy, his face lit by the yellow fire, peered into the blackness and patted the bulge at his side. A short, stringy man stepped out from a darkened doorway. "You stand in the doorways, the wind doesn't bite," he said with a French accent.

The man stepped forward and Andy could see him better: French cheekbones and eyes, a dirty, colorless beret cocked over half an ear—the other half rumored to have been lost to a German in the North African campaign—bloodshot eyes, and a mouth with only a few brown and pitted teeth. He spoke with such a strong accent that he was difficult to understand. "What do you wish?"

"You are Dominique?"

"What is the word?"

"Hummingbird."

"He's upstairs. That door over there. Room three hundreds and twenty-six." Dominique pulled a cigarette from behind his whole ear and lit it with the stroke of a wooden match. The sulfur cloud partially hid his thin face. "Three flights up. Room three hundreds and twenty-six."

"I understand." Andy handed the man a twenty. "*Merci*, Dominique."

"*Oui, m'sieu.* And I remain right here, until your departure. This time of night that is the only exit, *m'sieu.* You will give our mutual friend no trouble." The bill disappeared into a hand that pointed down the alley. He repeated, "Room three hundreds and twenty-six."

"Go back to your wind break, my friend. This won't take long."

They both nodded.

Andy walked away, leaving the Frenchman to his cigarette and the dark of the doorway.

He turned the knob and pushed against the door and it opened freely. He stepped inside a confined entranceway, with the stairway to his right, and closed the door, shutting out all light. Allowing his eyes time to adjust, he experienced the familiar anxiety of an unfamiliar place. He couldn't help but think of the two men in the park, and whether those same two—or even more— might be here, waiting to try again.

The stairway climbed straight in front of him, a crippled banister on the left, an age-cracked wall of crumbling plaster on his right. The steps were warped and bowed by years of traffic. He eased his foot onto the first and listened for the inevitable squeak, and as it occurred, began to sing an old sailor's song. His melody was off; his lyrics nearly unintelligible, but the drunken tongue quite convincing:

> *"Ayee . . . Swallow me down me grog and me mate*
> *Her puddin' is tastin' as sweet as a date . . ."*

He continued to climb the creaking staircase, continued to sing:

> *"'T' was the first time I'd sawn her*
> *To port I had come . . ."*

Up past the first landing, then the second with its stale beer odor and its broken window.

His heart raced ahead of the tempo, eyes on a string, back and forth, back and forth. He climbed toward the light on the third landing:

> *"Aaay, swallow me down me grog in the heat,*
> *When me bullion is heavy and me rum it is sweet . . ."*

As he reached the third floor he let his voice fade, then was silent, standing with gun ready, barrel pointing to the ceiling, staring at five well-spaced bare bulbs hanging on chains so covered with dust that they looked more like unsupported gray sticks nailed to the ceiling.

In the silence, the drumming of his heart thundered in his ears. His shadow changed from giant to midget, and appeared both before and behind him. To his right, number 322.

Two doors to go . . .

A cat screeched in the alley, its wail muffled by the roar of blood rushing past Andy's ears. With his back against the time-worn wall, he inched down the colorless hallway, the grays and dirt-whites blended into an unforgiving drabness. Alert for any sign of trouble, he passed 324, and stood before 326.

He wanted to trust Testler, but decided not to.

Inhaling deeply, he cocked his leg back, hoping the door would yield to his first hard kick. Nervously he counted: three, two, one . . .

He threw all his weight into it. The door tore open. He leaped into a somersault, smacking the floor, and then jumped to his feet, gun trained on Testler, who was sitting at a table, a game of solitare spread before him, clutching a Swedish pistol that he had aimed at the doorway.

"Don't, Nicky!" Andy commanded from the end of the bed.

With his gun and full attention still aimed at the door, Testler complained, "You're early. You scared me half to death. You broke my friend's door. What's wrong with you?" Then, trying to sound as pleasant as a shoe salesman, he said, "Hello, Andy."

"Let's put them down."

"Agreed."

Testler set the gun down on the table, well out of immediate reach; Andy returned his to his holster.

"You're angry. You think I arranged last night?"

"What the hell should I think?"

"I suggested you ride with me in the car," Testler said. Andy noted the undue amount of black curly hair on the man's neck, and the permanent suede color of his skin. And when the light caught Testler's profile, despite his pointed face, he appeared even handsome.

Testler explained, "I discovered the phone tap through a friend, fifteen minutes before I left to meet you. Then, you know, I was positive we had trouble. I tried to warn you." He lit a cigarette and exhaled toward the lamp.

Andy realized that Testler could have seemed casual with a soldering iron up his ass. He told him, "I won't believe you, Nicky, no matter what you say. We had better just get on with it. I'm sure you understand."

149

"Eh, fuck you, Andy. You never believe anyone. That's your problem." He sucked on the cigarette and said, "One thousand American, to be wired to a broker in London by ten tomorrow morning, New York time."

"Five hundred."

"Nine."

"That's a lot of money, Nicky. What makes you think I would pay such money?"

"It's nothing, Andy! Your opposition will pay that price for a phone number. You had better decide."

"Four."

"Six."

"I'll look into six if the information checks out. You know how it works."

"Agreed." Testler stuck out his hand, and the two consummated the deal with a handshake, Testler more heartily than Andy. Testler then searched the pocket of his jacket, which hung on the back of his chair, and located his wallet. From this he withdrew the broker's business card and handed it to Andy, who put it away.

Arrangements thus complete, Testler said, "He's been traveling with a woman."

"The woman, I know about. That's not worth even a hundred, Nicky."

"The girl is reporting on him."

"To whom?"

"A man named Tristovich," he said. "He sits on your *Dragonfly* like an old maid. And that's why I think something is wrong with the man."

"I don't follow you. Do me a favor. Try and make sense." Andy began to worry that someone else may have already paid Testler, and that for the second time in three days he had walked into a trap.

"His assignment is taking him into the United States."

"Not Canada? You're certain it is the United States?"

"United States. Absolutely. That's why they chose him.

He's Bulgarian, and he's good. If he fucks up, it's all blamed on the DS."

"What's the assignment?"

"No idea. None whatsoever."

"A lot of good you are."

"I do know that a Lieutenant Tristovich has taken over Rhinestone, and that he was also in Syria when the Beirut embassy was sabotaged."

"So what?"

"He seems to follow *Dragonfly* around. The two are very close."

"Meaning?"

"I know for a fact that they have both been seen entering the Neurosurgical Research Institute named by Polenov. It's on Mayakovsky Street, in Leningrad, near Nevsky Avenue."

"What are you driving at?"

"You know the place."

"Yes."

"Then you know this is also where most defectors are debriefed." Testler fished a piece of tobacco from his tongue; the spider web stuck to his lower lip and stayed there.

Andy said nothing.

Testler asked, "What if Borikowski's a defector? What if he's not Bulgarian after all? That would make some interesting situations, would it not?"

"Not if I don't know his assignment. Testler, this is trash!" But Andy had heard a rumor about Field Operative Major Percy Goldman, G-2. A diplomatic attaché had sworn in front of the Senate Subcommittee on Intelligence that he had seen Goldman in a swimming pool in a Moscow military club—ten weeks after his reported "assassination." This incident had never been confirmed by another source. "Trash," Andy repeated.

"An interesting possibility."

"It's idiotic. What good does it do me? I pass this along, Testler, and they'll have *me* in a mental hospital. *You* understand? No thanks. I'll pay two hundred for this. No more."

Somewhat desperately, Testler offered, "What if I told you that eighteen months ago there was an operation called Bookends that involved the abduction of Captain Andrew Clayton on the outskirts of Beirut?" Testler's narrow and oily face peered through the curtain of thick smoke, expressionless. He finally noticed the web on his lip and removed it. "Captain Clayton was secretly helping the Lebanese Army establish an intelligence-gathering arm."

"Bookends?"

"Clayton was lured out to a rendezvous, through misinformation, but the wrong Clayton showed up."

"You're on thin ice, Nicky," Andy said bitterly.

"And that the Kolyma division of Spetsnaz is in Detroit right now, trying to abduct Andrew Clayton again."

A thought struck Andy like lightning: He had been careful not to be followed last night, but what if the Kolyma knew about his former relationship with Mari? It was unlikely, but what if?

"What is it?"

Andy stood abruptly.

"Andy?" Testler hollered as Andy ran from the room.

His footsteps banged against the old flooring. Two steps at a time; three steps; landing; turn; two steps at a time . . . he passed the broken window . . . landing; turn; three steps—jump; turn; two steps . . . He opened the door and hurried into the alley before he should have.

The agents had followed him from Mari's apartment. One of them, a big man with a narrow head and a wide mouth, was positioned behind a crate, beneath the fire escape, next to a brown dumpster.

Andy didn't see the man. He turned to adjust course

and slipped on a frozen puddle, careening and tumbling to the far side of the alley, where he bounced against the wall. "Shit!" he shouted. He came to his knees slowly, inspecting his elbow.

The man, hidden by the dumpster, stood and withdrew a bulky handgun that had an enormous barrel diameter: an air-compression dart pistol. He edged a few feet along the wall, eyes on Andy, but the burning trash barrel blocked his shot. He edged quickly past the doorway Andy had just come out of and continued up the alley until he was in front of the door to the Pit Stop.

Andy stood up, visible through the dancing orange flames and resulting black smoke, rubbing his elbow.

The man raised the large gun and took aim.

At that very moment, Andy looked over his shoulder and saw the man. He should have dropped and rolled, taken possession of his weapon, and fired. Instead, he hesitated—yes, he froze—just as he had told Mari he might.

He knew who this man was, at least *what* he was. He also knew that for some reason he had acted too quickly, and that now it might cost him his life—and that the reason was Mari.

In an instant of time, Andy identified his gross mistake of hurrying into the alley, and looked into the man's eyes and awaited the shot. But the shot did not come. Instead, he heard a clicking of metal, and then the man's eyes rolled into his head, he released the gun, which fell noisily to the ground, his eyelids closed, and his head slumped forward.

He collapsed to the pavement.

Dominique stepped out of the doorway, a switchblade in hand. He was grinning toothlessly.

He lit a match in a practiced fashion—one could picture him standing before a mirror and doing this for hours—and touched the match to the end of the cigarette clutched in his teeth.

Andy heard the stiletto close.

Dominique said, "Guns make too much noise. This will cost you extra, *m'sieu*. Five hundred American . . ."

But Andy was up and running again, his only thought Mari.

"Heh!" Dominique protested softly, not wanting to draw attention to himself or the corpse. "Hey!"

Andy did not hear the man. His attention, his entire being was with Mari. If anything had happened to her . . .

He turned left at the end of the alley and saw into the front seat of a car where two more agents sat, looking right back at him. Andy sprinted down the nearly empty sidewalk.

The resulting scene was like something from a Marx Brothers film. The waiting agents, caught off guard, obviously mixed signals. The passenger flung open his door and then couldn't make the seat belt release. The driver, in too big a hurry, started the car, put it in reverse, and backed up. The passenger door then lodged against the sidewalk, opened too far and broke the hinge, causing a horrible scraping sound that continued until the driver stopped the car. By now his passenger had unfastened the seat belt, and attempted a daring leap from the car; but the driver changed gears and put his foot on the accelerator. The car lunged forward. The door slammed against the passenger, who screamed at the top of his lungs, ribs broken.

Andy turned left and pushed hard, crossing the empty street and making a right down another alley that led to a one-way street. He ran against the sparse one-way traffic and took a right at every intersection for the next three. On this last corner was a grocery store. Tucked in behind two brick columns that seemed a part of a building planned but never built was a pay phone.

She answered in a groggy voice.

Andy mentioned no names. He asked, "Can you get to a pay phone?"

"Yes, downstairs, but it's awfully late—"

"Pencil?"

"Yes."

He gave her his phone number and waited only minutes before the pay phone rang. He said, "There's reason for concern, and I've come up with a plan. I don't want a discussion. Agreed?"

"Don't make me play spy games. I've got the bed warmed up and I'm waiting."

"I'm serious."

"But are you committed?" she teased.

He ignored her. "You'll need a disguise."

"What I need is an explanation."

He didn't want to alarm her, but he had no time to battle her wit, so he told her, "Your place has been watched. I was followed and have upset someone's plans. If they have any sense at all, that will bring them down on your place shortly. It has to be where they caught onto me. You can pull this off without a second thought. . . ."

"I'm a social worker, love. Don't pull this . . . crap . . . on me."

"How about a cheap fur, short skirt . . ."

"What?" she snapped incredulously.

". . . spike heels, black stockings . . ."

"I don't own a cheap fur."

"Listen to me!"

"Easy! Just kidding . . ."

"You're making a trip, so take anything important—"

She interrupted, "Now wait just a minute—"

"But don't take anything more than a purse. Dress as I just mentioned. And remember, you *must* do this quickly! Call an ambulance."

"B—" She tried to cut him off but he continued.

"Tell them your husband has had a heart attack. Sound frantic. Give them your address, but with a room number a couple floors below you. Fifteen-thirty or something . . . doesn't matter. Then call a cab, name a time, and have them pick you up outside of Charlie's—"

"But that's three blocks—"

"I know." He paused, putting the puzzle back together in his head. "Okay . . . you wait for the ambulance to arrive. When it does, you run like hell down the stairs. Don't use the elevators—"

"In spike heels?"

"Enough! You go out the back of the building, into the alley. You try and walk like a whore, you posture yourself like a whore, you *are* a whore."

"Watch your tongue."

"Stop clowning around. Repeat it."

"Okay, okay. Ambulance. Stairs. Walk like a whore. Charlie's. Cab. . . and just where am I heading?"

"The airport. We meet at the airport at eight-thirty."

"That's six hours from now!"

"So what?"

"It'll be mobbed!"

"Exactly. We'll meet at United. Out in the seats."

"United. How appropriate. I'll be the whore with the big bosoms and not-so-cheap fur. And you'll be the . . . Forget it! I'm not waking up some friend and killing six hours. This is unnecessary. I'll be fine."

He had feared this reaction. "Make a deal?"

"Try me," she told him, smiling now into the phone.

"We meet in one hour at the Airport Inn. We'll kill the six hours together." He wanted to believe that this switching of plans was not typical of him. He saw himself more as a man who stuck to a single plan and carried it out to the best of his abilities. He knew his first ideas always were his best ideas. . . .

But then he included into the second equation his chance to be with her again and reminded himself that his chief priority had been to get her out of the apartment building in a hurry.

"A delightful compromise," she agreed.

"You'll do the whole bit?"

"For you dear"—again teasing—"anything."

"Anything?" he retorted. "You may wish you hadn't said that."

"I doubt it. Listen. What about your suitcase?"

"Oh shit! Leave it with Billy. If you can be quick, pack a small one for yourself too. I'll arrange for them to be picked up later tonight, but that will take me some time. You'll probably beat me there."

"Good. That'll give me a minute. So I'll register. For two." She seemed girlish. "This is exciting! I'll be Mrs. French. Mrs. T. French . . . the somewhat whorish lady with the nice walk."

"Are you all right?" he asked, hearing that other Mari.

"Scared to death."

"You sound it."

"I am. Guilty. I *hate* the idea of people watching me!"

"Maybe they're not."

"No. They are. I can feel them."

"This is easy."

"I know. Just a typical evening. Busy, busy, busy . . ."

And he smiled. "Did you switch on your light?"

"I was nude. Did you expect me to go to the pay phone nude? I switched on the lights. I put on a robe."

"When you get back, turn them off. Work in the dark. It's important you get the jump on them."

"Hey!"

"What?"

"This is the last time you come to my place unannounced. You bring me nothing but trouble."

"Agreed."

"Airport Inn. Mrs. T. French."

"You're a prize."

She hung up.

Sunday, November 23

1:27 A.M.
Detroit, Michigan

She was sitting uncomfortably in a chair when he knocked. She bent to examine herself in the mirror one last time, pulled on a strand of hair, and let him in.

He inspected the motel room, noting that it seemed somehow more a glorified hospital room than the place for a guest. Everything was new and color-coordinated, and though certain expenditures had been made to "liven up" the surroundings, these were mostly in the form of illuminated light switches and remote control consoles and a clock, which if allowed, would talk to you.

These did not interest him.

Feeling awkward, Andy finally turned to greet Mari, but she was pressed up against the wall, her hands knotting themselves hopelessly.

"I'm not so sure this was such a good idea," she admitted, and he could tell that she was holding back tears.

"You didn't disguise yourself!" he stated, outraged.

"Easy, Fred! I changed clothes after I got here. Jeeez, you're jumpy."

"Cautious. I'm cautious, that's all. What are you doing holding up the wall over there?"

"What are you standing there with your coat on for?"

He took the coat off and slung it over the desk chair he stood by.

She walked over, passing him, took the coat, and hung it up.

He admired her, and hoped she might sit down on the bed, but at the closet she turned and said, "So."

"So," he replied.

"Here we are. . . ."

"Yes."

"It's late." She glanced briefly at the bed and then to the floor.

"Yes."

"You know, Drew. I still don't know whether you hate me, or whether I'm forgiven."

"Either do I."

"That's a hell of an answer."

"That's the truth. Would you prefer I lie?"

"You're angry. You're still angry. What the hell are we doing here?" She crossed her arms and rubbed her shoulders with her hands.

"How am I supposed to feel? How are you supposed to feel? Is there a 'supposed to' that I don't know about?"

"I thought . . ."

"What? What did you think we'd do? I know what I thought we'd do."

"What?"

"What do you think?"

"I asked you."

"Jesus Christ!" he said, and started to walk about aimlessly. "I'm having trouble with everything we hid from each other. It's not healthy."

"But it's normal."

"Doesn't make it right, or easy to deal with, at least not for me." He noticed her clothes now, having paid no attention at first. She wore a plain white shirt of a flimsy fabric, which stretched tightly around her bust, giving her more there than she had. Her skirt was some kind of gray wool, hanging just below her knees. Her hair was brushed and full and her teeth shone.

"You said maybe we could continue."

"Yes I did."

"Where do we start?"

"Where would you like to start?"

"It's two o'clock in the morning. My legs are tired. I'd vote for either starting in the morning, over breakfast, or forgetting all the rules and kind of jumping into the middle somewhere."

"Meaning?"

She lowered her head and her hair fell forward and hung like a curtain behind which she could hide. She snapped her head backwards, and the hair followed, falling back into place fluffed and wild. "Meaning I'd like you to touch me. I want to touch you." She edged toward him tentatively, yet confident that this was something she had to do. It was her turn to instigate, not his, she realized, and so she boldly stepped up to him and stood inches away. She reached out and ran a finger along his jaw and traced the edges of his lips. Her hands slid down his chest, and he took her by the hips. She looked up at him and he bent and kissed her.

His fingers found her hair and pulled it from her face. They touched lips softly a number of times and then their kiss held. He hugged her tightly and looked over her shoulder, and there in the mirror, Andy Clayton looked back. And instead of disgust or contempt, the face in the mirror agreed with this, granting an approval he feared he might not receive.

"We don't have to go to bed ... I mean make love. ..." She tried to make it sound convincing.

But everything about both of them disagreed with this.

She disrobed. He watched. She let the clothes fall to the floor in a heap—not like Mari. As she unbuttoned his shirt, he was looking at her clothes piled on the carpet. He mocked, "What, you're not going to hang those up?"

But she had his shirt open now, and rather than answer, she hugged him warmly.

He was gentle with her. He remembered every touch she enjoyed. They spent hours this way: touching, whispering, kissing.

Then finally, as a pink blade of morning light crept over the horizon, they joined together blissfully, cradled in each other's arms, holding on as if they might never let go.

And they both hoped they never would.

Later, they lay on the bed, Andy with his feet hanging off the end, Mari holding a pillow across her chest, both staring at the ceiling. She told him, "We belong here . . . together. I know we do," without even a degree of reservation. "That proved it to me." Then she trembled from toe to nose. "Ohhh, that was nice."

He sighed and continued to stroke her hair.

"Can you imagine that . . . all the time?" She grinned and looked over at him. "What a thought!"

"Not for a week," he teased. "I need time to recover."

"How about fifteen minutes?"

"What you need is a good eighteen-year-old."

"Oh no. What you need is what a bureaucrat calls good lip service."

They both laughed and Andy turned on the light and went into the bathroom. When he returned, Mari explained, "I'll walk away, if you'll walk away."

"From what?"

"Our jobs."

He sat on the side of the bed and looked down into her speckled eye. "How?" he asked, entertaining the fantasy.

"We write our resignations on Airport Inn stationery, and we retire to some exotic place together."

"How do we live?"

She looked at him quizzically. "The trust is enormous, Andy. Believe me, the hardest thing we'd have to do is decide what time to eat our next meal. We could drive nice cars and travel often."

"Tempting."

She sat up, and he bent over and kissed her navel. She positioned a pillow behind her neck and head. "I think we should do it. You throw in the towel and so will I."

He was not about to ask, "Are you serious?" because he knew she was. Instead he asked, "Is this a standing invitation?"

"Do I look like I'm standing?"

"So this is a lying-down invitation?"

"Most definitely."

"And if I decline?"

"Then you have to catch a plane, and you miss out on some wonderful lip service."

"You drive a hard bargain."

"That depends on how good the lip service is," she joked.

They both laughed, mostly from nervousness and to release a tension that was developing.

He set his wristwatch to wake him in ninety minutes and switched off the light.

They fell asleep in each other's arms.

6:29 A.M.
Detroit, Michigan

He sat up in bed, startled, the alarm screeching at him. Mari rolled over and mumbled, "Turn that thing off!"

He did, and before climbing out of bed he gave her a kiss on the forehead.

Twenty minutes later they had both showered and dressed. Mari was brushing her hair endlessly.

Andy said, "I have you booked on a flight to the Yucatan."

"I'm not going anywhere."

"Mari. You're going to the Yucatan for a two-week vacation."

"No. I'll call the police or a private eye or something. They'll supply protection. You know that. There's no need for all of this."

"There is."

"No, Drew. You're getting carried away. Soviet agents read our newspapers and bribe our technicians. They don't hunt insignificant social workers like me. If they're after you, you're gone. There's nothing I can supply them with."

"But do you actually believe that?"

"Yes."

"You're being naive. They do whatever they have to do. Two weeks, Mari. It's not so much, given the alternatives."

"It's paranoiac. Are you worried because I'm a woman?"

Andy had half his lower lip pinched between his teeth in concentration. "No," he told her. "Because you're *my* woman."

She seemed touched by this, but still joked, "Who says?"

Andy missed the humor. "My friend then."

And now Mari wished she had not joked. She asked, "Trade?"

He said, "Try me."

"I'll give you the two weeks, if you'll give me two weeks after the assignment."

"After debriefing."

"Whatever."

"Deal." He offered her his hand.

But she pushed it aside and snuggled up to him and

placed her lips onto his and kissed him hungrily. "We didn't get much sleep," she reminded him.

"Doesn't matter. What we got was better."

"What are my orders, Captain?"

He told her about a woman he knew, Valerie Reed, who lived on an island off the east coast of Mexico and owned it outright. He gave Mari instructions on how to find the town of Sisal from the airport near Merida, and how to contact the woman once there.

They went over the details three times, until Andy was certain she would not forget.

"Fine. I've got it. Now stop with the business."

He hugged her, and whispered so softly that she could barely hear. "I've never stopped loving you, Mari. I haven't even touched another woman in the last two years. I've always regretted walking in, unannounced. I'm sorry for that."

Her crying acted as a release for all her pent-up guilt, and she held onto him tightly for several minutes, face pressed against his shirt. She choked out, "This is a crazy place to fall in love."

"No, not really," he told her. Then, biting back an Andy Clayton grin, he said, "Diesel fumes have a way of doing that to me."

**6:45 A.M.
Washington, D.C.**

"I told you. When the garbage disposal is working, you will get the check. This will be your third time out, and I am still without . . . No, it didn't work . . . No, it didn't. When it works . . . yes, that's right, and not until. Goodbye, Mr. Scharf." Stone rehearsed the coversation, trying to memorize his replies, perplexed by the need for even the simplest of things to go wrong. He would make the call tomorrow morning.

His apartment was on the fifth floor of an old brick building that overlooked the Capitol. The city was awakening.

Where are you, Josie? he questioned plaintively, still deeply saddened by his loss these many years later. She had been his love of loves, his wife, his best—his only *real*—friend. Melancholy swept though him, stabbing him. Oh, Josie.

He always felt this way in the morning. Especially Sundays.

Josephine Rutland Stone had stood to his left on June the fifteenth, nineteen hundred and twenty-three, a buxom, wide-grinning, yellow-haired woman, with big teeth and a surprisingly strong handshake. She had pep and vigor, and an inexhaustable well of goodwill and generosity.

The traffic was slight. He called Marvin, his chauffeur, and arranged to be met in front of the cemetery, after church, at 10:15. He wanted to walk to church.

He went to the sink and doused his face in warm water and tried the conversation with the repairman again.

The kettle cried from the kitchen. He fixed himself a cup of coffee—real coffee—and returned to the bathroom.

Whenever he brought images of Josie to mind, he most often saw her eyes before him. "The windows to her soul"—her "peepers," as he had called them. And she had given birth to Mark David Stone on March the ninth, nineteen hundred and twenty-four—a wedding-night child, she had called him—the love of their lives, the center of all attention, the "most important person" in her life.

He sipped on the coffee as his grandfather's clock tolled proudly from the corner. Through his bedroom window, winter's early morning darkness was broken by lights of all kinds: white headlights, red taillights, yellow office windows in the distance, and amber streetlamps. All glowing artificially. Amid all these lights, despite the early hour, people milled about.

As a child, Terry Stone had watched an ant drag a twig twice its size toward the nest, while other ants passed it by, hurried and without a care for its struggle. Now, with a dozen thoughts on his mind, Stone remembered and felt like that ant.

Josie. Why'd you do it? he asked her again, seeing all the people below and wishing one of them were her, wishing there existed even a possibility that one of them were her. But he knew better. He knew where Josie was; and after church he would leave a flower by her gravestone—if he could find a vendor. He blamed himself— this job—for her death. He always would.

Too many memories, he thought, feeling a twinge of loneliness and a degree of failure with his life. I lost the two people who meant anything to me: first Mark, to the war; then Josie, by her own hand. And then, years later, Andy walked through my door. Andy, with his moods, his indifference, his guts: just like my Mark.

And Friday night, *they* tried to abduct him.

And I'm not even sure who *they* are. . . .

I'm not sure of anything.

6:45 A.M.
Ada, Ohio

Liz Johnson opened her eyes. The opaque curtains held the Pine Ridge Motel room in a dark shadow. Dr. Alex Corbett's left arm lay across her chest, his right trapped beneath the small of her back and under her buttocks where he had last held her. Before dawn, he had awakened aroused, and they had shared in each other again. She felt his warm breath against her skin, and as she moved, he sighed.

169

Staring at his overworked face, at the dark semicircles of skin below each eye, she felt a tremendous amount of guilt for what she had done. Six months ago she had been given the assignment: Enroll second semester at MIT; locate Dr. Alex Corbett; lead him on. Then a month ago: Have him invite you to Ohio. And here she was. And they had made love last night for the first time.

And though their lovemaking had been only fair, she had played her role well; and to him, their loving had been immense and ardent.

And now . . . She slid away cautiously, slipping off the bed without disturbing him, in the same manner as a mother might sneak away from her sleeping child. The guilt found its way into her throat and choked her.

Corbett's hand caught her before she was fully off the bed. She tensed. He whispered softly, ". . . so many things I want to say, Liz."

She tucked her hands between her legs, leaned forward and squeezed her legs together tightly. In her nakedness she felt vulnerable. She wanted to tell him. There was still time to tell him.

Corbett continued blissfully. ". . . how nice it was . . . this is . . . how I've dreamed about it." He dragged a loving finger down the bumps of her spine, leaving behind a trail of standing hairs. "I thought the age difference—"

"Shhh . . ." She didn't want to hear about the years that separated them; she didn't want to hear about her beauty; she didn't want to hear about his love. Her chest heaved involuntarily and she choked on tears.

He noticed. "What is it?"

"Shhh . . ." She looked at the blank television screen. It was gray and dark.

She stood. "I'll be right back." She crossed the room to the bathroom door. He admired the dimples above her buttocks and the long line of her back.

She ran the water, blew her nose, urinated, and flushed

the toilet. She reached into her toilet kit and withdrew the syringe and the small vial. A moment later she watched the fluid jump from the end of the needle: no bubbles. She cupped it in her hand. She swallowed the lump in her throat.

When she came out of the bathroom, Corbett saw only her nakedness. He didn't see what she held in her right hand.

He watched her, boyishly: her thighs rubbed together as she walked; her tits bounced.

She stood next to the bed, bent over him, and kissed him. He closed his eyes and kissed her back.

First, he smelled it. Then he suddenly felt something sharp prick his skin, and he sat up quickly.

She lost hold . . .

The syringe dangled from his arm. He looked at her, stunned, his face drained of color, his eyes curious and then begging to be told he was still asleep, still dreaming.

He began to thrash.

She thought, Stop! You're going to knock the thing out of your arm and break it! Oh, shit. You're going to screw the whole thing up! All her months of preparation came down to this one split second, and again she considered allowing him to escape.

"You, Liz?" he questioned, his voice nothing but a wind.

The question stunned her. Me? she thought. Yes, me.

She smacked him hard across his temple with her open palm and propelled him to the mattress. The syringe bobbled in his vein. The drug took effect instantly.

Corbett slept.

She finished administering the full dosage, and then put the syringe away and dressed.

Once clothed, she monitored his pulse for five minutes. Then, from her suitcase, she withdrew a small canister of gas and, after attaching the mask to his face, opened the valve.

Anesthetized, his pulse leveled off a few minutes later. She returned the equipment to her suitcase and angrily banged it shut. She covered him with the bedding and stood shivering beside him. But the room was not cold.

Then, a single knock.

Two more knocks followed and, so, she opened the door.

Borikowski entered, looking like a confident general: arms crossed, leather gloves, sharp strides. He dumped his coat on a chair, his attention already on Corbett.

The room, still quite dark, made it difficult for her to see Borikowski's face. He switched on the lights and she gasped. "Impossible," she claimed, terror present in her voice.

"Yes," agreed Borikowski, knowing that his selection as the agent for Crown was based partly on the bone structure of his face and its resemblance to that of Alex Corbett's. "And with your cosmetic talent, I will match him exactly."

She did not comment; she wondered at his dead eyes: You look so dull . . . so permanently sad.

He thought, That's why this operation is going so badly: I shouldn't be here. This isn't my specialty. I'm a teacher of tactics, and yes, I have killed people too; but I'm not a thief. I'm not an impressionist, an impersonator; I'm an actor. There is a substantial difference. I don't like this. I'm nervous. I've never had to imitate an existing person before. Damn!

He walked over and measured Corbett at the temples with his open hand, and this nearly made Liz Johnson sick to her stomach. The dead trading minds with the sleeping, she thought, seeing it all as evil. This man is evil. She said, "He's a nice man."

Borikowski looked at her oddly but then said, "I read your reports. I've studied him carefully. I know he's a nice man. This has to be done. He'll be all right."

"No he won't."

"Whatever you say." He opened his suitcase and then twisted the latches and changed the combination so that the compartment would open. He removed most of the contents and walked into the bathroom.

Liz Johnson followed. It was her job to make the metamorphosis complete.

8:30 A.M.

Ninety minutes later, Liz Johnson stepped back and said, "I am amazed. It is a very good likeness." Her brow knitted disdainfully. She compared the face of the man on the bed with that of the man in front of her. "I wouldn't have believed it possible. It's uncanny."

"Do I sound like him?"

She gasped. Her face became a paste gray and she reached out for support.

He helped her to the bed, where she sat down.

"Please don't do that again. Yes. Exactly."

"The tapes you sent—"

"I understand. Please . . ."

"Are there any problems with the—"

"Stop it! Please!"

"All right," he said, more like Peter Trover, remembering she was an American sleeper. Peter Trover was American. "Are there any problems with the cosmetics?"

She regained some color and appeared more calm. She folded her hands together on top of her lap. "Yes." She looked him over. "The coloring under the eyes takes the light funny. We better try again. Also, your hair is too neat. He is kind of unkempt, you know." She smiled a quick smile reserved for herself. "His eyes are less steady than yours. It's not a perfect match. I would spot you. But people he has never met . . ."

"Fine." They went back into the bathroom.

Then she hated herself, and she began to attempt to reason. I'm a cheap whore, she told herself. A cheap whore and they've used me.

Borikowski waited. Then he asked, "You're angry with yourself?"

"Yes."

"It will pass."

"I wonder."

"It will."

"And what if that's what I'm afraid of?"

He looked into the mirror.

8:50 A.M.

Twenty minutes later he stood in front of her again. This time he looked almost exactly like Corbett, down to the doctor's tam, which he had "borrowed."

She said nothing.

He removed Corbett's wallet from the trousers by the bed and ransacked Corbett's suitcase, searching it for any other identification. Nothing. The wallet—the all-important wallet—was all he had. Borikowski transferred a number of plastic credit cards from his own wallet to Corbett's, removing those that were there and handing them to the woman. "You will dispose of these?"

"Yes."

A buzzer went off on his watch; he silenced the alarm and removed the watch.

She handed him a briefcase that in appearance was identical to Corbett's buffed aluminum case. She opened a small box and handed him what looked like two digital watches. He strapped one to each wrist.

She said, "The briefcase will open only once for you. Any attempt after that—"

"I know." Borikowski nodded, then asked, "How long will the drug last?"

She looked over at Corbett. "Fourteen to sixteen hours."

Borikowski was gentle with her. "You have done well. Thank you," he said as he slipped the special ammunition clip into the butt of Lydia's semi-automatic, replacing bullets with tiny drug darts. He checked the safety and handed the gun to her. He removed his holster and then put on Alex Corbett's heavy winter jacket. It was snug in the shoulders.

"You're all set?"

"I think so . . . all set." She explained, "The potted pine to the right of the door."

"To the right as you're leaving," he confirmed.

"Yes. As you're leaving."

"Very well. Listen. I will recommend they delay any reassignment. It's the best I can do."

She nodded reluctantly, eager to see him leave.

Borikowski patted his pockets as he walked down the well-lit hallway toward the lobby. He inhaled, holding his breath for a long count and then exhaled slowly. He pushed through the doors and into the office lobby, aluminum briefcase in hand.

The man reading the morning paper was not who he had expected. Instead, a younger man with short blond hair and narrow pointed ears stood near the desk, chewing gum and reading a newspaper. He wore a dark tan suit and a red, white, and blue-striped tie. Glancing up, he set the paper down and stood to greet Borikowski.

Borikowski was appalled. This is it! Another mistake! No one knows a damn thing! Ignorant fools!

The young man smiled and nodded.

Dr. Alex Corbett returned a nod and walked immediately over to the nearby men's room, pushing the door open as he entered.

The Plan. Their Plan. The FBI.

Only moments later, the young agent entered. "Dr. Corbett?"

They shook hands.

"Yes."

"My name is Huff. I'm your escort for your field trip this morning. Sorry about this, but you know the procedure."

"Yes." Borikowski allowed the man to pat him down, searching for weapons. And he knew how a nervous Corbett would react. He *was* Corbett now. "This is all a little bit like James Bond to me. You'll excuse me if I seem excited. I don't mean to sound rude, but could I see some identification? They told me to be very cautious."

"Of course." Smiling, the agent opened the small wallet, flashing an official-looking ID that placed him with a security company out of Columbus. Borikowski knew the employer was the United States Government.

Imitating Corbett, Borikowski shifted his eyes constantly, as nervous as a penniless man at the race track.

"Totally understandable, sir. Personally, I wish we didn't have to go through this. But that's all there is to it. After you."

Borikowski insisted, "No, please."

Huff led the way.

Who are you? Borikowski wanted to ask. We have no reports of any young agents connected with the Vaughnsville Project. The Franklin papers indicated the surveillance was Level Five, mostly electronic, and that the few agents assigned to Vaughnsville were in their sixties. How many more like you are there?

"Did you say something?" Huff asked as he led the way out into the cold.

"No," Borikowski replied, anxious for the man to turn around. The potted pine was only a few feet away, and there, at the far end of the parking lot, headed away from them, was the sexy walk of Liz Johnson.

Borikowski glanced back at the motel doors, making certain no one was behind him. He then looked ahead, to insure Huff was still walking away from him, which he was. At the potted pine, Borikowski bent quickly, took the gun from its hiding place, and stuffed it between his pants and shirt, continuing on without so much as a break in stride.

Huff tried several times to start a conversation as he drove Dr. Alex Corbett out of town, but the biophysicist professed to be studying for the upcoming meeting. He finally admitted, "You know, Mr. Huff, this is exciting for me."

Huff smiled. The ride continued for twenty minutes with Borikowski's head hung deeply in thought. He had memorized some key scientific phrases. He reviewed these now, in case he should need them.

Looking out occasionally at the unrelieved flatness, he admired the wintered fields and thought of the farmers in his homeland.

They drove through the tiny town of Gomer, and finally slowed to a stop, brakes singing, next to a small strut bridge that spanned the Ottawa River.

A white, stretch-cab pickup truck, its sides and tires covered with streaked mud, was parked in front of them. Huff threw his arm over the back seat and looked Borikowski in the eye. "End of the line. You want to get in the back door."

"Thank you."

A gust of wind nearly knocked Borikowski down. Pain stabbed his head and then disappeared. The aluminum briefcase swung away from him like a kite caught by the wind. He grabbed his tam just as Dr. Alex Corbett would, elbow tucked, head cocked, hair a shambles.

The truck's rear door popped open. Borikowski grabbed the handle and pulled.

As he climbed inside, he caught a glimpse of the silver-haired man who resembled Albert Einstein. He yanked the door shut and locked it. The howling outside was replaced by a delicate exchange between woodwinds and violas.

"Mr. Halleran, the music please . . ." Dr. Eric Stuhlberg spoke with a thick German accent.

Stunned by the presence of yet another unexpected agent—Halleran—Borikowski suddenly believed he was being led into a trap.

They're going to drive me right into a jail!

Stuhlberg's eyes were the color of faded denim; his voice sounded like sandpaper being rubbed against concrete. "I'm Eric Stuhlberg. Thank you for coming, Dr. Corbett. I appreciate your valuable time."

"Call me Alex, please. It's certainly a pleasure to meet a man I have read so much about, lectured so much about . . . I am honored to be invited . . . excited!" Borikowski finger-combed his coarse, wigged hair, pushing a clump to the other side of his head.

"Alex, I'm afraid I must ask you to wear this blindfold," Stuhlberg explained regretfully, handing him what looked like ski goggles painted black. "Mr. Halleran will insist on it."

Halleran's smile filled the rearview mirror.

Stuhlberg continued, "And he makes the rules."

"I understand, Dr. Stuhlberg." Borikowski stretched the elastic band around his head and pulled the blindfold in place.

Halleran turned up the music; the sad plea of an oboe filled the vehicle. Violins and cellos conversed. The truck bumped, but not in time with the music. Borikowski rocked back against the seat, his head strangely sinister in the black blindfold.

The executioner's hood.

Flutes echoed, timpani rumbled and quieted. Stuhlberg knew exactly when the pause came and how long it would last. His salty voice took a solo. "Please excuse my silence. I dislike that blindfold, and I would prefer to wait until we can see each other. . . ." His words faded into the waterfalls of cymbals and trumpet melodies chased by French horns.

Borikowski waited patiently in silence. The quiet before the storm. He could sense that Halleran occasionally looked at him in the mirror.

For Borikowski, habits, schedules, surveillance techniques, number of personnel, performance characteristics of environmental monitoring equipment all came into play now. A critically timed operation, Crown's success now relied heavily on the accuracy of the gathered intelligence. Seeing both Huff and Halleran had done little to sustain Borikowski's confidence in the quality of that information. He thought, What else don't I know?

He counted one turn after the bridge: a left; then three rights. Halleran, however, had done two clever loops and had fooled a veteran fooler.

They traveled down a series of country roads—the last two miles dirt. Large signs repeatedly warned trespassers in bold letters to STAY OUT—LIABLE TO CRIMINAL PROSECUTION. STATE PROPERTY.

It was Federal property.

The trip took less than twenty minutes.

The overpowering smell of raw cow manure wafted in through the truck's vents. Borikowski heard a large door shut electronically.

Stuhlberg said, "You may remove the blindfold now, Dr. . . . Alex."

"Debussy, isn't it, Dr. Stuhlberg? But I can't seem to place the . . ."

"*La Mer: 'Jeux de vagues'* . . . Play—"

"—of the waves. Yes, of course. Lovely."

Surprised, Stuhlberg replied, "Ah, you speak French!"

Halleran's eyes filled the rearview mirror; and Borikowski cursed his overactive ego.

Borikowski knew that, in fact, Corbett did not speak any other languages. And surely Halleran did too, for his eyes reappeared in the mirror, intent and anxious. He made no effort to leave the truck, now that they were parked.

Borikowski explained, "No. I'm just familiar with some of Debussy, that's all."

Halleran seemed satisfied with the reply, though still mildly curious. He asked, "If you don't mind . . . What was the color of your maternal grandmother's house, Dr. Corbett?" and removed and unfolded a piece of paper from his breast pocket.

Thump . . . thump . . . thump . . . Borikowski's heartbeat intensified.

"Frank!" Stuhlberg objected.

Borikowski interrupted, "No problem here, Dr. Stuhlberg. I understand such precautions." He looked at Halleran in the mirror, and then he recalled. "My mom was born in that house, you know: a big old blue three-story, with black shutters, two chimneys, and a tall elm out back that died of Dutch Elm disease when I was six . . . or was it seven?"

Now Halleran was satisfied. He climbed out and opened the door for the two.

Feigning surprise, Borikowski said, "A dairy barn! You've been working in agriculture!"

Stuhlberg's lips pursed and then curled. "No, my friend. You know the government. Always tricks."

"Like working on Sundays?"

"We've been working six days a week for months. Tuesdays are our day off here—though not this Tuesday since we have the opportunity to work with you." He smiled. "I am sorry the support teams aren't here today. Sundays we strip it down to only a few diehards. There will be four of us today; five if possible. You'll meet the rest tomorrow."

"Sorry I stole your Tuesday."

"It's not the first, I assure you. Nor the last. We're having some problems. That's why we've called on you. We're happy to have you here."

They were standing inside the dairy barn. The truck, parked next to them, blocked the door at this end. Another truck blocked the far door. More than twenty cows stood in tight stalls as electronic milkers emptied their udders. Plastic umbilicals carried the milk away. Three older men were performing light chores: two checking lines; the third shoveling manure into a wheelbarrow. These were the men Borikowski had expected.

Stuhlberg's voice bounced aimlessly through the barn and a bird flew from one rafter to another. The old scientist followed its flight. The bright overhead lights sparkled in his eyes. "I can't tell you how I've looked forward to this." He walked around the truck. "Your research is what impressed me—your articles. This way," he explained, jerking his head toward an area filled with sacks of grain. Borikowski followed. "Specifically your antigen research. Remember, Alex: salt. Our first problem is salt." Stuhlberg turned, stopping Borikowski. His eyes were young, his skin loose on his bones. Like the cows' udders. "I have some projects here, Alex. I have some projects that I am very proud of. A little help is all I ask.

Creative help. In order to win some traits we had to lose others. With your help, I hope we will reestablish some of that which we have lost."

Borikowski avoided the shop talk. "The blindfold, the dairy barn. It's all so new to me . . . so strange."

"Our research money is half government, half corporate. In its present stage, some of our bugs are very toxic. This fact is central to our problem. We are toxic under the wrong conditions; we are made ineffective by others. Final touches are all we need. Final touches. Please, step in here."

He led Borikowski through a door and into a small storage room, its shelves crowded, its floor hosting sacks of grain, which filled the enclosure with the pungent smell of molasses.

"Close the door, if you please."

Borikowski pulled on the rusty handle, shutting the two men in the tiny room.

Stuhlberg motioned for him to step closer. "We are in an elevator. Stand in the center, please."

Borikowski watched Stuhlberg's right index finger closely, waiting to see which switch he used. The computer rotated the operable switch daily. Only the doctors knew the correct switch. Any of the others would trip an alarm.

Stuhlberg pushed a middle button on a very small panel that was hidden well within a shelf. The room dropped with a silent suck to the stomach. "Level One is fourteen meters below the surface. Levels Two and Three are not in use at this time."

Borikowski continued his rehearsed Corbett role with perfection. "But why?"

Stuhlberg's hoisted brows answered the question.

Corbett would be shocked, Borikowski thought. "It's that toxic?! Is this military? Doctor, I was assured I would not be involved with any—"

Stuhlberg interrupted, smiling as he spoke. "Nor would I!"

The elevator stopped.

Stuhlberg surprised Borikowski when he tripped another switch—one that the Durzhauna Sigurnost had not gleaned from its inside sources. A wall rolled aside, revealing glass and aluminum: a House of Mirrors. Small outer room; tan security box mounted to the wall. Decontamination booth the size of three phone booths straight ahead. The lab, only ten feet away, visible through thick glass.

Two people waved: a woman in a blue surgical uniform and thin paper hat and face mask, and a man in green scrubs with the same protective wear. Their faces were hidden, but their eyes smiled.

Dr. Alex Corbett offered a layman's salute, also smiling.

Stenciled on the glass doors next to the security box, were the words: LEVEL ONE.

This was one of the most important moments of the assignment. Borikowski could no longer rely on his acting or his cosmetics. Now he had to rely on a small piece of plastic—an imitation credit card that Soviet Military Intelligence technicians had provided him—a piece of plastic carrying a computer-coded magnetic strip containing a recording of *his* voice speaking the three words: "Dr. Alex Corbett." At the motel he had placed five such cards into Corbett's wallet, aware that the computer also daily rotated the security cards. To use Corbett's cards—cards with the wrong voice recorded on them—would trip the computer's alarms. So, he watched Stuhlberg carefully.

The scientist withdrew a Gold American Express card from his billfold and inserted it into the tan box, face up. A tiny red LCD light changed to green. Stuhlberg spoke at it carefully. "Dr. Eric Stuhlberg."

An odd electronic voice—nothing but a series of taped

words strung together—replied antiseptically, "Sun-day
. . . Twenty . . . Three . . . November . . . Zero . . . Nine
. . . Twenty . . . Nine . . . Hours . . . Welcome . . . De-oc-
tor Stool-bug." Stuhlberg pushed one of three buttons
atop the machine, all unmarked. The box responded,
"Con-diz-un-al." Stuhlberg told it, "Host." To which the
machine responded: "Guest?" Stuhlberg stepped out of
the way, allowing Borikowski to use the machine.

As Borikowski—Corbett—slid his card into the small
slit in the security box, heat ran up his spine. He waited.
It seemed like forever. . . .

The red light finally changed to green.

"Sunday . . . Twenty . . . Three . . . November . . .
Zero . . . Nine . . . Thirty . . . Hours . . . Welcome . . .
De-oc-tor . . . Keh . . . Orbit . . . This is your first visit . . .
Do you wish instructions? . . . Push the third button . . ."
But Stuhlberg pushed the second button. From the box
came, "Thank you. You may continue."

Seconds later the doors hissed open.

He was inside.

The men's locker room, identified by a stick figure, was
to the left. To the right, the woman stick figure wore a
skirt.

Borikowski asked, "If not defense, or agriculture . . .
then what . . . medical?"

"Pardon me, please," Stuhlberg answered, a coy grin
playing across his dentures, the dull blue eyes glinting. "I
had been asked to wait until we were actually inside the
laboratory. Now we are. The project I most need your
help on is in the energy field, Alex."

They entered a white-tile locker room, sterile and so
well-lighted that it nearly blinded. A door closed behind
them.

Stuhlberg told him, "For experimental purposes, and
due to toxicity, we attempted to safeguard our test bacte-

ria using pressure. The process was relatively easy—we engineered the cell walls to collapse given a certain change in pressure. But, of course, this triggered the release of endotoxins, and we ended up with more problems than we began with. What we were after was a monoclonal antibody. Rather than recombinant, we have been working in the more cost-effective cell fusion. Hit and miss. We maintained the safeguard of pressure, but were hoping for a specfic monoclonal to develop through transduction. What we hit upon two months ago was a set of bugs that cause cellulose hydrolysis on biomass at a high rate, with a high yield. And what we hope for is another bug to then chain n-alkanes."

"Petroleum?"

"Exactly."

"Incredible."

Stuhlberg smiled proudly. "Our problem," he continued, "is that our monoclonal antibody recognizes sodium chloride as its antigen. For both national security and laboratory health hazards, during early development, such an antigen was useful. If our pressure system for containment failed, we could resort to salt water. But this is clearly an obstacle now. We hope, with your expertise, to attempt recombinant procedures and alter the bugs one last time. We need to change the antigen reaction without losing the specific function of the bug. We can't have salt water eliminating our bugs. For our purposes, that is now unacceptable." Stuhlberg did not tell him the rest. He decided to wait. No use frightening the man.

"Fascinating."

"I was hoping that would be your reaction. I am extremely proud of this work. It represents a dream I have held for quite some time. This discovery will contribute to our country's indepedence—energy independence. What could be more important, Alex?"

"Energy from biomass?"

"Exactly."

"But is it cost-effective?"

"We hope so. We're much closer than anyone else. Our hydrolysis rate and yield are outstanding, tenfold over any other fermentation process."

"But that would mean it's toxic: it would react on any organic matter, would it not?"

"Yes, extremely toxic in its present form. That is another problem. But of course a good dose of salt water kills it instantly."

"But if it were to escape?"

Stuhlberg cocked his head. "Impossible. Each internal section of the lab is individually sealed off, in the event of contamination. There are seven independently controlled sections, each with its own sensor and enviro-sealed doors." He added, "No chance of escape."

Borikowski thought, That's what you think. He knew of the microbiological sensors placed throughout the complex. He also knew that if anything went wrong now, he would be sealed inside without means of escape.

Only suicide.

And it was for this reason he hoped there would be no problems.

The two removed their winter overcoats, placing them in electronically accessed lockers.

Borikowski left his sport coat on, unnoticed by the excited Stuhlberg, covering it with a medical-green scrub jacket. He sat on a small aluminum mesh bench and slipped into the surgical scrub pants.

Both men obtained disposable shoe covers, hair covers, and facial masks from labeled blue-and-white cardboard boxes, which were lined up on a glass wall shelf. They donned the protective gear, checking in mirrors for loose hairs, and carefully molding the thin metal strips of the masks over the bridges of their noses. They looked exactly like surgeons.

Stuhlberg said, "Today, I wanted to get you acquainted with the procedures, introduced to my two colleagues, and caught up on some of the technicals. One hour lunch at one, on site. Antigen demonstration following lunch and then an informal discussion, question-and-answer period for you. We'll have you back by cocktails." He smiled.

"Busy," replied Borikowski.

They left the locker room, doors closing behind them. Passing through each sealed doorway, Borikowski felt more and more isolated.

Then, the sliding door to the decontamination booth opened, and Borikowski entered alone, at Stuhlberg's request. He closed his eyes—as another electronic voice insisted—and felt a quick pulse of heat surround him. A strange smell filled the tiny area, followed by the same recorded voice okaying entrance to the Vaughnsville Project's "clean room."

The thick glass door slid quietly aside. Two voices came alive, the words welcoming a man who was not here, a man lying unconscious, deeply drugged, in a motel room.

Borikowski shook their hands, acknowledging and returning introductions: Dr. Alan Nostravich and Dr. Mellissa Sherman. The two he had expected. Stuhlberg followed him into the lab. It happened so quickly, no one even heard Stuhlberg's greeting.

Borikowski unbuttoned the lab jacket and withdrew the silenced weapon. Then he began firing. Nostravich took a drug dart in the thigh, but fell across the countertop, breaking beakers and test tubes and causing a tremendous roar. Mellissa Sherman screamed and Borikowski quickly shot her in the chest. She fell to the tile floor, bleeding slightly from her right breast and thinking she was dying. But she was not.

Nostravich was. Although Borikowski's DS superiors had insisted there was to be no killing, they did not know of Nostravich's bad heart. For him, there was indeed no hope—his horror was quickly hooded by the darkness of death.

Stuhlberg rushed the intruder, his head low, arms out straight. He careened into Borikowski and pushed him to one side. Then he lost his balance and fell to the tile. Borikowski was more shocked than anything. This was the last thing he might have expected. He bumped into some equipment and spilled it onto the floor. Stuhlberg was up again and charged straight ahead. This time Borikowski fended him off effortlessly. He took hold of Stuhlberg's left arm, twisted it behind the man's back, and shoved him to the floor. But Stuhlberg continued. He spun quickly and was ready to try again when Borikowski kicked him violently in the stomach.

The doctor vomited and sat down on the tile, defeated.

Borikowski looked at the old man with a peculiar expression. He waited, but the fight in Stuhlberg was used up. Borikowski headed for the stainless steel refrigerator across the room. Next to the refrigerator was a computer console.

Stuhlberg uttered faintly, "No!"

Borikowski ignored him, taking a moment to inspect his victims quickly. Mellissa Sherman was fine except for her neck, which was twisted awkwardly to her left; he moved her head so that she might breathe more easily. When he touched Nostravich's neck and found no pulse, he shrugged. Everything else has gone wrong with this assignment, he thought. No reason this should have gone smoothly. Fuck your mother, Nostravich! Now I've murdered an American scientist!

He located a box of latex surgical gloves amid the beakers and test tubes scattered by Nostravich's fall. He snapped on a pair.

Eric Stuhlberg quivered against the white wall, where he now sat with his knees tucked up under his chin. He said, "I should have guessed a Sunday. Frank knew," referring to Halleran's earlier questioning in the truck.

Borikowski glanced at him coldly. "They're only drugged, Doctor," he said, lying, but trying to stabilize Stuhlberg, who appeared to be working himself into a stroke or heart failure.

Stuhlberg's face reddened. His jaw trembled, and then he roared, "*This is scientific research! You have no business here! You . . . bastard!*" He continued to stare at the wall in front of him, rather than at Borikowski. "*This is non-military! Who are you? Who are you?*"

"You're an old man, Doctor. Old men do stupid things sometimes. Your niece is young. Keep that in mind. Before you attempt being a hero, look at these." He reached into his coat pocket and withdrew the Polaroids. He dropped them onto the floor and kicked them toward Stuhlberg, who picked them up.

Ellen Bauer was tied to a kitchen chair. She was naked and her lip was bleeding.

Stuhlberg looked away, but he had already seen her face. "Ellen? You took Ellen? You involve my family!? *Who are you?!*"

Borikowski tugged at the rubber of each glove, pulling them on even more tightly. They snapped in place. "She is our hostage. You will remember this, Doctor. You will cooperate with me fully; if you do not . . ." He paused. "I'm certain you have a fertile enough imagination."

"Corbett, you're a traitorous monster."

"If the operation goes correctly, she will be freed unharmed. Clear?"

Stuhlberg glared.

Borikowski bent over and jerked Stuhlberg's chin to afford them eye contact. He repeated, "Clear?"

Stuhlberg yelled, "You must not proceed with this! This is *my* project! You don't know what you're—"

"Quiet! You must think of Ellen."

Stuhlberg looked as if he might attempt a fight. He struggled to his feet. "Are you insane? Do you know me? Do you know Eric Stuhlberg? Obviously not!" The hunched, white-haired man approached the agent, step by heavy step. "You assume I will obey you in order to protect my Ellen." Stuhlberg was breathing heavily and staring at the intruder.

"Doctor!" Borikowski barked. He entered a cipher into the computer's keyboard. The green screen cleared and then displayed a menu of possible commands.

Stuhlberg hesitated and stopped his approach.

A cursor blinked on the first choice.

Borikowksi selected the third choice on the menu, and when prompted, entered a second alpha-numeric code, which resulted in a short, high-pitched beep. The stainless steel storage compartment could be opened now.

"This is impossible," proclaimed the stunned Stuhlberg.

Borikowski took hold of the handle. If either code was incorrect, then by turning this handle he would seal himself inside his own tomb.

"Don't do that!" demanded the old scientist. "You must not—"

But then Borikowski lifted the handle, and the refrigerator opened.

He stared in at six shelves, each holding eight aluminum containers stacked in pairs. The containers were the size of a college dictionary and each was held shut by a series of clip latches. There were twenty-four numbered series, two boxes to a series; an alpha-numeric, five-digit filing code facing out, and written by hand.

Borikowski selected two of the boxes, and withdrew them gently, placing them onto the counter. He then shut the door and entered another command into the keyboard.

A single ping rang out. Like a doorbell.

Borikowski, one small container in each hand, faced Stuhlberg. "Let's go." He motioned his chin toward the exit.

"You have underestimated your oppenent, Corbett," announced Stuhlberg. "Yes. You have underestimated Eric Stuhlberg."

"Stop there," Borikowski demanded, seeing the rage in Stuhlberg's eyes.

"Two lives are nothing when compared to this project." He looked around the laboratory. "This . . . this is *my* project!! And *you* will not take it."

Stuhlberg again charged Borikowski like a speared bull and slammed into him with enough force to knock him to the ground. The containers crashed to the floor and this stole both men's attention, for the latch on one of them had popped open and the seal was cracked. While Borikowski's attention was fixed on the container, Stuhlberg took hold of a beaker and attempted to smash it into Borikowski's face, but the agent moved his head, and the beaker broke in Stuhlberg's hand, slicing two of his fingers. A glass fragment cut Borikowski's neck. Borikowski rolled out from underneath the man and crushed the sole of his shoe onto Stuhlberg's throat. The doctor's eyes widened, and his face turned fire engine red. Borikowski held his foot there, pushing even harder. Stulhberg was attempting to hold the foot back, but was losing. He was being choked to death.

"You stupid old man." Borikowski reached for his

weapon and fired a dart into the man's chest. Stuhlberg's right arm lurched up, then fell slack to the tile.

Borikowski touched his neck and felt the blood. He bent down quickly and latched the lid to the container closed, sealing it.

He pushed a button on the wall and the decontamination booth opened. He set the containers on the floor inside and dragged Stuhlberg into the small booth with him, before shutting the door with another push of a button and awaiting the completion of the fast decontamination process. Then the recorded voice thanked him and the door opened.

It required two trips to move both Stuhlberg and the boxes of bacteria safely into the locker room. He dragged Stuhlberg over the slick tile floor, through the air-sealed doorway, and leaned him against the lockers, as he continued his work.

Borikowski opened the briefcase Liz Johnson had given him at the motel. He then placed the numbered containers next to the briefcase, taking care to inspect and to adjust the graduated dials that fronted two electronic boxes, both of which were held snugly inside the briefcase's custom-cut foam rubber lining. One of these—the transmitter—monitored atmospheric pressure, and if triggered, would radio an alarm to both of the wristwatch devices he wore. The other piece of equipment, a receiver, awaited a signal from these same two wristwatches—modified Japanese jogging watches that measured Borikowski's heart rate and blood pressure—and was wired to a small amount of plastic explosive. Borikowski gently placed the boxes containing the recombinant bacteria into their respective holes in the foam rubber, and after checking the dials once more, closed the briefcase, locking it.

Then the alarm went off.

Borikowski looked around and saw nothing unusual. Then, from the door to the locker room, he saw a red light flashing above the entrance to the laboratory. A second alarm and light began flashing above the decontamination booth.

He worked quickly, fearing he might be sealed underground at any moment. He faced the far wall, where an unseen camera recorded his every movement. He held up his wrists, displaying the devices to the camera. To the blank wall he said, "My pulse is being monitored electronically. If you kill me, or sedate me, an explosion will open the briefcase and release its contents into the atmosphere. Dr. Stuhlberg is my hostage. No harm will come to him if you cooperate."

Hurriedly, he checked the clip to the gun and then slapped it into the butt of the automatic: four darts remained. He removed his scrubs, shedding them onto the tile, and then, briefcase in hand, dragged Stuhlberg to the elevator.

A third alarm sounded, and the doors to the laboratory swished shut behind him.

He hit the button. The elevator's doors opened.

Borikowski was but two steps into the barn when he realized the alarms were not ringing up here yet. He reasoned that this was, after all, supposed to be a dairy barn, and perhaps for reasons of security, the alarms would not ring here. He did not know.

He caught one of the older agents by surprise, and silently shot at him. The tiny darts had an accurate range of fifty-three feet. Still, this shot missed the man's chest and embedded in the fat around the stomach. The drug took an extra few seconds to take effect, and in this time the sixty-year-old agent/farmer completed two full strides toward Borikowski. An arm's reach away, he tumbled to the dirty cement floor and slept.

Halleran calmly entered the area with a cup of steaming coffee in hand, but then saw the unconscious man and Dr. Alex Corbett holding a gun. His reactions immediate and professional, he dropped his cup of coffee, quickly withdrew his weapon, and fell to the manure-and-hay-covered floor. Halleran aimed. The puddle of spilled coffee snaked toward an elbow.

Borikowski, shielded behind the wood of a stall, fired first, sighting ten inches above Halleran's head to accommodate the dart's poor trajectory.

The dart embedded in the man's cheek.

Halleran fired wildly, hitting a truck headlight and spreading the glass.

Borikowski fired again and hit him in the shoulder.

The deafening report of Halleran's gun brought another of the older men into the area. Borikowski thought, Only one dart remaining.

He fired carefully, before the man saw him. The last dart lodged in the man's thigh and he staggered drunkenly before falling forward, impaling his neck on a upturned hay fork. His throat gurgled and sucked for air. He twitched liked a fish out of water, and then became still.

Leaving the briefcase on the floor, Borikowski hurried to open the barn's door. It was operated by a switch to the right, which Borikowski threw. Then he ran back to the truck. Some rain and wind found its way into the widening crack of the rising door.

He dragged Stuhlberg from the grain room to the truck, and placed him face down on the floor behind the front seat, covering him with a canvas tarpaulin that he found in the supply room to his left.

Borikowski was not concerned with being some distance from the briefcase—the transmitters worked efficiently up to a quarter mile away, and even then, would beep for fifteen seconds prior to detonation.

Stuhlberg's body covered, Borikowski placed the pickup in reverse and his foot on the accelerator.

And then they drove away.

1:03 P.M.
Washington, D.C.

His green phone rang.

Terry Stone pulled the receiver to his ear and said, "Go."

"ORANGE! The store has been sold. Repeat. The store has been sold."

Although the line remained open, whoever had spoken was no longer there.

Stone tilted back in his black padded throne, the phone receiver still in hand, waiting for the trace to go through as Code Orange dictated. He loosened his tie, amazed at how light-headed he was. His heart hurt. He sucked for more air, suddenly feeling suffocated. Terry Stone called it indigestion.

Janie finally said, "ORANGE back, sir: Vaughnsville, Ohio; rated Level Five."

"Thank you. I'm locking in," he said, pushing a button beneath his desk's center drawer, which threw a bolt on his door, assuring privacy. He sipped his decaf and waited for his chest pain to subside, which it did.

He knew little about the Pentagon's Vaughnsville Project, only that a Level Five rating classified it as an important laboratory that few people would even know about. All detailed information would have been stored in two separate databases: one, a government computer center in Ohio; the other, a data center at the Pentagon.

His call to Secretary of State William Daly was placed immediately. "Bill? Terry Stone here."

"Yes, Terry."

"We have an international violation here."

"In the form of?"

"A scramble is not possible."

"Can you stop by?"

"I think it had better be a room over here, if that's all right."

"Two hours?"

"I should have something by then."

"See you then."

4:09 P.M.
Montreal, Canada

The cab pulled to a stop in front of the phone booth, and Andy climbed into the back seat. He slammed the rear door, saying, "New Holland, please."

The knitted cap nodded and the cab began to move forward. The rearview mirror was aimed at the seat again. The meter was running.

The cabbie began. "I insisted on speaking with you because I have confirmed that the Soviets have moles in both the NSA and the SIA, and this information is critical to your assignment, and I didn't want to risk compromising the information because that would leave my own position tentative at best. Do you understand?"

Andy admitted, "I had wondered. Yes. I understand."

"The woman you're looking for checked in last night. She's in Sault Ste. Marie, Michigan. I don't know which hotel, but I do know for a fact that she's on orders not to leave the room."

"You're certain? That's very importa—"

"Yes, absolutely. By the way, you—or whoever—did well in blowing his cover to the press. The Uppers raised hell! He's forced to keep her nearby now, in case he

196

needs another face change. And because the press reported him traveling alone, they will travel together, so you had better find her. And you better be quick about it. They'll move fast now."

Andy didn't reply to this. He watched as hordes of well-dressed people exited a church via a set of steep stone steps. The ringing bells reminded him of other years. It was a Sunday wedding.

The informer said, "If you're who I think you are, you had better be careful, too. They missed you in Detroit, but they'll try again, given an opportunity."

"Have you heard anything about Kolyma?"

"Yes. Several have arrived on the continent. I also know about Tristovich."

In order to protect Testler as a source, Andy did not reveal that he had already heard about Tristovich. "Which is?"

The cabbie corrected him. "No, *who* is." The car swung left, then left again quickly, and traveled down a narrow alley. The man continued. "A recently arrived KGB bureaucrat who has taken over Rhinestone for a while. He's also in charge of the Kolyma. And, as I understand it, their main concern is the abduction of a Captain Andrew Clayton. Is that you?"

"Why Clayton?" Andy answered.

"No idea."

"Does Washington know?"

"How the hell should I know? *Baisse mon cou!* I haven't been in years, friend."

Andy stared at the knitted cap and actually saw a face looking back at him—a face that had to belong to that voice: The man was clean-shaven and had a firm jaw, a pug nose, and dark, beady eyes the color of old tires. He had a crack down the middle of the left front tooth with the finest line of gold filling the crack that had ever been put into a mouth. He probably worked in a clerical or communications department of the Soviet Embassy, and had a cousin or a friend who drove a cab. He was definitely caught in the deadly trap of working both sides, where he trusted no one, no machines, no wires to be listened to. He demanded meetings on his terms, driving cabs along city streets with his mirror aimed down at the front seat. He would return the cab, then be driven back to his embassy desk job and, once again, excuse his absence. And then one day he would be followed, and his own precautions would hang him.

"I have two of *Dragonfly*'s identities," the informer continued. "They are out of date, of course, or I wouldn't have seen them, but they may help. Ready?"

"Yes."

"Franz Vogel and Peter Trover."

"V-O-G-E-L?" Andy spelled.

"Yes."

"T-R-O-V-E-R?"

"Right."

"Got 'em."

"Do you have any Canadian money?" the cabbie inquired.

Surprised by the question, Andy replied, "Not much. I jumped a plane."

"Then I'll drive you to the airport."

Before Andy could say, "Thank you," the cab lurched left and up a ramp, and the accelerator kissed the rubber mat. They pulled out onto the autoroute.

Andy cracked the window.

The cabbie said, "One other thing. There's a rumor that Tristovich is connected with the NRI in Leningrad."

"Meaning?" Andy leaned forward intently. Testler had vaguely mentioned the same connection.

"They do brain research there: surgery, that sort of thing."

"They also debrief defectors there."

"Then you know about it?"

"A little."

"It makes for interesting possibilities."

"Such as?" Andy asked.

"Who knows? It's not confirmed anyway."

"But it's interesting."

"I just said that, friend. I just said that."

Monday, November 24

The ship jerked. Gears suddenly screamed loudly and the hull vibrated.

He felt it pull away from its slip.

The sound of the engines was deafening, and so, after a few minutes, he abandoned the captain's quarters, walked up to the main deck, and leaned against a bulkhead where no one noticed him. Cold wind slapped his face; squawking gulls spinning loops around the ship, dizzying and frantic, sang the same chorus in toneless harmonies.

The ship motored noisily away from the shore, blue exhaust rising above its boiling wake. A few of the crew freed Stuhlberg's sleeping bag from the tangle of netting. One of the men took his pulse, after which two of them carried the scientist below deck.

Borikowski edged over to a chain rail supported by stanchions and watched the hull push back the water. With Stuhlberg along, this was the only safe way to cross back into Canada. And in a few hours, his rendezvous with Lydia.

A growing wave curled away from the ship, and a small wake began its long and predestined journey, out and away.

Out and away.

The lobby was nearly empty and no one stood behind the registration desk, but even so, Andy hoped he might catch the day manager before he left for home. And he did.

He was an overweight man in his mid-fifties: thick but flabby neck, jowls, and a bowl of black, oily hair surrounding a vast expanse of shiny bald skin. He appeared with a handkerchief in hand, and kept it close by at all times, blowing his nose in little spurts, so much and so often, it seemed, that his upper lip was a permanent bright pink.

Andy's shoulders slumped, his clothes were wrinkled, and his eyes drooped. He smelled something like a gymnasium.

"What can I do for you?" the manager growled.

"I wonder if we might speak in your office?"

"This is my office," he declared, stretching his arms out to encompass the registration desk and perhaps the entire hotel.

"Some place private then."

"Just kidding." When the big man smiled, he tilted his head back as if to hold in his teeth. "You take a left up there," he said, pointing, "then another left through the door marked Private. Say! That's appropriate, isn't it?" He winked and grinned, and again leaned so far back that it appeared he might fall over.

Andy followed the directions and the two met in a hallway outside the office. The man blew his nose and then led the way in and waddled over to a much worn desk chair, collapsing into it.

Andy took a chair in front of the desk. His body was of such a size that he rarely, if ever, looked comfortable when sitting. "I'm a Federal agent assigned out of Washington. I'm interested in seeing your guest bills for the last day or two. Specifically, I'm interested in a single woman who is charging her meals to room service."

"Is this a joke?"

"No."

"You know, I thought it was a joke, except that you look exhausted. Can I offer you a cup of coffee or something?"

"Thank you. In a while maybe. I *am* exhausted." Andy had spent the better part of the night waiting for a plane at Mirabel airport in Montreal, and had consumed this entire day questioning five other hotel managers, all of whom had taken their time.

"Important, is it?"

"Yes."

"Well, I have to tell you this is the most unusual request I've ever had as manager, and not at all the kind of service we provide. Obviously, I will need some identification, as well as a reference or two whom I may call to confirm your authority on such matters. I'll also have to check with our home office in Los Angeles and receive at least a verbal approval. I should wait for the telex, but that might take forever."

"I don't carry identification," Andy told him.

"Oh my." The big man tilted back in his chair. "That is a problem."

Andy noticed a candy bar wrapper lying dead in the wastebasket. He said, "There is a number you can call."

The man rocked forward. "Well. That's a start. Let's have it and we'll see what we can do."

While the manager made the call, inquiring about a George Baker, Andy looked about the office. Besides a couch, a low table, and two guest chairs, there was precious else. No plants, few wall decorations, no filing cabinet. Bland. Blaaa . . .

The fat man hung up and said, "Yes. I suppose I believe you. But the fellow who I spoke with said that your wife has taken ill and would appreciate a call."

"Pay phone?"

"You can use this one. . . ."

"No. Sorry. It has to be a pay phone."

"Around the corner and down the hall, left, down the stairs and there you have it. Follow signs to the pool."

"Will you help us?"

"Yes. Of course I will. I'll get all the billings for you immediately, and I'll place a call to the home office and see where we stand."

A few minutes later, following a brief exchange, Andy hung up the pay phone and waited for it to ring. When it did, he introduced himself as George Baker.

Parker Lyell's voice responded, "Oh yes. Terrific! Are you secure, George?"

"Yes, are you?"

"Not to worry. All's fine. Here's the gist: Our friend has hit a store in Ohio. Unfortunately, the computer data-storage has been erased, and so access into the area is still not possible. It's sealed tight as a drum. There are backup computers over at the Pentagon, but the brass is dragging its feet. We still don't know what, if anything, he took with him. The place was riddled with video cameras though, so at some point we'll know the whole story. Meanwhile, it is essential you stay in close contact. But on that note, we have other problems. Listen up. Interpol has uncovered a sabotage plot aimed at destroying Canadian communications. We have no idea how serious the threat is, but should communications be lost, we will go to CROSSWORD CODE, RIGHT. Copy?"

"RIGHT."

"Correct. Otherwise, check in midday tomorrow. We expect to know more by then."

"Okay. I've got it."

"News?"

Andy found himself tempted to tell Lyell of the almond-eyed woman he was stalking; but, recalling his cab ride of the day before and the warning of leaks, thought better of the idea, and instead told Lyell that he was tired, hungry, and dirty.

"Remember to keep us up-to-date."

"Yes."

The two hung up and Andy returned to the office.

The jowled manager had on his desk a tidy stack of guests' bills. Andy entered, closed the door, and sat down with a sigh.

The manager said, "Take a look at these. Three single women out of two hundred and two beds filled! How do you like that? And only one who has ordered meals from Room Service. She checked in yesterday." The man slid the chit across the desk to Andy. A line of computerized charges filled the right-hand column.

Andy waved the bill in his right hand. "This is as close as I've come, but I'm faced with a bit of a problem."

"More?"

"I don't dare tell your room service personnel what's going on, or who I am, because they'll act differently— no matter what they may think—and that could foul this all up. But it is imperative I match descriptions of the woman. I wonder . . ."

"Yes?" the manager asked, leaning forward intently.

". . . If you could discretely make some inquiries for me, we might achieve the same results."

"Such as?"

"Is there any way to tell who has delivered to her, and who hasn't?"

"Yes. No problem. The individual orders will be initialed by the waiter or waitress. May I ask a question?"

"Certainly."

"Is the hotel in any immediate danger? This isn't a terrorist or something like that. . . ."

"No danger."

"Oh good."

"Then perhaps you could approach one of your older waiters who has delivered to her and pretend you're infatuated with the woman in"—Andy checked the bill—"four-ten."

"I can certainly do that with no problem."

"What I'd like you to do, is pose it as a question. Her outstanding feature is her eyes. You could ask, 'Say, is that woman who has the eyes and the dark hair, like Sophia Loren, the one in four-ten?' Something like that."

"Oh yes. I see."

The manager appeared excited by it all, and this worried Andy. "You must not seem too excited. Only interested. You understand?"

"Mr. Baker, we talk about beautiful women everyday. Shop talk. It's nothing new. I'll check the charges and see if I can't find one of the waiters. We're just switching shifts and there should be someone here who served her last night. Just a minute." The man forced himself up and out of the chair and waddled to the door, closing it as he left.

Andy sat restlessly for nearly ten minutes before the man returned with a tight-lipped smile pasted on his face. It had seemed more like half an hour. He said, "Peter agreed she's the prettiest we've had in six months. The eyes and hair match. What now?"

Andy sighed. After seven hours of this, he had been ready to give up. "Thank you. Thank you so much. I'll take that coffee now, if I may? Oh, and I'd like to take a look at your phone system, if I could." And then he added, "And I'd love a bite to eat."

The fat man chuckled. "And a hot shower, I'll bet."

"Yes. A shower would be wonderful."

"Which will mean a room." He leaned across the desk. "Will that be cash or credit card?"

7:23 P.M.
Lake Huron, Across the Canadian Border

He had been on board ship for twelve hours when it approached the old fishing town of Blind River. A Canadian wind stirred the night air, and where Borikowski stood, overlooking the dark shoreline, the wind stung his cheeks.

Finally, the *Ciel Rouge* banged into the old wooden docks, which complained in muted creaks, and the crew made her fast.

This leg of his assignment caused Borikowski additional concern. Here he was to wait for a contact, something he never liked because it left him under the control of others. Yet this stop would also temporarilly rid him of Stuhlberg. The scientist was to be turned over to the Kolyma for the next part of the operation. If all went as planned, then Stuhlberg would be shipped to British Columbia, and for a few days, Borikowski would be rid of him.

A few days.

Meanwhile Borikowski would travel with Lydia, and he looked forward to that with heightened anticipation.

When the expected agent was an hour late, Borikowski became concerned.

By the end of two hours, his lungs hurt from smoking and his stomach growled angrily at the black coffee. The sailor who was standing sentry at the bottom of the ramp pounded his feet on the dock to fight off the cold. Borikowski did the same as he paced the stern deck, listening to the hypnotic slap of water against the hull, annoyed once more by the assignment's share of problems. He lit another cigarette and continued to pace.

"Psssst." The sentry caught Borikowski's attention, then cocked his head toward the dim glow of a cigarette in the shadows of one of the nearby warehouses.

Borikowski nodded and struck a match, but the wind blew it out, so he cupped the next and it stayed lit.

The visitor approached the ship cautiously, was searched, a gun taken from him—much to his objection—and then joined Borikowski on the stern deck.

"I am LeClux. You have had some difficulties."

Borikowski spoke through his stuffed nose. "I hope they warrant your being two and one half hours behind schedule. It all goes in my report, LeClux. Certainly you realize that it all goes in my report."

"Fuck your mother with your report."

Borikowski struck the man across the face.

"What the fuck!?" LeClux touched his pained cheek.

"You may be accustomed to a certain casualness around your colleagues. However, I will not tolerate it. You will observe rank, soldier, or I will have you reduced to a citizen. Do I make myself clear?"

"You cannot demote me, *m'sieu*. Yes, sure, you can strike me; but I am not your soldier! The man you were to see was badly injured in Soo. The Security Service raided your safe house earlier today. It was a disaster!

"I did special favors for your agents," the man continued. "We have some of the same long-range goals. The man you were to meet here trusted me to assist you. He said it was important you be informed. I am telling you, he is hurt badly, *m'sieu*, and has taken refuge in a small cabin up near the ski area. I wish to help you, *m'sieu*, but I will not be treated like this. *Non!* Henri LeClux is a man of principles and of honor."

Borikowski took a drag off the cigarette. "Forgive me. I appreciate your help. Please explain the raid." He stared out into the dark.

LeClux explained, "Three of your agents were arrested. Two of theirs were injured. My friend and I made it out. He asked me to tell you that the SS took the medical supplies intended for your delivery." He rambled on, nearly hysterical. "I am late because I had to be extremely careful of tails. The SS is good you know. . . ."

"The exchange?" Borikowski inquired, unimpressed by the typically frenetic Frenchman.

"Yes. I can take you to the exchange, but the medical supplies—your contact was to bring them along."

"Is there nothing you can do?"

"Such goods are black market, of course. But I would need to get back to the city to make the necessary arrangements . . . and I would need to be paid, of course." He looked quizzically at Borikowski, wondering what his reaction would be.

"That's no problem. But I am on a schedule. You will take me to the exchange. I will have two of these sailors with me. Once contact is made they will return for the cargo and bring it to us. When my responsibilities are fulfilled, I will be on my way. You and . . . and the people I'm meeting can work out the details."

"Whatever works the best."

"That's the way we'll do it."

"Okay. Fine with me."

Borikowski picked up his suitcase and nodded to shore. LeClux proceeded down a steep metal stairway, which led to the shore ramp and then to the dock. But as Borikowski, suitcase in hand, placed his foot on the first step, he slipped on a thin layer of ice, which had formed only minutes before. He threw the suitcase forward, and miraculously LeClux, who had heard the slip and turned, caught it. Borikowski, who was worried more for the suitcase and the enclosed bacteria than for his own safety, banged his head against the metal steps and slid, face up, crashing into LeClux. His head had smacked the fourth and fifth step severely, with such force, in fact, that it tore loose his wig. Dazed and briefly unable to stand on his feet without support, he was helped into the Jeep by a deck hand and LeClux and driven away, bleeding only slightly from his nose.

Reattaching the wig proved no problem, but the lump on his skull told of the force of the fall. And now a headache ran wild, as if a hundred head of cattle were stampeding toward his eyes. Every little bump in the road magnified his pain tenfold.

To his alarm, his nose continued to bleed, and easily qualified as the worst of his life.

They drove to a house on the north end of Blind River. It was Tudor and in need of fresh stain, as well as some masonry work. The nosebleed finally stopped a few minutes after their arrival. Borikowski changed his bloodied shirt and then lay down on the couch to allow his nose time to fully clot.

He was up and about when three Kolyma arrived at the house on schedule, twenty minutes later, and took over.

Borikowski had never met a single member of the elite squad who was, in his opinion, worth knowing. He was happy to be continuing on without them, aware that in a few short days, and a few thousand miles, he would meet with them again.

For now, Borikowski was free of Stuhlberg, and to him, this was all that mattered.

One of the Kolyma entered the living room. "Fuck the old German bastard!" the man directed at Borikowski.

"What is it?"

"We changed the dressing on his hand and everything was fine."

"Yes?" Borikowski inquired.

"Now he has a nosebleed! And the damn thing won't stop!"

Andy enjoyed the hunt now. This was as close as he had come to Borikowski yet: a real, live, living-and-breathing connection, and he wasn't about to lose her.

He had taken a room—cash—eaten and showered. He wore a new change of clothes: blue shirt, blue jeans, and a corduroy sport coat.

Downstairs, in the small underground garage, a rental car awaited him. Inside were two ice chests filled with fruits and dairy products and bags of ice. Binoculars, road flares, a compass, a hunting knife, a high-powered flashlight, thermal socks, long underwear, a winter parka, and felt-lined boots had been on his list as well. At a Sears he had pick-pocketed three men all within a matter of a few minutes. Two of the wallets he merely dropped onto the floor as if fallen from a pocket. The third he kept. Unlike the others, no photograph showed on the identification. Instead, this man, Ted Welch of Dearborn, Michigan, had recently been issued a temporary driver's license, and owned three credit cards, one of which had been used to rent the car. Andy felt this necessary, because he knew the KGB had moles in the offices of every major credit card company and most banks, and he was taking no chances of his location being discovered through a credit trail. His suitcase, now filled with his dirty clothes, lay on the floor of the back seat, and the blue car's gas tank was filled with unleaded.

Most of this was typical solo surveillance precaution. If the woman left the hotel and traveled to any form of public transportation, train, bus, or air, Andy could follow, leave the car behind, and take the same means of departure as Lydia. If she left by taxi or a car of her own, he was prepared to follow her, even if it took days.

The styrofoam ice chests were not original either. He

213

had learned this trick years before from a crusty old intelligence officer named Ralph Plank, a man who could not be without food for more than an hour.

For now, though, he sat in an uncomfortable chair, on the landing to the fourth floor, the door to the fire stairs cracked open with a pencil. He had a good view of the elevators and much of the hallway.

The combination of the rental car, keeping an eye on the hallway, and the cordless phone in his coat pocket, which was bridged to her room's extension, offered him security. If a call came to her room, he could listen. If someone arrived, or if she left without a call, then he would see.

Trapped, that's what she was. Trapped.

So he leaned forward, eye to the crack, and waited.

8:22 P.M.
Washington, D.C.

Scrawny Chris Daniels had found time to race home, shower, and change. So had Terry Stone for that matter, but he didn't look at all different.

Daniels now wore khakis, a buttoned-down oxford shirt, and a black silk tie. He entered the office pushing his glasses back onto his nose.

Stone was accustomed to the habit. He thought, How many times have I told the boy to get those damned things fixed? "You ought to get those damned things fixed," he said stridently.

Daniels announced proudly, "I believe we may have something here," and sat down facing Stone.

"In what form?"

Daniels' exceptionally long fingers guided a stapled group of papers across Stone's enormous desktop. "The Canadians sent it telex to Central. It's in the computers now. This is your copy."

Stone reached for it and studied it in a cursory manner. "I'd rather an explanation, if you don't mind." He lifted his glasses off the desk. "I refuse to wear these another minute."

Daniels nodded, nervous by the intimacy. These last few days had shown Daniels a glimpse of the other Stone: the human side. Daniels started in. "The Security Service turned up certain medical supplies in their raid this afternoon on a Sault Ste. Marie safe house: lactated Ringer's solution, surgical tubing, some syringes—"

"I've already read that report. And we've already discussed it." Stone toyed with impertinence.

"True. Well, sir, a few hours ago, a hospital in an exurb of Sault Ste. Marie, Ontario, was robbed. The stolen items match those confiscated this afternoon."

Stone perked up and leaned forward. "Run that by me again, son."

"The same items."

"Someone's injured?"

"Certainly a possibility. Perhaps injured . . ."

"Or illness. Stuhlberg would have a hell of a time holding up as a hostage. He's an elderly man, for God's sake."

So was Terry Stone, but Daniels hardly felt it an appropriate time to make comparisons.

"You don't agree?" Stone asked, detecting reservation in Daniels' face.

"It's hard to say. Any number of possibilities exist: coincidence, decoy, injury, illness . . ."

"But . . ."

"But I can't help but be reminded of the Hutchinson kidnapping, sir. The similarity of the medical inventories is astounding."

This triggered a laugh from Stone. Sometimes Daniels was too bright for his own good. "Refresh my memory on the Hutchinson kidnapping, would you please?" He scratched his nose in order to cover his mouth, for he was grinning, and although he did not mind laughing with people, he disliked laughing at them.

"An FBI case—"

Stone then interrupted, and snorted, for the joke was on him: he did remember. "Of course! They buried the daughter alive for something like fourteen days! Texas, wasn't it?"

"I'm impressed," Daniels conceded.

"Bullroar! If I hadn't remembered, you'd have been disappointed. There's a difference, Chris."

Daniels continued. "Remember how they kept her alive?"

"IVs and an oxygen tank . . ." Stone clicked his tongue to the top of his mouth.

Daniels continued for him. "Lactated Ringer's solution to prevent dehydration and supply food to the blood, and an oxygen/nitrogen combination fed through a gas mask." He waved the stack of papers in the air. "Same gear."

Terry Stone slapped the desktop. "Nice job, Chris! You anticipate that they'll try and ship Stuhlberg?"

"It's certainly what I would expect. And it creates two interesting possibilities. First, that they will keep both Stuhlberg and Borikowski together, so that, as we said before, Stuhlberg's presence increases our losses if we attempt to take Borikowski. Second, however, is the possibility that they merely want to render Stuhlberg useless, and divide and conquer, if you will. If they are separated, then each has his own chance of escaping detection, and the odds increase that one or the other will get out of the country. Separation also frees *Dragonfly* of a cumbersome package."

"They'll use a casket?"

"Yes, that would be my guess. If not an actual shipping casket then a crate of equal size. A shipping casket would be easier and draw less attention." Then he added, "And a shipping casket would allow the use of detonation devices."

"That's a morbid thought. . . . You mean rig it to blow up the doctor?"

"It *would* discourage us from opening any and all caskets."

"Would it?"

"Wouldn't it?" Daniels asked heatedly.

But Stone did not answer. Instead he asked, "I suppose they'll try to fly Stuhlberg out, eh?"

"I doubt it. The enhanced airport security would all but rule out air shipping. You've heard the news reports. Air traffic has been slowed by the thorough searches. Federal Express and Emery both have filed suit against the FAA, claiming their companies should be exempt from the searches. Caskets have always been a favorite of gun runners and dope dealers. . . . The Canadians and the FBI have both stopped a dozen air shipments in the last four months, so the DS would anticipate caskets being searched."

"So they'll try something else."

"That's my guess."

"And we wait and see."

"Yes. And we put men on rail and trucking routes in both Canada and the U.S. That, I think are their likely choices." Daniels added, "I've also alerted Naval Intelligence."

"For what reason?"

"Because of what Stuhlberg's assistants told us. I think it safe to assume *Dragonfly* took a sample of the bacteria. If true, then he must avoid flying with the bacteria because of its extreme sensitivity to pressure change. We'll know more accurately what we're up against once the brass lets us look at that data; but if he can't fly out, then he's headed for one coast or the other, and it may involve a rendezvous with a ship."

Stone, intrigued with this notion, again sat forward. "That's good thinking, Chris. Yes. Soviet ship movement—including their fishing fleet—may indicate which coast he's headed for." He leaned back in his chair. "That would lead us to him, wouldn't it?"

"It is certainly a strong possibility."

"Yes." Then Stone's face held a wise expression. "You know something?"

"What's that?"

"You'd make a hell of a strategist."

Daniels blushed. "Sir, perhaps it is time we passed on our hunches to Parker Lyell. He could relay the information to Clayton when they next speak. After all, Stuhlberg's assistants warned of the bacteria's toxicity. . . ."

"I agree completely, and as a matter of fact, I've already spoken to Lyell. He'll pass along the information tomorrow at noon. We will maintain Clayton, however—much to the protests of GH4—on the off chance he can uncover Borikowski. He'll be on orders not to shoot."

"Will that make any difference?"

Stone, surprised by the question, smiled bleakly. "I hope so," he said.

11:55 P.M.
Sault Ste. Marie, Michigan

Andy Clayton sat in a chair, straining one eye to see through the thin crack of the stairway door, which allowed him a view of the hallway of the fourth floor.

The simplicity of the hotel's semi-automated phone system had made it easy for Andy to connect the Sears cordless phone he had bought to Lydia's room extension. He had also performed surgery on the phone's receiver, disabling its microphone by snipping two thin wires, so that he could listen in, but not be heard. And so, a few hours ago, when she had ordered dinner, he had listened to her conversation with room service and had been pleased with how well the system worked. The hotel operator would ring his extension first, then seconds later would connect Lydia's phone, thus eliminating the quiet pop of Andy's receiver being connected. Now, four hours after that successful first test with room service, his cordless receiver rang again and he switched it on.

"*J'ai perdu ma montre. As-tu le temps?*" a male voice asked, and Andy's heart raced.

"*De temps en temps.*"

"*Quel temps?*"

"*Chaque fois.*"

Andy began scribbling a cryptic shorthand onto a piece of paper resting on his thigh.

The male voice—Borikowski—asked, "Have you any travel plans?"

She asked, "How's your weather?"

"Blue sky."

"Sounds wonderful."

"It is."

And they both hung up.

Andy immediately shut off the cordless by setting it on the floor, and just as quickly it rang again. He picked it up, put it to his ear, and heard two lines connect again.

"Room Service," a young voice answered.

"Brandy please. Four-ten."

"Any particular brandy, madam?"

"Your most expensive . . . and a cup of hot water to rest the snifter in."

"Yes, madam. That's room four-ten."

"Yes."

"Thank you."

"Thank you." She hung up.

So did Andy, realizing that she planned on leaving— "Have you any travel plans?"—yet deciding it would be later than sooner—because a brandy was a before-bed drink.

Taking no chances, he pocketed the cordless phone and headed to the underground garage, deciding to park across the street from the hotel, where he had both a view of her lighted window and the front—and only—hotel entrance. Here, he waited out the night.

At half-past midnight, her window went black.

Tuesday, November 25

6:47 A.M.
Sault Ste. Marie, Michigan

She came out of the hotel's front door looking as beautiful as any fashion model. A doorman carried her bag, and she, her purse. A cab was waiting, and only seconds later it pulled out into a light traffic, Andy's rented Citation following.

He had remained awake through the night, sitting in the rented car watching the hotel's front door, cordless phone resting on the dashboard, his fingers drumming on the steering wheel. His new parka had ten pockets and was reversible from beige to dark brown, and he played with velcro for something to do. The parka and new boots had helped to keep him warm; but even so, the cold Canadian air had forced him to run the car's engine periodically to warm himself.

He wondered why she had not departed at three in the morning—as he had expected she might—rather than now, when heavier traffic made it more difficult for her to spot someone following. He knew this was no doubt part of a plan—the phone call, the timing of the departure, the rendezvous—devised and conceived by Borikowski or even higher-ups, and now set in motion despite the flaws born into it.

He shrugged and turned left, following a good distance

behind her cab, rubbing his eyes and trying not to feel tired.

The morning air warmed the sky, a tinge of orange brushing a few clouds to the east. Two pigeons settled on the roof of a nearby building.

Her cab headed straight out of town and across International Bridge.

Using George Baker's credentials—but still in possession of Tom Welch's temporary driver's license he had pick-pocketed the night before—Andy passed through the border checkpoint without any trouble. But as the Customs man handed back his identification, Andy realized that others could also be aware of his George Baker identity, just as the Montreal mole had known of Borikowski's Peter Trover and Franz Vogel identities.

He slipped the driver's license back into his wallet and drove away, restless and annoyed at himself for not using the Welch identification.

And then he started looking in his rearview mirror.

The cab dropped her at a Hertz agency, where she rented a large dark blue four-door. Within minutes Lydia left the city and found her way to the Trans Canadian Highway.

Andy's Citation remained well behind. As he devoured an apple from a cooler, he checked his map and began his own patented brand of surveillance. Because she would be watching for any tails, he had to be extremely cautious. He settled on the Kreuter plan: dropping well behind the suspect until visual contact is lost; keeping a careful eye on both the odometer and the map, only closing the gap between the two vehicles when—according to the map—the suspect approaches the next upcoming exit.

This was an American Intelligence surveillance technique developed by Harold Kreuter in the mid-1960s, and worked on any major limited-access highway. Back roads, with their numerous intersections, would have forced Andy to keep too close a tail on her, and more than likely, she would have spotted him. But there were no such back roads west of Sault Ste. Marie. Instead, the Trans Canadian Highway cut through thickly forested, lush green mountains, snaking through the hills like a ribbon dropped from the sky.

He checked his watch, turned on the radio, located some loud rock music, and settled back, prepared for a long drive.

He thought about his earlier conversation with Mari, her arguments against his continuing the assignment. And though he wanted to believe he would not attempt to kill Borikowski at the first opportunity—as he had told her—he was not absolutely certain what his reaction might be.

He argued with his conscience throughout the drive. He was afraid of Borikowski, if for no other reason than that the man had compromised Duncan—and Duncan had been rated as one of the country's top five field operatives at the time of his abduction. At the same time, Andy feared the sloppiness that might accompany his own unrelenting desire for vengeance. There was no room for mistakes now. Borikowski was on unfamiliar ground, on what was obviously a complex operation, and Andy held the element of surprise.

If he could find him.

2:03 P.M.
Wawa, Ontario, Canada

He drove past Lake Superior Provincial Park and closed the gap he had allowed between his car and Lydia's, following her off the highway when she exited at Wawa, a modest town that welcomed tourists past a tremendously large bronze statue of a Canada goose. He allowed a car of hunters to pass him and pull between him and Lydia to help shield him from her view.

She drove north out of town, a few minutes later passing a spectacular waterfall, and finally turned into a motel complex.

Andy, still behind the hunters, slowed to take a good look, drove a hundred yards past the motel's entrance, and parked across the road, pulling the vehicle into a stand of pine.

Only a dusting of snow covered the thick floor of frozen needles. The closeness of the trees made the forest extremely quiet, and the lack of wind kept the chill at bay. He hiked with thermos and binoculars until directly across from the motel's entrance, but thirty yards in from the road. The forest floor inclined steadily up from the road, and the motel, which sat in a bowl-like hollow between two hills, lay below him. The best view required he climb a sticky pine tree. And so a few minutes later he sat like a bird, perched halfway up the pine, his newly purchased binoculars aimed at the motel.

He crouched in the tree for what seemed like an hour before she finally appeared beyond the far side of the motel, edged alongside the pool, and climbed the broomed steps terraced into the snow-covered hill, banging her suitcase on each step.

Andy had carefully scanned the grounds through his binoculars and had seen no one. So he was surprised when now he spotted the white mist of someone's breath coming from under a huge pine that shaded the middle chalet. He looked more closely and saw a brown winter jacket pressed up against the rough bark. He touched the breast pocket of his new parka, reassuring himself that his wallet was still there, and watched the almond-eyed woman gain entrance.

Another guard inside, which brought the count to two.

Now he was certain he had found Leonid Borikowski, and the awareness both stimulated and frightened him, for his immediate reaction was that of the hunter who sees the rabbit heading into the trap and knows inside that the prey is finally his. . . .

Lydia Czufin had painted a picture of how their reunion was going to be, so when the stocky man holding a silenced automatic opened the door, she was disappointed. She recognized the man, knew he was a member of Spetsnaz's elite Kolyma squad, but couldn't remember how or even where they had met. He was a pleasant-looking man for his size, his voice as low as the growl of a bear. "Greetings. Enter," he told her, eyes studying her body.

Typical of the Kolyma, she thought. Animals.

She stepped inside. He shut the door behind her. They chatted mindlessly, until, when it seemed appropriate, she asked where Borikowski was; and the man, shaking his head slightly—as if disgusted—said, "He's upstairs. But I had better warn you. He is not well."

"What is it?"

"Headaches. Nosebleeds. He took a bad fall. Whatever he did . . . he did not sleep well last night. He kept us all awake with complaints and demands."

She looked at the man curiously, almost as if he were to blame, and then hurried upstairs.

Borikowski didn't hear her until she said, "Hello."

"Hello," he offered with a strange expression on his face.

They were quite far apart, she propped in the doorway studying him, and he on the bed with his hands on his head. The large and open bedroom and its bath were the only rooms on this upper floor, and the A-frame's ceiling veed above them. His cosmetics, left unattended, had

227

streaked and mixed, and these colors and shadings made him appear old and haggard.

"How are you?" she asked, still posed in the doorway. Looking more closely, she noticed that the discoloring across his forehead was not failed cosmetics, but an oblong bruise. In fact, most of the cosmetics were off, she realized, taking three more steps toward him. His wig had been removed, and in place of wavy hair was a head closely shaven; and in the center of his skull was a bump so big that it looked more like a child's shoe hiding under a rug.

What both surprised and frightened her was the demonic look carved into his eyes. A sheen, like a stretched thin plastic, jumped out of the black pupils. Eyes looking at her, but never focusing. He held a handkerchief in his hand, which was stained with dried blood.

Since he did not answer her, she said, "Do you need a doctor? Your head looks . . ."

"No." He continued to grind his knuckles into his temples.

She approached cautiously, as one might approach a stray dog. She touched his shoulder.

He looked up. The woman he had murdered at Dorval stood in front of him, her face as bloodless as snow. She was spinning the hat pin behind her ear, and at the same time sticking her tongue in and out like a venomous snake. He glanced into her eyes, but she had none. Only empty sockets, crawling with hungry black flies.

"Leonid?"

Now Lydia stood before him. He stopped rubbing his temples. "Sorry. It's better now."

"You look like you tried to stop a train with your face."

He attempted a smile, like a defeated boxer might.

"What is it?" she asked with a more frightened voice.

"I slipped and fell." He rubbed his head. "Down a

flight of stairs. I'll improve. I need some time, maybe some sleep."

Something crawled around in her stomach every time she looked at his face. She kicked off her shoes and sat next to him, turning him around and trying to work out some of the knots and cables in his neck.

He groaned. "The nosebleeds come and go. This feels good. Ohhh, that feels better. Yes. Ohhh, right there . . ."

She kneaded his right shoulder with her fingers and felt his whole body relax. She pushed him onto his face and made him lie down and continued to rub. She rubbed down his arms and unbuttoned his cuff and began to unstrap what looked like a watch on his wrist.

He yanked his arm away and shouted angrily, "What are you doing?"

She sat back, shaken by his abruptness. "Taking off your—"

"You must be crazy!"

Dumbfounded, she stared.

Then he remembered she had no idea of any of this. "Oh! I'm sorry."

"Crown?"

He smiled thinly, trying to be nice. "These have to do with Crown's security," he said, strapping the watch back to his wrist."

"Two of them?"

"Each backs up the other."

Looking at the watch more closely, she asked, "What does it do?"

"Monitors my pulse and blood pressure."

"Both of them?"

"I told you: One backs up the other. If both fail . . ." He trailed off, not knowing whether to tell her.

"Was it successful?" she asked.

"So far. Yes." He removed his shirt with her help and

lay back down. "Since we'll be traveling together, you might as well know what you are a part of."

"I don't have to . . ."

"Over there in my suitcase is a briefcase, and inside this are some biological experiments made by the United States Defense Department."

"Germ warfare?" She was horrified.

"No. But in its present form, it's just as dangerous. It can't be flown out, due to the effect pressure has on the bacteria. To help protect it, the briefcase is slightly pressurized, but orders are to keep it with me and make a rendezvous in a few days. That's fine with me. I hate flying. If they kill me, or if they force me to kill myself, or even if they sedate me heavily"—he hesitated in thought—"these devices on my wrists detonate the briefcase using radio signals, and the explosion releases the germ. Simple. The germs are toxic. These devices are deterrents. Always deterrents."

"And it kills people?"

"Don't sound so concerned."

She stopped rubbing his neck. "Does it?"

"I don't know. No one will bother us. I know that much."

"I don't believe that. Besides, what about accidents?"

"I don't understand."

"What if you die in an accident, or of natural causes . . . or of falling down a flight of stairs. . . ?" She was somewhat panicked. He rolled over and gazed at her. But she could hardly look back into those eyes, and her mind was reeling with various possibilities, all of which frightened her.

"I won't. Why do you think they chose me?"

"I should contact Rhinestone. . . ."

"No! I'll be fine. All I need is a little rest."

She said, "You look horrible, Leonid. You need more than rest. You need some X-rays and a doctor."

"Out of the question."

"But . . ."

"No!" he hollered. "Let me rest."

She rose from the bed and paced the room.

Twenty minutes later she sneaked out while he slept. He was mumbling unintelligibly and tossing and turning.

The idea of some form of germ warfare in a nearby suitcase, rigged to this abnormally behaving man, did little to boost her confidence in the assignment.

She placed her call from the pay phone by the pool. It was cold, but private, and she could see around herself in all directions.

General Gustav Molière's communications staff, having intercepted a shipment of electronic gear at Mirabel airport six months ago, had known for several weeks which scramblers Rhinestone used. They also knew that the United States had broken the Executive Code earlier this week and so they were now busy making three separate tape recordings of the entire unscrambled conversation, for shipment to Washington, D.C.:

Tristovich: "Hello?"

Woman's voice: "He has taken ill. He's in pain."

Tristovich: "How ill?"

Woman's voice: "A head injury."

Tristovich: "Anything else?"

Woman's voice: "Nosebleeds."

Tristovich: "Impossible! Nosebleeds!" (Pause) "How much has he told you?"

Woman's voice: "Very little."

Tristovich: "Did he tell you about the watches?"

Woman's voice: (Pause) "Yes."

Tristovich: (Grunts)

Woman's voice: "I can take care of him. I'm not worried."

Tristovich: "You are to remain with him for the duration of the assignment. And remember, as long as he is wearing those devices, he must not take any drugs! If the situation worsens, you must take over. Remove one of the devices. Strap it to your wrist and make certain the dot in the upper right-hand corner is blinking. Then repeat the procedure with the other watch. Do you understand? It is very simple."

Woman's voice: (Pause) "Make certain the dot is blinking, then transfer the other."

Tristovich: "Yes."

Woman's voice: "I understand."

From his post, Andy saw her hang up the phone and head back up the hill. He looked at his watch and shifted his ass on the branch, not knowing how much longer he could remain in the tree. In the cold.

He removed his automatic, checked the clip and chamber, wishing it was a high-powered rifle, and returned it to his holster.

Then he trained the binoculars on the chalet's second-story window and waited.

2:23 P.M.
Washington, D.C.

After a series of formal protests, the withheld data arrived at the SIA and Chris Daniels began to analyze it. Stone's septic mood had isolated him, and everyone was avoiding him.

Chris Daniels was the exception. He was sitting across from Stone, dark suit, blue tie, with a ream of computer paper on his lap and no less than six folders on the small table beside him. At Daniels' request, they had both viewed the videotape of Borikowski's warning, twice.

Stone stopped the tape and said, "Let's start all over. Is that sort of thing possible? Do such things exist?"

"Yes. It's entirely feasible."

"So, we're supposed to just allow him to take it, or else we risk spreading this stuff?"

"That's up to you."

"Fill me in on this bacteria, eh? You seem convinced he hasn't already flown it out of the country, and I find that difficult to believe."

"I'm convinced, owing to the nature of the bacteria. The bugs are susceptible to a change in pressure. In any flight situation the bugs would die without a doubt. That much we know."

"And what was the other thing?"

"Saline solution. Salt water. From what we can tell, they've developed an extremely efficient microbe, but it's unable to survive in a saline solution. Stuhlberg used this as a safeguard at first, knowing full well that eventually this condition would be unacceptable. Then with the help of the Center for Disease Control, they discovered a much more significant problem and brought in Corbett to help."

"But let's go over this again. . . . If Borikowski ends up over salt water—which indeed he must if he can't fly out—we may still have a chance at him."

"Yes, all the data support that. The bugs die in salt water."

"Good! Then we attempt to locate and stay with him if we can. We maintain *Baker*2, but alert him to the new dangers. And if it looks like *Dragonfly* intends to release the bacteria, we make every effort to stop him and take our chances with the bugs. Now, exactly how dangerous is this . . . bacteria?"

"The Pentagon, in what turned out to be a struggle, forced Stuhlberg to send a sample of all research microbes to the Center for Disease Control. This all happened nearly a year ago, partly because of the public outcry surrounding any genetic testing. The Pentagon wanted to know what they had and whether or not it represented any immediate health risks. If our initial identification of the substance Borikowski stole is correct, then he has taken a volatile bacteria that might be extremely dangerous if released into the atmosphere. Using the bugs—as well as Stuhlberg—as a hostage was clever. We'd be making a terrible mistake if we allowed the bacteria to escape into the atmosphere."

"I thought you said that there was evidence the lab was already contaminated."

"Yes, I did. The sensors indicated contamination. However, one thing in our favor is that Dr. Sherman was not contaminated, which may mean it's only transmitted by physical contact."

"So it's not as dangerous as we think?"

"We're collecting opinions on that. The fact remains that Dr. Sherman was wearing a mask that would screen out the bacteria. So it's highly possible it's as dangerous as we think, but that she was lucky. CDC in Atlanta confirmed that if physical contact is made, it will perform somewhat like a germ warfare bug. It 'feeds' off organic matter. That's one of the grave concerns. They have a nickname for this particular bug at CDC, sir. They call it 'the Desert Maker,' fearing the possibility of it wiping out all vegetation in a brief amount of time, if it ever escaped. Incidently, they recommended destroying the bacteria, but this was only in part because of its 'Desert Maker' reputation. The other problem is that it reacts strangely with blood." He thumbed through the stack of printouts, and his head remained lowered as he read and then explained. "Any living organism is composed of organic matter—protein chains. In laboratory rats, the CDC found that when the bacteria enountered an organism's immunological system, it secreted an enzyme that turned out to be a fibrinolysin: enzymes that digest fibrin, which is, of course, the primary component of blood clots. Bacteria do exceptionally well in mucous membranes because they thrive on moisture and warmth: eyes, ears, nose, throat . . . vagina. Although the lab rats' immune systems killed the bug within forty-eight hours, rendering it noncontagious, the fibrinolysin broke down their bodies' ability to clot blood. One of the first symptoms in rats was nose bleeding and serious bruising. This was followed, some seventy-two hours later, by massive hemorrhaging and death."

"In its early stages, would it be treatable?"

"It's possible that during its contagious stage—the first forty-eight hours—massive transfusions might work. As I said, we're collecting opinions. After that, I doubt it." He wanted to say, "The only thing for us to do is let Borikowski flee unharmed. Contamination will mean genocide." Instead he told Stone, "We now presume that Stuhlberg has been taken hostage in case we do obtain an antibody that is capable of neutralizing the bacteria."

"You mean they've upped the stakes," Stone grunted.

"I assume their reasoning goes something like that, yes. They expect we might take action against a ship that Borikowski was on—and that's his only available means of escape, unless we've overlooked something. But will we take action that risks the life of one of our leading scientists, who just happens to be a close friend of the president?"

"I'd forgotten about that."

"They went to UCLA together, sir," Daniels reminded Stone. "Stuhlberg returned to Germany until shortly after the war with France broke out. He escaped to England, from where the president, then a senator, helped him emigrate to the U.S. in 1943."

"Oh Christ! Wouldn't you know?" Stone thought for a moment and shuffled some papers around on his well-organized desktop. Then he asked, "What was the purpose of all these experiments?"

Daniels leafed through several folders and opened one up. Reading, he pushed his glasses up his nose. Then he looked up and recited: "Vaughnsville had three separate long-range goals. The first involved producing a microbe capable of increasing food protein in cultivated plant life. The second group of experiments was aimed at developing several microbes to be used in neutralizing toxins such as chemical or micro-biological waste. The third bug—the one we think Borikowski took—was aimed at energy independence, by speeding up biomass conversion—the fermentation process—resulting in ethanol production and eventually a light crude. His targeted biomass was garbage and human waste."

"Energy independence? That explains it, doesn't it?" Answering his own question, Stone said, "Yes. I see. No wonder they're playing hardball."

Stone became quite pensive for the next five minutes and scribbled a half dozen notes to himself. He placed a phone call and arranged a meeting with GH4 for later in the day. Then he asked Daniels to review the laboratory break-in. "You mean to tell me that once the GRU had broken the voice code on the credit cards, all they needed to do was walk on in?"

"Not quite that simple. First they had to locate someone who looked like this Dr. Alex Corbett. Then they had to record and code his voice onto a card. But they clearly knew quite a bit about Corbett—we've put out an all-points for a woman named Elizabeth Johnson, a graduate student at MIT who was close to Corbett and has disappeared. The DS also knew that a Sunday was the best day to attempt the operation. There would have been many more people around on any other day."

"They used Borikowski as Corbett," Stone stated, but Daniels knew it was also a question.

"Yes, despite the fact that this is not a typical assignment for Borikowski. They were lucky, sir. There's no question about that. Luck. That's all it was."

"Their good luck. Our bad luck."

"Yes, sir."

"Any field reports on *Dragonfly?*"

"None."

Stone said gravely, "I keep coming back to the possibility that Borikowski may try *using* this stuff. I don't know where the Pentagon thinks leaving him alone will get us. I told Tom Fenton that we were attempting to make contact and he nearly hit the roof. Everyone over there is scared silly."

"It's their project. If this blows up in their faces—if it becomes a health hazard—some people will have some serious explaining to do."

"Yes, indeed. Well! As far as I'm concerned, we treat this like a combination of a security theft and a kidnapping. I want the Canadians informed, in case he makes a run through Canada."

"Yes, sir." Daniels pushed his glasses up his nose and looked back into some more paperwork.

Stone said, "I don't like hostage situations."

Daniels eyed Stone.

"They have a habit of going bad."

"Perhaps it's time to call in Central, sir?"

"No. We've been over that. Besides, now the Pentagon would never approve it. They're determined to leave Borikowski alone. They even want me to call off Andy."

"And you, sir?"

"I beg your pardon?"

"What do you think? Wouldn't you advise pulling Clayton given the present circumstances?"

"No. You know where I stand, Chris. You don't have to toy with me. All I can do is get mad. But no, to answer your question. I believe it would be a bigger danger to allow Borikowski a free rein than to keep one agent out there looking for him. After all, if we can locate Borikowski and stay with him, we might be able to stop him somehow. Putting Naval Intelligence on this was a bright idea."

"Thank you."

"I don't believe in quitting until it's time."

Daniels read the statistics from the CDC once again, silently, and wondered what it might be like to die from hemophilia. Bleeding to death. He wanted to say, "It's time." Instead, he said a prayer, hoping that Andy Clayton would never find the man.

Stone's phone rang and he answered it. His brow knitted and the skin of his face seemed to hang more heavily from his bones. "Thanks." He hung up and quickly switched on his television set. Then he turned the knob to Channel 9 and sat back.

On the bottom of the screen, red letters flashed LIVE.

On screen, Karen Kwang sat a desk. "This just in: Responsibility for the attack has been claimed by the Arabs for a New World. To repeat our Cable Watch Special Report: Royal Canadian Mounted Police confirmed just moments ago that there's been a staged terrorist assault on Canadian communications." She read from a slip of paper: "Two-thirds of Canada is presently without phone service, and apparently will be for several days. The entire province of Manitoba is without electricity. Three people are known dead as a direct result of the staged assault. In all, at least seventeen microwave towers have been destroyed by synchronized explosions across a two-thousand-mile area: what law officials are describing as the largest single terrorist effort in Canada since the natural gas catastrophe three months ago, in which eighty-six people were killed.

"Five major switching stations were also destroyed in this afternoon's attack, leaving Montreal the only major city in the entire country with phone service. The group claiming responsibility, again, the Arabs for a New World. The Canadian government has had no immediate comment, partially, I might add, because all the phone lines into the province of Quebec . . . are busy." She grinned. "We will have more on the terrorist—"

Stone shut off the set.

Daniels was already pulling the large atlas from Stone's library of reference material. He found the page he was looking for and said over his shoulder, "Where did she say?"

"Didn't she say everything west of Montreal?"

"No. She said Montreal was the only city with service."

"Same thing. Damn press can't ever get a single detail straight! Where are they when you need them?"

Stone's intercom buzzed and his secretary said, "General Gustav Molière. Canadian Security Service. Line Four. Scrambled."

Stone picked up the phone, waving for Daniels to remain in the room, for the gaunt man was moving toward the door. He obliged the agency chief by taking his seat again.

Stone said, "Hello?" He paused as he listened, nodding in agreement. "Yes, we just heard"—nodding—"yes"—looking to the ceiling—"I see. I hardly think that's—" He stopped and wrote something down, concern sweeping his face. "Yes." He listened. "No, General. That's certainly not—" He stopped talking and placed the receiver back down.

"You look distraught."

"He hung up on me." He tipped his coffee cup to check inside and, seeing it was empty, said, "He confirmed the terrorist attack. He also had two other tidbits for us."

Daniels allowed the older man time to collect his

thoughts, well aware that Terry Stone, rarely, if ever, had been hung up on.

"He informed me that he has issued an arrest order for George Baker. He was briefed earlier by *our* Secretary of Defense, Collier Nast. Their mutual decision was to leave Borikowski alone and allow him clear passage."

"What does that mean? What if he intends to *use* the bacteria? Did they mention that?"

"Now you're beginning to think like me, Chris."

"Heaven help me." Daniels smiled, and was rewarded by a contagious grin from the Old Man, who had not smiled in days.

Stone re-thought the chain of events that had led to this, and shared it with Daniels, who sat listening intently. "Molière spoke with Collier, who would have informed him of the biological risks the bacteria presented, along with, I presume, a detailed account of Borikowski's warning and those whatever-you-call-'ems on his wrists. Perhaps then Collier mentioned Andy's cover name, since I doubt Collier Nast has been briefed of his real name and refers to him as a 'thorn in everyone's side'"—he said, using his fingers in the air to indicate the quotes—"and explains to Molière that Baker is after *Dragonfly*, possibly to kill him.

"He then mentions my old age and my reluctance to pull Baker . . . Andy . . . from the case, and generally discredits me."

"I would certainly doubt—"

"—Molière knew that Baker entered Canada at International Bridge early this morning," Stone continued.

Daniels said, "That's not possible. Canadian Immigration does not operate that quickly—"

"Possible?" Stone asked incredulously. "Don't you see, Chris? *We* gave him that information; probably Collier Nast. Only U.S. intelligence has the information on Andy. We've been compromised by our own people!

"No," Stone continued to ramble, "this is not coincidence that Collier should be privy to such information. Quite the contrary, someone supplied it to him. We're victims of an intentional conspiracy. Defense is afraid of the repercussions, that's all. This is just another attempt to hide a screw-up. Who can blame them? When they remove Andy, they free Borikowski. It's that simple. They play it safely and hope to hell that Borikowski will slip quietly away. Foolishly, they ignore his previous record and the chance he might intend to use the chemicals to do harm. Foolishly, they ignore the incredible political ramifications of losing an important step toward energy independence. And since the White House is directly connected to Stuhlberg via the president's friendship, and Stuhlberg is connected to GH4 via funding . . . add to that that this is an election year!"

"Why should they risk having to explain anything at all."

"Precisely." Stone looked at his sailboat sailing across the wall, at the books stacked neatly in rows above the small bar; he smelled the leather of the furniture and the aroma from a hundred cups of coffee. "With the phones out, Andy's on his own. He won't be able to check in, so we'll have to go to the Crossword Code." Disappointment pursing his lips, Stone lamented, "We won't be able to warn him in time. Molière will have him by dinner." Stone looked up. "He also read me a section of a transcript they're wiring down here. What it boils down to is that Borikowski is ill."

"Ill?"

"You're not going to like this, Chris. I suggest you take that pen out of your mouth, or you're likely to bite it in half."

Daniels fumbled the pen and dropped it onto the carpet. He brushed some lint hairs from it as Stone continued.

241

"She mentioned headaches . . . and nosebleeds."

Daniels' eyes widened and he dropped the pen again. "He's contaminated?"

"If he is, what does it mean?"

"Oh my God! Do you think he's contaminated?"

"Chris! What does it mean?"

"It means that for the next two days every Kleenex he discards, every fork he uses, may carry the bacteria. It means that come hell or high water, we *absolutely must* know exactly where he's been. And it means that he has somewhere around seventy-two hours before he dies and those devices explode, releasing it into the air and contaminating God only knows how many people. And then those people contaminate others, and those others—"

"Chris!" Stone had never witnessed his assistant this out of control. The young man's face blanched, and his hands were shaking. Stone thought, I'm glad I don't understand all this crap, or I'd be as scared as he is.

"You have to reach Molière," Daniels instructed, which was completely out of character. "And you have to convince him of the severity of the situation. Borikowski must be kept track of at all costs. It's possible to reduce the chance of contamination, but it will require professionals and a great deal of attention to detail. It's no easy task to clean up after a contaminated person who is on the move."

"I can try Molière, but I can tell you right now, that's a losing proposition. He doesn't trust us. He'll be convinced we're making the whole thing up in order to save Andy's assignment."

"But this could be epidemic in a matter of days if it's not controlled!" Daniels was shouting and leaning toward Stone, shaking a fist. "Epidemic!" His face was bright red.

Andy knocked his boots against the tree, sticky gloves balled into a fist, back pressed against the bark of the trunk, binoculars around his neck. He had emptied the thermos an hour ago. His buttocks were numb, and he worried his nose might be frostbitten.

During the past hour he had occasionally lifted the binoculars and focused on the yellow rectangle of light that filled the second-story window. Perhaps Borikowski had yet to arrive? Did her earlier phone call mean something had gone wrong, or was it perhaps the signal that she had arrived?

If you stay here through the night, I'll have to change plans, he thought, still banging his feet. I can't endure this cold forever. I wish Lyell had arranged a backup.

However, his patience paid off moments later when one of the guards walked to the parking lot, returned in what looked like a new Porsche, and left it running. With another agent's help, the two strapped skis and poles to the trunk's rack, their movements caught in the harsh light of overhead streetlamps, which moved in the wind and aggravated their motion like the strobed antics of actors on the silent screen. Then the almond-eyed woman emerged from the chalet alongside a man, each carrying a suitcase, and she her purse as well.

Andy reacted immediately by quickly descending the tree, despite his uncooperative muscles. Branch by branch he lowered himself, finally dropping awkwardly to the ground.

Through a thickly woven maze of trees, he raced toward his car.

He heard the Porsche's doors bump shut and its engine rev.

He sprinted, dodging his way through the thicket, chin

243

tucked into his chest, arms pumping, knees high. Slowly, blood returned to his extremities, bringing with it the imagined sensation that he had dived into a swimming pool full of thumbtacks. Overhead branches caught the sweep of the headlights as the Porsche pulled away from the motel. Gears changed down.

Andy reached the parked car, slammed the door shut, started the engine, and shifted into reverse. The machine slalomed backwards through the copse, out onto the pavement, and then sped away, lights off. The moon played hide-and-seek behind a checkerboard sky, and the first hints of an impending snowstorm did battle with the windshield.

Following the Porsche with his headlights off reminded Andy of Duncan, of summer evenings when they had played this same game on bicycles: chasing a tiny red light and reading the bumps and turns in the road by its movement.

He kept up the game for several miles, the whole time convinced that this had to be Borikowski, that he had finally caught up to the man; that now, after years of dreaming about his chance, it was his. And all reason left him, his imagination running wild with a hundred different ways of killing the man. Memories of Duncan flooded him: running in the surf; sliding down a mountain in Colorado; his face; his monstrous laugh; his smile. He felt as if Duncan were right here, next to him perhaps, coaxing him along.

But Duncan, in typical twin brother fashion, was insisting Andy call Terry Stone. And Andy agreed.

As they reached the outskirts of Wawa, waiting until he was hidden by a curve, Andy switched the headlights back on.

The Porsche hummed past the statue of the giant goose and entered the westbound entrance ramp of the Trans Canadian Highway.

Andy turned right, into a jammed truck stop. He pulled up to a pump and hurried out, thermos in hand. An attendant was already waiting to help, dirty rag clutched in his hands, acne from ear to ear. "How much?"

"Fill it!" Andy shouted over his shoulder, heading for the building.

The restaurant, an open room filled with dozens of booths and smelling like coffee and cigarettes, had a counter that serpentined along the far wall. Andy stepped into line behind a trucker who was paying ʕ ʾr his meal. When the trucker had taken a toothpick ana left, Andy looked into the thickly painted eyes of the woman there and handed her the thermos. Without so much as a word, the woman turned and handed it to another waitress. "Black?" Ms. Mascara asked.

"Cream please," Andy replied.

"We don't use cream," she told him, apparently disgusted by him. "Half-and-half or non-dairy creamer?"

"Half-and-half," he replied amiably.

"Half-and-half," she passed along, though the waitress who was filling the thermos at the industrial-size coffee maker had heard perfectly clearly.

"How about a pay phone?"

"Geez, where you been? Phones are out. More terrorists! They blew up the phone company this time! No phones for a few days."

"What?" Incredulous, he dashed off to the pay phones by the bathrooms. He lifted every receiver and listened.

A man came out from the men's room and, seeing Andy frantically going from phone to phone, said, "The phones are out of order." He started the message again in French, but Andy nodded and the man stopped.

When he returned to the cash register, Ms. Mascara asked rhetorically, "They didn't work, did they?"

"What's the closest town with phone service?"

She laughed. "Montreal. Back that way." She pointed.

"Perfect," he gibed sarcastically. "How much American?"

"One dollar and eighty-six cents, please."

He fished out two bills and some change, leaving a tip, and hurried back to the car.

When he paid the gas jockey, he noticed a twinkle to the boy's eyes, a cunning to the smile. He thought nothing of it, consumed instead by the frustration of not being able to alert Stone.

Fifteen minutes out of Wawa, the engine began missing badly. A dash light proclaimed: ENGINE. No fooling, he thought. He shouted, "Fuck off!" But as he coasted into the breakdown lane he understood. This was not coincidence. This was sabotage!

If his guess proved wrong, all was not lost. It would be difficult, but not impossible, to make up lost time, especially given the thousands of miles that he anticipated Borikowski had yet to travel.

Better safe than sorry. If it was sabotage then someone would be arriving any moment.

He knew KGB agents, even the Kolyma, would not attempt abducting him in a crowded truck stop. But they did have a reputation for using clever tricks—cagey bees—like rigging an engine to die fifteen minutes from nowhere. Caught up in the chase, Andy had paid little attention to his rearview mirror while following the Porsche.

He had heard too many stories of captivity.

He hopped out as the car rolled to a stop. In the trunk, below the spare, he found three flares and stuffed them into one of the many pockets of his new parka. Swiftly, he ran out into the snow field, headed toward a stand of fir forty feet away. He then quickly retraced his steps, taking great care to make it appear someone had headed for the trees. In the dull night light the illusion worked perfectly.

Now back at the car, he checked his watch: two minutes had passed since the breakdown. As yet, no cars. Improvising, he unfastened the gas cap. Removing the scratch-top from the flare's tip and tossing it into the snow, he carefully inserted the dull-orange tube into the opening. He toyed with it until it rested inside, only its tip protruding. With his ears atuned to the silence, he heard the distant whir of tires long before he saw any headlights. A small rise in the highway did not yet allow a view. He hurried to the median, planting himself down into the snowbank. Headlights cracked over the rim. He withdrew his gun—hating the weapon for some reason—and made sure he had a clear shot at the flare, though in the darkness it was difficult to see.

A light snow continued to fall. The car whisked past.

He held his position, rocking side to side to further bury himself. His jeans became wet. Fucking cold! A second car approached and passed. The third pulled over.

It was a dark brown four-door, new enough to be a rental or government-issue. Andy hoped the driver might attempt to offer help and drive on. But instead, a tall man climbed out of the passenger seat. Even in the dark, Andy recognized the man as the person who had greeted Lydia at the chalet.

Bump . . . bump . . . bump . . . his heart rate increased. He had been followed, and he had never even suspected it.

A third man left the idling car and joined the other, who was just now peering inside the driver's window.

As Andy had hoped for, and expected, both men walked past the capless gas tank, none the wiser. When this second man withdrew a tremendously large handgun from under his jacket and pointed out Andy's tracks in the snow, Andy was faced with an immediate decision: if he waited too much longer they might get too spread out, or worse yet, they might notice the flare in the gas tank.

Outnumbered and losing precious time, he made up his mind. He aimed carefully at the flare and fired three consecutive rounds. The first two missed, but following the third, as the agents turned around and took aim on him, a soft *pufft* occurred simultaneously with a yellow flash of light, and then, so quickly that it seemed impossible, the car blew apart, scattering debris and tossing the men in the air like weightless puppets. The resulting inferno swallowed them.

Andy instinctively shielded his face from the roar of flames.

The driver of the other car jumped and rolled onto the pavement, carrying a large rifle at his side.

Andy saw the man and pulled himself from the snow, waving his gun in the man's general direction. But then a thick cloud of black smoke enveloped both, covering the highway and making it impossible to see. Each knew the other was only yards away, but neither could see well enough to risk a shot. Andy backed up and fanned the smoke with his left hand, hopelessly trying to cut a hole through which to see. To make matters worse, the snowflakes were larger and falling more heavily, swirling and obscuring his vision as well. Then, like the flicker of a candle, a gust of wind washed the smoke away. The agent was standing up, eye sighting the rifle, and facing Andy, who was looking too far to his left.

The man squeezed the trigger and the rifle discharged.

The concussion lifted Andy off his feet and knocked him backwards, stealing his wind. Yet he felt no wound; and as quickly as he pounded to the pavement, he returned fire.

A piece of the man's shoulder tore loose. The force of the shot spun him around and he fell, screaming, into the spreading gasoline fire. His shoes caught fire first and then, in one quick flash, he became a scarecrow afire. He thrashed and flailed his arms and, blinded, ran further into the consuming fire. Soon, his screaming ceased.

A car's headlights appeared in the opposite lanes, still a good distance away. Then another vehicle crept over the rim behind Andy, and without a second thought he climbed into the driver's seat of the idling car and drove away, choking on the smoke and the smell of burning flesh.

The only damage that he could see was a slight crack to the front windshield. Moments later, when he was up to speed, he switched on the interior light and looked down at his chest, expecting to see his own blood, for he assumed the bullet had merely numbed his chest. Astonished, he saw only a stainless steel cartridge with a fluffy white tip: a tranquilizing dart that had embedded into his coat's breast pocket . . . the pocket containing his wallet.

He yanked the dart free and stared at it. And then he began laughing, partly from fatigue, partly from the tension of having just killed three men. He kept seeing the first two being lifted into the air by the explosion; and he heard the screaming of the third man as he watched him be swallowed by flame.

Hell.

I'm sorry, he told them. You were pawns in the way of the queen. I have no intention of losing Borikowski now.

5:16 P.M.
Washington, D.C.

Daniels entered the Old Man's office without warning. "An item of interest."

"I'm listening . . ."

"Naval Intelligence reports an unscheduled assignment for a Class-2 nuclear submarine out of Kamchatka, bearing east-southeast. It departed Thursday night, and if they've plotted its course correctly . . . it should be one hundred and fifty nautical miles off the coast of Vancouver Island in just over three days."

"In international waters?"

"Yes, sir. It could be the rendezvous. That close to shore, Borikowski would only be over water for a matter of hours. Once he's transferred to the sub, they know we're not going to strike. And of course the submarine could have equipment on board to further pressurize the bacteria."

"It'll be tricky," Stone acknowledged, rolling a pencil between thumb and index finger, "for both of us. Those are rough seas to make any kind of transfer in." He grew pensive for a moment. "Good work, Chris. I'll set up a meeting with the vice president. You contact the Coast Guard and have them be on the lookout for any Soviet trawlers straying toward the coast."

"Yes, sir. Oh, one other thing."

"What is it?"

"As you requested, I generated a Crossword Code to inform *Baker2* about the bacteria and its susceptibility to salt water. Because the phones are out, the crosswords will have to be flown in, and I need your approval for that expense." He handed Stone a paper to sign, which the Old Man read quickly and signed.

"Will these hit all the Canadian newspapers?"

"All but a few small ones. The syndication people were cooperative as always."

"And what about those devices? Did you warn Andy about that?"

"Yes. I hope he understands the message. As you know, the Crossword Code is rather cryptic. What about Molière?"

"No luck. They still intend to arrest him."

"But *Dragonfly* may be contaminated! Did you tell him that?"

Stone puckered his mouth into a disquieted frown. "Yes, I did."

"And what did he say to that?"

"He laughed."

7:37 P.M.
Thunder Bay, Ontario, Canada

"From behind, Leonid. Take me from behind," she pleaded as she let go of his waist, rolled over, and tucked her knees under herself. He gripped her on either side of her hips and they joined. She groaned approval, and then he reached forward and pulled her hand free and guided it toward her crotch so that she might masturbate at the same time.

He loved it.

Soon she was engulfed in pleasure, writhing fervently, moaning with each thrust, head bowed low, one hand pulling on the mattress.

He grunted and slammed into her so hard that she hit her head on the headboard; and now she bit firmly on a pillow and screamed, collapsing to the sheets and panting heavily.

A few minutes later he was smoking a cigarette, clad in trousers, sitting at the small table in the motel room. His nose had not bled for nearly two hours, but the previous nosebleed had caused both of them great concern, for it had lasted nearly thirty minutes.

He looked to the phone. "They're far too late. They should have called. We'll change plans." He slipped a timetable back into his coat pocket. "We'll go by train instead." The motel room's color television, used for back-

251

ground noise, was tuned to a cable station that ran advertising billboards and local radio music.

They had been waiting at Thunder Bay's Nu-View Motel for an hour, expecting a call.

Lydia attempted to cover her surprise, but failed.

"What is it?"

"It's just that I thought trains were considered an unnecessary risk. They offer no chance of escape, should anything go wrong."

"Yes, this is true. But Vladimir knows we are here, and he knows we are planning to drive the rest of the way. If he's been taken prisoner . . . if he should talk. No! We change plans now. Besides, we're behind schedule and I'm not feeling well. You can't possibly drive this alone. And what of this storm?" he asked, parting the curtains and looking out onto a parking lot collecting snow. "It's a blizzard! What if the storm closes the highways? What do we do then? I am on a tight schedule now. No, the trains will continue to run even through a snowstorm. We'll change identities here—both of us—and we'll board the nine o'clock for Winnipeg."

Her spectacularly shaped eyes were softly illuminated by the changing light of the television set, and her mood was subdued and enchanted. Her arms were crossed, and she continually rubbed her hands against the cotton of his man-tailored shirt, which she left open and unbottoned. The shirt and a pair of silk panties were all she wore. She smelled of perfume and of their lovemaking, and to him, it was wonderful. "Do you feel any better?" she asked.

He attempted to forge a smile and reached across the table to touch her cheek. She offered him her hand with a reluctance she didn't fully understand. For some reason she was reminded of a wedding she had attended recently. The holding of hands seemed more a finality. A commitment.

He said, "We must change our faces quickly, if that's possible. I'll help you however I can. This train is the only one with private cabins until tomorrow. Still we must be extremely careful with our cosmetics. We must be convincing." He pinched his temples between his hands. "They may have agents on the trains. With your help, they'll never recognize me. I have saved my most convincing identity for last. Do you have a sister?"

"No."

"You do now."

"A woman?"

He nodded.

She smiled. "I wish we did not have to change your face. I like you as you. You're very handsome, you know." She squeezed his hand tightly and then let go. She wanted to say, "I'm worried for both of us. Where are the others? Why have they not called, as they were supposed to?" She said nothing.

He stood and turned to pull the curtains entirely closed and she gasped. He spun around quickly. "What is it?"

A trembling hand covered her mouth, tears glassed her eyes, and she appeared both shocked and horrified.

"What is it?" he repeated.

She stood, the open shirt revealing her smooth dark skin, and led him by the hand over to a chest of drawers that fronted a large mirror. She spun him around.

There in the mirror, on his back, at his waist, he saw two perfectly drawn bluish hand prints, exactly where Lydia had held him during their initial lovemaking only minutes earlier.

Only the hands had not been drawn on.

They were bruises.

Sitting across from the Nu-View Motel, Andy was thinking how lucky Borikowski was, considering the DS agent had spent the better part of his intelligence career underground, invisible—stalking victims, sleeping in dives, traveling less than third class—and now he was courting a beautiful woman; and here they were sharing a room and God knows what else.

And here I am, freezing my tail off, sitting in a car in the middle of a Canadian blizzard.

It had taken him three hours to catch up to the Porsche, finally spotting the closely set taillights. Two hours later they had exited at Thunder Bay and had driven directly to the motel.

Room 7.

The windblown snowfall obscured Andy's view of the two as they left the motel, and he might have missed the couple entirely had they not returned to the Porsche, and if Lydia's hips had not swayed the way they did. When two *women* left number 7 he was nearly fooled; but he knew from his own observation that no one else had entered the room since Borikowski and Lydia had. So, either someone had been waiting in 7 for them—and had now taken Borikowski's place—or this was, in fact, Borikowski dressed as a woman. He favored the latter possibility, because it seemed a typical *Dragonfly* trick, and because the new woman carried the same red suitcase Andy had seen being loaded into the Porsche back at Wawa.

She/he was a slightly overweight, middle-aged Ms. Bland, an enigma whose demeanor suggested overwork mixed with disappointment, even through binoculars. She slouched as she walked, her head hung in boredom. She seemed plain and innocuous.

Andy slouched down behind the steering wheel—although the two were careless, walking away from the motel in conversation, paying little attention to their surroundings.

The Porsche made second gear as it whined by Andy, who lay across the front seat to avoid being seen. He waited and then followed them, remaining close behind. In this snowstorm—this blizzard—spotting a following car would be difficult, if not impossible. The road demanded full attention.

When the Porsche parked in front of the Thunder Bay train station, and the two hurried inside—bags in hand—Andy was caught completely off guard. Unable to locate an easy parking space, he double-parked and crossed the street, snow whipping around him.

But the two had cleverly timed their arrival, and the train was prompt; so by the time Andy entered the station—looking like a bum—they were nowhere to be seen.

The dull and lifeless young woman selling tickets explained in an apologetic tone that Andy had just missed the train: an "overnight coach" with private cabins, headed express for Winnipeg where it would pick up a first-class dining car and two scenic coaches, and then continue on to Vancouver with several stops in major cities.

Andy read a schedule and felt nauseated. He had had too little sleep, too much NO-Dōz, and now had too far to go. The idea of racing an express train to Winnipeg, alone in a blinding snowstorm, seemed ludicrous. So he hurried to the phone booths, hoping the lines had been repaired, hoping to reach Parker Lyell; but the lines were not repaired. They were dead.

From behind him a low voice asked, "George Baker?"

Andy turned around. The man was in his early forties and wore a conservative dark suit. His shiny shoes held glossy beads of melted snow and his smile was vague and

255

filled with mystery. Andy felt strange next to this man. "No, the name's Welch. I'm sorry." He turned to leave.

"Could I see some papers please?" the stranger asked.

Andy thought, Oh shit, they've caught me again. But they won't dare try for me until there are less people around.

He turned, now a few feet further away. "Certainly not. At least until I see some identification. Who the hell are you?"

"I'm sorry." The stranger unfolded a leather billfold containing an impressive-looking shield and an official-looking card, complete with a color photo. "Robert Stevens, Assistant Deputy, Royal Canadian Mounted Police Security Service, Ontario Province headquartered at Thunder Bay. Mr. Baker, you're to come with me, if you don't object."

"The name's Welch," Andy insisted, handing the man his borrowed driver's license.

Stevens studied the paper, but looked dubiously at Andy. He leaned forward and covered his mouth while whispering, "Listen, I don't know what you're doing, but I know who you are. I'll play along, but we meet outside immediately, or this becomes embarrassing for both of us. Don't make me chase you, Baker. That would be a mistake." Then more loudly Stevens said, "Oh! I am sorry, sir. I hope you'll forgive the confusion," and he walked out of the terminal, turning to keep an eye on Andy's next move.

Andy might have welcomed contact with the Security Service—since they would be the agency to assist in Borikowski's abduction—but Stevens had not mentioned the code.

When Lyell had rated Andy HOT, he had assigned him to the Crossword Code in the event the phones were sabotaged. If the rating was now changed, then the code word was JUMBLE. Even though Stevens' identification had appeared authentic enough to Andy, the man had not used the code word. Wrong.

Guardedly, Andy walked outside and met up with the man. Stevens explained, "I don't want to make this into a problem for either of us. The deputy director would like to see you."

"What the hell is going on here?" Andy looked around. Stevens didn't appear to have any backup. He had probably been sitting around the station most of the day.

Stevens was restless. "Your assignment is canceled. I'm not familiar with the details. You're to come with me, if you please."

Andy's car was double-parked across the street. A quick glance revealed no attended cars in the immediate vicinity, so if Stevens planned on using force, he would apparently be acting alone. To be safe, Andy asked, "Your car?"

This question confused Stevens, who relaxed, thinking Andy had decided to cooperate—not at all what he had been told to expect from Baker. He pointed to a black car not five feet away. It was empty. "It's open." He stepped in front of Andy and opened the door for him.

"What about my car?" Andy inquired, pointing across the street.

Stevens turned sideways, holding the opened door with his right hand.

Andy made up his mind.

He kneed Stevens below the ribs, grabbed the man's hair, and slammed Stevens's head against the metal door-jamb. Stevens collapsed, unconscious. In the same motion, Andy stuffed Stevens into the front seat and closed the door. The Canadian was bleeding from above his right ear.

Someone shouted through the storm.

Andy ran across the street, hurried into the double-parked car, and drove away, angry and confused. Why was Stevens here? What am I up against? He suddenly wished he had tried for Borikowski at the motel—when he had had a chance—despite his orders. Now what? Had Stevens actually been waiting for him at the station? Were others waiting at other stations? Airports? Service stations? Bus stations? What the hell was going on?

Turning the car onto the westbound highway, he switched the wipers to high. There was an inch of fresh snow on the pavement, and more accumulating with each passing minute.

Wednesday, November 26

12:47 A.M.
Upsala, Ontario, Canada

Having trouble staying awake despite the NO-Dōz, Andy rolled down his window and let the cold air slap his face, pulling his mind back to the road and away from the temptation of sleep. The train tracks ran parallel to the highway and twice he had caught a fleeting glimpse of the train, only to fall behind again. Exceeding the speed limit in order to keep up, he fully expected he might be pulled over by the Mounties at any minute. He didn't know quite how he would handle it. "Sorry, officer, I'm chasing a Bulgarian spy who killed my brother, a man who is presently dressed as a woman, and is riding the Winnipeg Express. And when I catch him I'm going to . . ."

His attention drifted again, off to no place in particular—like a dream with a snow-covered highway running through it. He wondered if catching Borikowski would indeed be as sweet as he imagined, or if the fun was in the chase.

Is the chase all I live for? he asked himself again, not wanting the answer.

The storm would close the highway soon if the drifting continued. He had already passed three cars that had skidded off the road.

In his fatigued delirium, his imagination ran wild.

Racing down the highway, feeling two steps away from abstract, he heard Mari's voice say repetitiously, "Hearts, eternity." Repeatedly, the same two words. Then a vision: Mari beneath him, naked and trembling, her one speckled eye staring back at him, her smile sincere.

He thought, Sincerity is the endangered species of the twentieth century.

The radio returned his attention to the car. The band, Red Light, was attempting to rip apart the car's small speaker. Mixed with his own fatigue from having been awake for the past forty hours, the angry music and NO-Dōz left him dulled.

The disk jockey proudly announced the next forty-five minutes as commercial-free air time devoted entirely to Red Light. Andy sang—screamed—along with the music. He began smashing his hand against the steering wheel in time with the drums. Yeah, yeah, yeah.

He felt oddly evil now, and terribly alone—he fancied himself a misunderstood hero, but saw himself more as a heartbroken twin attempting to be his brother's keeper.

I will settle this for you, Duncan.

I will settle this.

> The Man said, "Look out boy,
> better lay that weapon down;
> that gun is not a toy;
> that cap is not a crown."

His hand bounced off the wheel, his heart raced from the NO-Dōz in his system.

> I need my pills
> Got my eyes propped open: my heart alive
> Got my mind still hopin' . . .

He had stopped for gasoline as he left Thunder Bay,

but had not left his car, had not gone into the restaurant, for fear of encountering more Security Service agents. The result was now a burning stomach and a near-empty fuel tank.

His head hurt.

It's the music, he thought; no, it's the fucking pills, the NO-Dōz. See what you've done to me, you bastard?

> One thing's for certain,
> The only constant is change. How strange . . .

He left the radio loud for the entire forty-minute set.

Then a heavily accented English voice advertised loudly and enthusiastically, "Virgin snow-covered hills bathed in a magenta sunset serve as background as a herd of elk drink from the crystal running stream below you. Off to your right a flock of geese take wing and disappear into the melting horizon. Whether hunter or photographer, adult or child, Purdy Wright's Air Wilderness Excursions will show you the way it used to be: Nature at its best. Call Wright's Guided Air Tours in English River today. And, if you mention this advertisement, you will receive an extra ten minutes in the air, courtesy of this station."

Andy had given the idea of a plane flight serious consideration, but due to the weather, and the possibility that the Security Service was watching the airports, had decided against it.

He pulled into the breakdown lane and checked a map he found on the floor, a heel mark covering most of the eastern provinces.

English River was not far away.

He dry-swallowed three more NO-Dōz, his seventh and eighth and ninth. He urinated by the side of the road and thought he felt better, thought that maybe this time the pills would stay down. But as he sat behind the wheel, he felt it coming. Leaning out the car door, he vomited violently in three long heaves, and continued wretching in spasms for another few minutes, his head tingling from the drug, eyes hot and dry, worms crawling inside his skull.

Hands shaking, he resisted the stomach seizures, aware that the manufacturers placed a trace amount of a vomit-inducing chemical in over-the-counter drugs to prevent misuse and overdose.

I have no choice, he reminded himself, disquieted by the drug, jumpy and nervous.

He gagged down two more, knowing these would stay put where the others had not.

And they did.

Purdy Wright's Air Wilderness Excursions was listed in the Yellow Pages, complete with an insert map showing the way out to the field. The wind had increased dramatically in the last ninety minutes and the snow was drifting badly. As Andy left the roadside phone booth, he saw a bundled Mountie closing off the entrance ramp to the highway, using a wooden barricade that carried the bold capital letters: CLOSED.

So now he had no choice and little time.

It was two o'clock in the morning when he reached the Quonset hut on the outskirts of English River; a snow-covered sign rocked in the wind. A double-wide house trailer sat off to the right. A relatively fresh set of tire tracks led to a hefty truck parked by the trailer, and Andy knew that, given the present rate of snowfall, it had not been parked for more than an hour.

Andy pounded on the door and waited. A light appeared at the end of the trailer; then another, closer. The door cracked open. "Yeah?" complained a firm man in his mid-thirties, wearing a T-shirt with the faded letters

CUNY across the front and a pair of white long underwear ripped at the crotch.

"Purdy Wright?"

"Might be."

"I'd like to hire your services."

"Tomorrow, buddy. Come back tomorrow." He began to shut the door but Andy stopped it with a hand that held a one-hundred-dollar bill.

"Tonight."

Wright flicked on the porch light and took a good look at Andy's face, and at the bill. He then poked his head out of the door—his hair tossed by sleep—and examined the weather. He yawned. "Not in this shit. Come in a minute and we'll work this out; but let's make it fast, shall we?"

Andy accepted the invitation to warmth and followed Wright inside.

Wright, however, had headed into the small kitchen area immediately adjacent to the equally small living room. When he turned around he held a long-barreled pistol in his hand, aimed at Andy. He waved it, until Andy saw him, and then said, "No, no, no. Don't even flinch, Baker."

"Oh shit!"

"Hands against the wall, there . . . that's good." Wright patted Andy down and withdrew the two wallets—Andy's and Welch's—and the silenced automatic. He tossed the gun into a padded chair behind him and motioned for Andy to sit down. Wright sat in a worn sofa-chair facing Andy. "They've been looking hard for you. They've come here twice." He stood and went into the kitchen, still training the gun on Andy, and retrieved a piece of paper—a flyer. He handed it to Andy, and sat back down.

The xeroxed page showed a recent photograph of Andy—most likely taken by a hidden camera at the Security Service offices—and also listed his physical description with a brief warning at the bottom.

Wright said, "Listen up now, friend."

Andy listened.

"I don't know what it is you've done, and just maybe I don't give a shit. Just maybe the Security Service has hauled my ass in a bunch of times on trumped-up charges that never stuck—you follow me? Maybe that's because—because of certain things. Maybe there's other reasons. One thing is for certain: you better have a lot of money on you, or you just ran out of luck." He searched the contents of Andy's wallet, counting.

"You're American?" Andy asked.

"I might have been. Once."

Andy explained directly. "I need to reach Winnipeg by six this morning. If you can't offer me that, then by all means, turn me in. They'll send me home and everyone loses."

"It won't work."

"What's that?"

"The sympathy routine."

"Is that what that was?"

"Yeah."

"Six this morning. Can you fly in this storm?"

"In this storm? Are you—"

"Yes. This storm. If you can't—"

"Mister. Purdy Wright can fly in damn near any weather. I fly a ski plane. Snow doesn't bother me."

"How about a storm?"

"Tricky winds tonight. Risky. But I've flown worse. It'll cost you more." Wright put down his weapon.

Andy relaxed, thinking, His button is money. "You're instrument-rated?"

"How else could I fly at night. Jesus Christ, buddy, you think I'm stupid?"

Andy asked, "How much?"

"Where do you want to land?"

"Away from people, but close to the city. I'll pay extra for that."

"You're damned right you will, buddy." He rubbed his face. "Twelve hundred American."

Andy could hardly believe the figure. "Six."

"This particular excursion package comes complete with a private landing strip and ground transportation into the city. Eight hundred. That leaves you four and change."

"You're all heart. Okay. Deal." Andy pictured Mari.

The two shook hands, leaning from their chairs. "You get the weapon back at the end of the line. You pay the cash up front," Wright explained, while fishing the bills from both wallets and counting out the eight hundred. "And you agree to letting me tie your hands. Otherwise, no deal."

Andy pondered the offer. With his hands tied, the man could knock him out, empty both wallets, and leave him in a snowbank somewhere. "What if I don't agree?"

"Then you're stupid." Wright picked up Andy's gun and carried both weapons with him as he walked into the confined kitchen and located a ball of thick twine. "It's that, or the SS. Your decision. But either way . . . first I tie your hands."

Andy was not in the habit of finding himself in these situations. He was nonplussed. He debated attempting a struggle with Wright, but to what end? To win the fight would lose him the flight, and therefore his chance at Borikowski. He turned around and offered his wrists. "Get dressed. The sooner I'm in Winnipeg, the better."

Purdy Wright smiled, and searched for the end of the twine.

When Andy awoke, Wright was speaking gibberish into the radio. It was some kind of crude code Andy did not understand. He soon realized Purdy Wright was far from the model citizen.

The plane dove at an unbelievable speed.

Andy closed his eyes and thought, All I've been through . . . and now I die in a plane crash.

Then the plane leveled off.

He glanced at Purdy Wright and saw a devilish grin. Andy did not particularly care for show-offs.

Wright switched off the wing lights, his eyes trained on the instruments. The plane was now less than twenty feet over the dark, dense sea of treetops—dangerously low.

"Hey, what the fuck?" Andy questioned.

And then, eyes still glued to the dash, Wright shoved the wheel forward, dropping the plane so quickly, so severely, that Andy lifted from the seat and his raw stomach nearly emptied again. Wright dropped the plane into a tiny opening in the forest, a snow-covered lake or small pond. The narrow opening was barely wider than the wings of the plane.

"You should try this in a wind!" the pilot suggested comically.

The landing strip, a title that dignified the snow-covered lake, had been lined with flaming-orange auto flares, placed intermittently every ten yards for the length of the pond. Andy could find only one explanation—Purdy Wright was a part-time smuggler.

At the last second, the pilot switched on one lone spotlight, pulled to a stall, and landed gracefully. Practiced. "A friend of mine lives here," he said, pointing to a large log house at the far end of the otherwise uninhabited lakeshore. "So you don't get the wrong idea . . . if it makes any difference . . . we occasionally run executives out here. Their wives think they're on fishing or hunting trips . . . you follow me?" he asked, flashing his eyebrows. "It's a very exclusive club. The girls here are the best in Canada. I get my air fare, and a small kickback . . . it helps pay the bills." He smiled.

"And taxes," Andy offered, returning the grin.

"Yeah. That too." He reached out his hand, waited for Andy to turn around, and cut the twine from his wrists. "There, you're on your own. Unfortunately, I must take off before the flares die. A commercial flight goes over this area in ten minutes." He winked. "I wish my friend would pay me in merchandise. He's a careful man. Don't make trouble."

"One question."

"What's that?"

"Were you a draft dodger?"

Wright studied Andy thoughtfully. "Do I fly like a draft dodger? No. I hope not. I was Air Force. I went AWOL after the Tet Offensive, hopped a freighter in Saigon, and ended up here."

"We could have used you."

"No doubt." Wright hesitated and then said, "I was young. It seemed like the right thing to do at the time. Now, I must be off. For one hundred American, Jacques will see you eat and clean up. You don't smell too good." He grinned. "They'll supply transportation into Winnipeg. Ask him for my good suit. We're about the same size. It's yours."

"I thought you said you never come here."

"I thought you said your name was Welch."

Purdy Wright performed a beautiful nose turn and faced the plane back down the strip. A few of the flares had already died out. Wright saluted properly. "Good luck!"

Andy nodded rather than compete with the noise of

the engine. He climbed out onto the wing and jumped to the hard-packed snow. Two dark figures ran toward him and guided him over to a parked truck. They watched as the plane took off. Fifty feet into the sky, the plane's lights came on and it banked to the right and vanished.

The fee was two hundred dollars, not one, but bought Andy the pin-striped suit, a brown leather briefcase, which he stuffed with his winter coat and smelly clothes, a Bogart hat, a trim to his beard, breakfast, and an offer of their best whore. He accepted a ride to the train station instead.

He arrived at six o'clock as the express pulled in—the hour the ticket office opened. Adding the dining car and scenic coaches required twenty minutes and in this time Andy bought a private cabin ticket to Vancouver, keeping a close eye on the one man who could have been a Security Service agent. Andy looked much different in gold-colored wire-rim glasses, a fresh suit, and a Bogart hat, but even so, did not press his luck. When his business was through, he hid for ten minutes, sitting on a toilet in the far stall of the men's room, window cracked, keeping an eye on the coaches.

Borikowski and his almond-eyed woman had not disembarked, so Andy, ticket in hand, boarded.

He looked out his window for any last-second departures, wondering if they were still on the train.

None.

As the train rolled out, Andy shut his eyes and fell asleep, hat tilted over his head.

Shades of Humphrey.

9:03 A.M.
Washington, D.C.

Terry Stone said, "The White House has agreed to try to stop him."

270

Chris Daniels' relief was apparent. "How will they do it?"

"They'll arrange a joint operation between Navy UDT and the Coast Guard."

"Underwater Demolition. . . ?"

"Exactly. They'll have two options: one is to blow it outright; the second is to sabotage and force it to drift into our waters, much the same as is done for drug smuggling off Florida."

"And how's that?" Daniels asked.

"They drop a UDT some distance in front of the plotted course of the vessel. The UDT is in dark rafts that utilize powerful electric—and therefore silent—engines. As the ship approaches—usually just before dawn—the UDT approaches the vessel and sabotages the drive shaft or steering mechanism. Timers are used, which gives the UDT time to escape detection before the sun comes up. Then, sometime later, the charges, which are exceptionally quiet and made just for such purposes, leave the ship helpless in the water. At this point the Coast Guard happens to wander along and offer assistance, or in this case, board the ship and make arrests on whatever charges they can find—and there's always something. In the case of the drug smugglers, they are often outside of our waters, so the idea is to render them helpless when they're in currents that will drag them into U.S. waters, and therefore under the jurisdiction of the Coast Guard."

"I always wondered why so many of those busts were made on ships that were floating helpless at sea. It never occurred to me that we had staged the whole thing."

"We often do."

"It's an interesting strategy."

"Yes. Once they float into our waters, they're ours."

"So they'll need to determine exactly which ship Borikowski is on, assuming we've guessed right. . . ."

"Yes, they will. But it shouldn't be as difficult as it

271

sounds. They have radar stations all along the Vancouver area and though the merchant traffic is heavy there, they should be able to locate a Soviet trawler; and even if he's on an American trawler, they should be able to figure out which ship is headed toward the area of that submarine. It may not give them a hell of a lot of time to react, but the UDTs are highly trained and should be able to handle it."

"So . . . what now?"

Inside his head, Stone recognized his own depression of the last week. I'm too old for this, he told himself, recognizing it as the truth. I'm far too old, and tired, and opinionated. And discouraged. I don't believe in it anymore. Now I see it as only a game, like so many other games, whereas before I felt it was so serious and important. But when you're eighty-some years into life, international intelligence isn't as important as the last few years. No. I want to live out the last few years my way. Like Sinatra sings, "My way." Boats and warm breezes and long afternoons and rum and fishing. That's what I want.

Knowing he had too many plans mid-stage simply to walk out, he resolved to see the *Dragonfly* operation through and then retire. He had Parker Lyell all picked out to replace him.

Oh, Josie, he thought sadly, if only you were here to spend my last few years with me. I would like that more than anything in the world. More than anything else. I still love you, I still love you so much.

Feeling good, exceptionally good, with this decision, and promising himself to stick with it, he turned to Daniels and asked, "Did you know I'm a gourmet cook?"

"No, sir."

"Are you hungry?"

"Always."

"How about I cook for the two of us?"

"Seriously?"

"Very. We'll stop by the market, have Marvin do a little shopping, and drive over to my apartment for the best lunch you've ever had."

"No argument, sir. I'm honored."

"By the way, Chris . . ."

"Yes, sir?"

"What do you know about garbage disposals?"

Thanksgiving Day, November 27

1:36 P.M.
New Westminster, British Columbia

The arrangements had been quite simple. He had instructed the parlor coachmen to wake him ten minutes before each of the four stops on the nearly thirty-one-hour trip. They had not left the train at Regina, or at Calgary, or at Kamloops. Andy had maintained nighttime surveillance and relied on his watch's alarm—which he had set as a backup—or the coachmen to wake him before the train's next scheduled stop.

He had tried to catch up on lost sleep between Kamloops and New Westminster.

And the rest had been a dream.

The Crossword Code he had deciphered was so confused he was still not convinced it was accurate. A RIGHT code, which this was, operated off all right-hand numbers in the crossword. The first number that had a black space or a border to its right provided the number of words to be skipped in the columned clues. In this morning's crossword, which Andy had finally received at Kamloops—closer to noon than morning—the first RIGHT was the number four. Four words into the clues was the word *bacteria*, found in 5 Across, which read, "Yogurt bacteria." He had worked through the entire puzzle and had come up with:

BACTERIA ALUMINUM BRIEFCASE
EXPLOSIVES RIGGED
MUST BE STOPPED SEA ONLY
CONTAMINATED
CONTINGENCIES ARRANGED
HOSTAGE
ABORT OPERATIONS

He cracked the door open.

"New Westminster, next stop. Still nothing."

Andy shut the door and imagined he could see through the walls.

1:40 P.M.

Borikowski had worsened.

He was lying on the bed, his head dipped back over two pillows that lay under his neck. His nosebleed had stopped.

The bruises were everywhere, dark and foreboding: the back of his neck; the insides of his elbows; underneath both arms. Common movement now caused an immediate blue-brown that settled into an amber-rust a few hours later.

Lydia had not mentioned her own nosebleeds to him. Both had occurred while he had been sleeping, and she saw no reason to burden him with her plight as well.

He had agreed to switch the devices from his wrists to hers, worried that despite the fact that he felt fine, he was not well. It did not take a medical genius to know that something had gone wrong with his ability to clot blood, which meant a simple pinprick might kill him. Tristovich had explained the procedure to Lydia over the phone when she had called from Wawa, and Borikowski knew it anyway. All that was required was to remove one of the devices, strap it to Lydia's wrist, run it through its self-check, and then repeat the procedure using the other device. It had required five minutes and had not detonated the briefcase, which they had both watched intently during the whole ordeal.

Now her pulse protected the germs.

She had him sit up and worked with alcohol and cold cream on his face. "I think you are wise to do without the cosmetics."

"It's too time-consuming. I could not possibly sit through a session now."

She looked at his rugged but pale face, and helped him to lie back down. "How do you feel?"

"As I have already told you: I feel fine. It's strange."

"I am worried for you, Leonid."

"You are kind."

"No. I am worried."

"Don't make me smile. It bruises my cheeks."

"That's not funny."

"That's the truth."

"Turn around. I must hide this bruise on your neck. It draws attention."

He obeyed and she dabbed him with creams and powders until she was able to match his orginal skin tone. "There."

"Thank you. How long to go?"

She checked her watch: 1:41 P.M. "Ten minutes. You rest. I'll arrange for a coachman to hail us a cab."

1:51 P.M.

If Andy hadn't seen her hips swaying, he might have missed her. He had expected them to disembark together, arm in arm perhaps; but it was not to be.

She swayed over to a bench and sat down, and even through the safety glass of the train, Andy could feel her sorrow. Something was wrong.

The train terminal was large and congested. Hundreds of people milled about in search of friends or their ride out of town. Children ran; old people shuffled; steam rose from the tracks.

Moments later, a male Borikowski—whom Andy recognized by his suitcase—left the train and walked past Lydia without looking at her.

Never look back.

Briefcase in hand, Andy headed for the exit. Can this actually be happening? he wondered, or is it some kind of trick?

He hurried to the door, where several older people interfered with a quick departure. He rudely pushed past. Clap, clap, clap: he descended the train's metal stairs.

The woman was gone.

He looked around the terminal.

There! Walking toward the exit . . .

He briskly walked across the terminal, hat pulled over his face, anticipating trouble from the Security Service. He spotted two agents by the main exit.

Lydia entered the women's room.

Borikowski was nowhere to be seen.

Andy hurried to the ticket counter, pushed a man out of the way—to objections—and told the clerk, "Please page all Security Service personnel to track five immediately. Thank you!" He disappeared into the thick of people.

Then he spotted Borikowski. He was just leaving the men's room. He was holding a reddened handkerchief under his nose, which appeared to be bleeding badly.

"Your attention please . . ." rang out the page, the voice echoing through the building. As the message was completed, the two Security Service men Andy had spotted, and one he had not, all rushed toward track number 5.

The exit was clear.

Lydia appeared suddenly behind Borikowski, and the two went out into the street.

Andy ran to catch up with them. As he stepped through the doors, a cabbie was placing their bags into the trunk of his hack. Andy set down the briefcase and reached for the automatic, waiting to draw it from the holster.

The crowd moved between him and the cab.

Confusion.

Then a glimpse of Borikowski's profile. Andy thought, Here's my chance. Now I blow his head off.

The cabbie slammed the trunk.

The crowd thickened, eliminating any chance of a shot.

Andy flagged the next available cab, which was several back in line.

Borikowski had never even looked at Lydia, who now climbed into the back of the cab and tapped him on the shoulder.

Never look back.

Andy managed to stay with them. In downtown New Westminster they rented a car, as did Andy from the competition across the street. His rental was ready before theirs, and so he was idling on the corner when they left the parking lot, a light drizzle beginning to fall.

Ten minutes later they were parked in a line of cars waiting for the ferry that shuttled both people and automobiles across the Strait of Georgia to Vancouver Island.

His car was four behind theirs.

Once parked inside the ship's hold, Andy elected to remain inside his rented car and wait out the ride—a difficult decision since he knew the combination of stale air and confined space might cause him to be seasick, an affliction that had plagued him since the age of ten. Still, it had to be: This was the one place even a careless Borikowski would be watching for tails.

Fifteen minutes into the ride, he threw up—for what seemed like the tenth time.

The ferry docked at Nanaimo. By the time it was unloading, Andy had changed back into his smelly clothes he had kept in the briefcase. He inspected himself in the rearview mirror and approved.

The sun, held low in the sky by winter's feeble fingers, shadowed a handful of litter that scattered across the pavement, finally falling into the choppy water. A line of cars waited to leave the island. Two children played with a ball.

Andy was sitting in his foul-smelling car, waiting for the other drivers to come below. When they finally did, he watched carefully as a man unlocked the door to Borikowski's rental, two cars up. He didn't believe his eyes! The man had used his right hand to turn the key, had used the index finger of his right hand—a finger Leonid Borikowski had no use of.

This man was not Leonid Borikowski.

3:15 P.M.
Nanaimo, Vancouver Island

Frantically, Andy searched the two rows of vehicles through the dim light of the hold of the ship. Happy tourists and Vancouver Island natives walked with some difficulty between the tight aisles created by the parked vehicles. He could only think of two possibilities: one, Borikowski was leaving on foot; or two, as a final precaution, he would switch vehicles here. There was a surprising resemblance between the man who had just taken over the rental and Borikowski's most recent face, so Andy favored the switch. He continued his search for

Borikowski, knowing there was at least a chance the agent had altered his looks yet again—possibly in the ferry's restroom. The traffic of people eager to depart had swelled to a chaotic proportion, making his job increasingly difficult.

A gangling man with sun-bleached blond hair hung his weight from a chain and opened the large door at the stern of the ferry. As the ribbed door slowly lifted, allowing a pale yellow light into the hold, Andy spotted the common denominator. Only two of the twenty-odd drivers reached to adjust their rearview mirrors. One was the man two cars ahead, Borikowski's impostor; the other was behind the wheel of a shiny new pickup truck to Andy's left and further up the line. In that instant of time, Andy strained to see whether or not the driver used his index finger, but could not see clearly. His instincts jumped to believe it was, in fact, Borikowski.

But where was the woman?

This, now, was his final choice. Not unlike a difficult moment in chess when faced with anticipating an opponent's next move—the strategy—he was reduced to an educated guess. He didn't believe the agent would leave the ship on foot. Too easily spotted, he told himself. He chose the man in the shiny new pickup truck and decided to follow.

Engines revving, the ship rocking slightly in its slip, the cars began to leave, two by two. Light sifted through the thick blue exhaust, casting zebra shadows throughout the hold.

He wasn't certain until the small truck stopped in front of the clapboard terminal and picked up the almond-eyed woman. She carried an aluminum briefcase.

He followed the pickup—and most of the other cars— south on 19; but at Qualicum Beach the pickup exited onto 4A, and turned again onto 4 West, following signs into the sleepy town of Port Alberni. Andy played his fa-

283

miliar game of falling well behind the vehicle. He allowed a Mazda to pull between the pickup and his rental on the way into town.

His heart began to race. It couldn't be much longer.

He managed his first good look at Borikowski when the agent and his woman entered an inexpensive restaurant situated in the center of town. Now he was *certain!*

Fifteen minutes later, precisely at four-thirty, Andy watched as the two left the restaurant. At that exact moment, two cars slammed into each other up the street, forcing a truck loaded with large logs to come to a stop in front of the restaurant. The accident pulled Andy's attention away from the two.

The move deserved an award.

The drivers of the two dented vehicles jumped out and began a convincing fistfight in the middle of the street. Bystanders rushed to drag them apart. Andy quickly glanced back to the sidewalk, but all he saw was an aluminum briefcase being yanked up into the passenger side of the tractor trailer by a slender arm. They had switched again!

Andy unconsciously checked an inside pocket of his multi-pocketed coat and touched two clips to his automatic. He knew Vancouver Island well enough to know what the logging truck meant—this was the end of the line. He assumed the truck was headed for the thickly forested section of Vancouver Island to the west. Several small fishing communities dotted the isolated shoreline there, tucked into small rocky inlets—all ideal locations to board an agent onto a waiting ship. The trucker would know the idiosyncrasies of the labyrinth of unmarked rugged dirt roads that webbed the forests; a fine plan that would insure no one could follow on this last leg.

But the diversion worked against them by lasting a few seconds too long. Positioning himself behind the waiting truck so that neither mirror would show him, Andy walked carefully ahead to the trailer of stacked logs. With everyone's attention drawn to the fight, Andy ducked under the piled logs, climbed over the rear axle, and pulled himself up onto the boom of the trailer. Heavy chains held the logs in place. He took hold.

Gears complained and the rig slowly rumbled forward.

Twenty minutes outside of Port Alberni the road changed to dirt and the driver turned on the speed. Where the hell was the hostage? Andy wondered. He hung on, bouncing viciously against the boom, bruising his back, knuckles white. His empty stomach left him little reserve strength. The wet, freezing wind iced his exposed skin. Frostbite patches settled into his cheeks and hands. A tremendous bump! The boom slammed against his testicles. He thought, Maybe I'm supposed to fight like hell and still lose—get mowed over by a truck in the middle of fucking nowhere, never found, never missed. No. Not like that. Please God. Not like that.

He gripped the chains more tightly.

Then a cold rain began to fall.

Had it been hours? Minutes? It felt like days. Time had no meaning here, hanging by a chain beneath a thundering logging truck. The water soaked him in no time. His groin throbbed with pain.

Shifting gears and a flicker of lights through the smoke-like dusk of a cloud-covered sunset. Then, so suddenly, so loudly that he nearly lost his hold, an incredibly high-pitched whine pierced his ears. The truck whisked over an extremely old pivot bridge, a turnstile bridge meant to rotate on a center axis, not a drawbridge as he had first thought. As the tires hit dirt again, Andy lowered his head to see off to the side, spotting a small wharf area and cannery. A cul-de-sac. The driver downshifted to make the turn. Andy loosened his grip, heaved with his remaining strength, and rolled like a son of a bitch.

The crush of the fat, black, twin rubber tires missed his left shoulder by only a fraction of an inch. He continued rolling, over and over, until he heard the soft crunch of pine needles, and then, after another fifteen feet, hit the base of a pine. His face was scratched and bleeding, his hands scuffed, his shoulder aching as if partially dislocated. He smiled. Lying perfectly still, his eyes searched through the encroaching darkness, studying the surroundings. Through the copse of pines, he saw the truck come to a stop out on the pier. Beside it, the superstructure of a towering crane, once used to hoist fish from a ship's hold, jutted into the sky, its metal dark and old. Behind it lay the time-worn tin walls of the cannery. Andy sat up slowly and carefully, checking for broken bones. His nose, ears, and small fingers were numb. Over the groan of the semi, he heard the diesel of the crane start up. It belched exhaust into the veiled sky. He crept twenty yards on hands and knees to the far edge of the trees, an area cluttered with several dilapidated cabins.

The ship, a hundred-foot ocean trawler, had twin booms that held netting lines and veed above either side of the vessel like long fingers. Andy watched the crane remove the two topmost logs from the truck and set them on the pier. Then he watched as the crane's cable was reattached and a casket was hoisted into the air. The hostage? Dead?

He sprinted in a shadow along a seawall toward the pier, head tucked low, moving with long strides. He edged along the wall and ducked under the pier as all eyes followed the suspended casket, which was placed safely on board.

It was even darker under the pier, which reached a good twenty yards into the water, supported by clusters of pitch-covered pilings. Salt-encrusted conduit pipe hung from the underside. Water splashed four to five feet below the pier. Andy gripped the conduits, tucked his body into a tight ball, and began swinging, hand over hand like an ape, toward the waiting ship. Then, as he was halfway to the ship, a line fell in the water and was drawn up the side and out of sight.

The ship was leaving.

His hold, in fact the entire dock, shook as the trees were returned to the logging truck, which was about to back up. Andy hurried. Arm over arm, he raced back to land. Over his shoulder the ship pulled away from the dock. Faster! he coaxed himself, building up a rhythm, now only yards from the seawall. Hand over hand.

The engines of the ship sped up. Finally, he reached the seawall, ducked his head out, and peered into the blinding lights of the dock area where two men were busy fastening the chains back around the logs while the crane held them in place. The ship headed away from the dock toward the mouth of the narrow harbor. An angry depression gripped him. To come so far, only to lose—again!

He was looking at the departing ship, cursing their perfect timing, when he saw the small lights of the aged pivot bridge in the distance. It might work, he thought, already moving, deciding it was his only option. No other way. The bridge.

Andy clawed himself along the seawall and belly-crawled into the darkness. Rain hurried the men on the dock. Andy, crawling, watched them over his shoulder until they blurred into the darkness. Then he stood and sprinted like hell.

The trawler moved through the snaking channel, headed toward the turnstile bridge.

Andy followed the degenerated outline of an old path running parallel with the shore. His heart pumped, his arms threw him forward, carrying the extra weight of his saturated clothes with difficulty. He had missed running his daily nine miles for the past few days. Still, his legs carried him well. He ran strangely on the edge of tears, afraid of failure.

He squinted to his left, seeing the trawler making good time, and he leaned into the steady sheet of water, increasing the length of his strides. He heard a coach from long ago shout, "Reach deep!"

Two loud blasts bounced off the shore, signals between ship and bridge.

One hundred yards! He pushed hard for extra inches, chin high, arms thrusting forward and back. Forward and back. He heard the heavy clunk of steel I-beams disconnecting as the bridge rotated open on its axis.

Fifty yards and closing!

The bridge moved away from the shore like a huge propeller beginning to turn.

Ten yards!

The steel supports were now five feet from the road, six, seven, eight. . . . Andy sprung toward it like a cat in flight, body fully extended, arms stretching, fingers pointed. His hands smacked against the cold metal, groping for purchase; his face slammed into the steel and crushed his nose. He struggled to hold on. The bridge groaned, widening the gap between it and the shore.

With his nose bent and bleeding and angled to the left, the skin surrounding his right eye swelling, he pulled his soaked and beaten body up. He crawled to the suspended catwalk and pulled himself to his feet.

The ship waited for the bridge's signal.

The pivoting stopped with a tremendously loud thud. A horn sounded twice, and the trawler approached.

As it motored forward, taking the bridge's center support and control tower to starboard, Andy dropped from the catwalk, tiptoeing across the precarious struts that supported the steel mesh overhead. The vessel passed directly below him. The rain had cleared the decks of people. Andy was above, yes, but still had a fifteen-foot jump over water to reach the ship.

A hell of a jump, he told himself, knowing if he didn't time it correctly, using the piled fishing nets for padding, he would more than likely break his legs on the steel deck, or miss completely.

With precious little time available for calculations he looked and thought, *Just maybe.* Bending his knees into an angry crouch, he spit blood into the water below, and jumped.

To him it felt like slow motion as he fell through the rain. Then he heard himself say, "Shit!"

He wasn't going to reach the ship.

He plummeted toward the water. All at once, his hands hit and took hold of a line suspended from one of the booms. Instinctively his fingers wrapped around the wet line. He slid down, down, skin burning off his hands. He squeezed with all his strength and finally stopped eight feet above the churning water, his hands raw and bloodied.

He fought against the pain as he pulled himself back up the line, hand over hand. The ship bucked and groaned as it slipped out of the narrow mouth of the fishhook cove and into the violent sea. He climbed the line until he was level with the deck and then swung himself over and took hold of a cold stanchion. He peered over the edge of the deck and, seeing no one, pulled himself up. The windows of the wheelhouse glowed ivory.

He felt as if he weighed tons. His head ached—his whole body ached. Both hands were badly rope-burned and bleeding, the salt stinging the wounds. His lower lip was split open, his nose broken and cocked to one side. He had been so obsessed with catching Borikowski that he had not considered the consequences of boarding the ship. What now, he wondered, watching darkness steal over the sea. What now?

9:30 P.M.
Washington, D.C.

"May I ask?"

"About that phone call?"

"Yes."

Stone took a piece of paper from the desk top and wrote a quick list. He said, "It was SeaSec, Seattle."

"And?"

"The UDT missed the ship. Rough seas. We lost him." He stuffed the paper into an inside pocket and sat back down at the table.

"Damn it!" Daniels barked. It was the first time he had sworn in front of the Old Man.

Stone sat in the straight-back chair, rigid, stately, a glint in his pale blue eyes. His face seemed holy. Behind him and over his left shoulder on the wall there hung a photograph of a much younger man in a robe. And if it had been color, the sash would have been the regal red of a fine wine, the sky an indigo blue; and had one been there, one would have smelled the sweet damp fragrance of fresh-cut grass.

In the picture Terry Stone stood shaking the hand of a young John Fitzgerald Kennedy, who was in attendance to deliver the commencement address. Behind them the American flag was frozen in mid-flap.

Chris Daniels could hear the flag. He looked down at Terry Stone's nearly empty plate as Stone stabbed another brussels sprout and rocked it back and forth, inspecting.

"What is it?" Stone asked.

"Mind you, I'm not complaining. But I wondered . . . frankly, sir, my second meal with you, and in two days.

290

We've never even shared a cup of coffee. . . ."

"Ah. I see. Yes. You're quite right you know. Well, truth is, I liked our lunch together. This meal came off a little late. Oh well—"

"It's delicious."

"The company is nice. . . ."

"Yes."

"Just now I was remembering our discussion last week."

For a moment the brussels sprout looked terribly much like a human head. Daniels wondered why he allowed himself such an image. Then Stone stabbed the poor fellow. And ate him.

Daniels thought, We've had a dozen discussions this week.

Stone continued, "I'm a selfish old man, just as everyone jokes."

Daniels dared not interrupt.

"I've always wanted a double in the DS, you know that."

"Yes."

"Always. And well, Borikowski would be a dandy. He's been privileged—part of their top assignments. He would know them inside and out."

"Yes."

"But I've screwed up. We should have heard from Andy by now. He's had plenty of time to enter the States and make it to a phone that worked. He should have read the Crossword Code. He should have aborted."

"Yes."

"But he won't. He's too driven."

"Yes, sir." Daniels placed his fork down onto his plate and started comparing the man before him and the man shaking JFK's hand. Clearly the same man, only now a face with the skin of an onion.

"I heard the truth about Bookends shortly after Major Clayton's abduction." He paused and looked up at Daniels. "There are some things that appear important to

291

keep to oneself. Especially if they are seen only as a tool for confusion. Especially if they are too painful to face. I have held such a secret for quite some time now. It was stupid to do so."

Stone lifted his knife gently and sawed the next brussels sprout in half, holding it down with his fork. As he finished, one half scurried across the plate and nearly went off the rim and into his lap. He hoisted a cloth napkin and dabbed one edge of his lip, though it was not showing any food, then stuffed the napkin back down and out of sight. "I didn't want to hurt him anymore than he already was. . . ."

Before lifting his fork he steered a wrinkled hand to the wineglass, which he took hold of and dragged across the place mat. Then he lifted it, sipped, and said, "Never did see any reason to reveal it. After all, Andy was driven to catch Borikowski because the man had killed his brother. That's potent motivation for a man like Andy. His world was based on love and Borikowski shattered that love. I saw no reason to further destroy the man."

Daniels had not missed the tone of voice. He said nothing. He kept looking up at the picture and back to Stone and after half a glass of wine began to relax.

It was then he asked, "What is it, sir?"

Stone looked up. The brussels sprouts were gone. With one last long sip, the glass was empty. "You're a smart bugger, Chris. You use that right and you'll be happy. I guarantee you that. You abuse it, and you'll grow lonely, friendless, and in much despair. I should know."

Daniels felt his heart in his chest: What are you trying to say?

"What I'm getting at . . ." Stone leaned forward to grab the wine. He caught the bottleneck with the tip of his finger and managed to get hold of the bottle and pour another glass for them both. He was very graceful with it, and not a drop hit the table.

292

"You're retiring," Daniels stated.

"Yes. Fact is, I'm not going back. I have a list." He reached inside his coat and withdrew the slip of paper folded neatly in half. "I thought I could bribe you with a late Thanksgiving dinner into retrieving a few things for me."

"Never?"

There was a long silence. Then Stone said, "I've informed the president and all the rest. It is official. No. Never. Not again." He swallowed deeply, his wineglass on the table. He rocked his head from side to side. "I can't, Chris. I withheld vital information from the intelligence community for far too long. If I don't retire they'll throw me out anyway. No. Don't shake your head. It's the truth. I found out a few months ago from a very reliable source who disappeared four days later."

"*Canbeck3*, sir?"

"Yes. It was *Canbeck3* as a matter of fact. How did you know?"

"The timing. You said the agent disappeared."

"That's right. It was *Canbeck3*." Stone drifted. "I'd advise you do the same, son. Disappear. Teach at a college. Something different. It's not right for you." He laughed. "If anyone heard me say that they might lock me away for treason. You are an asset to your country, Chris. They need you."

"But . . ."

"But, you need you, too. All I ask is you give it some thought."

"And of course I will." Daniels stood, dramatically kicking his chair back and out of his way. He held his wineglass out and said, "Here's to the Old Man, sir. Here's to one hell of a service record."

"No, son." Stone paused dramatically and spoke his next words softly and carefully. "He's alive, Chris. Duncan Clayton is alive." He lowered his eyes to his empty plate. "He was abducted and taken to the Neurological Research Institute in Leningrad. His death was created by the Soviets as a cover. All made up. They broke him—which is how they knew the particulars of the Beirut embassy meeting—how they pulled off the bombing. Duncan knew all about the meeting. It was Duncan who told them. They've been after Andy ever since. I assume they thought that if they could break one brother, well, birds of a feather and all that." Tears formed in the pale blue eyes. "For months I had Andy write that damned report to keep him pinned down. I knew they wouldn't try for him here. But now . . . now he hasn't reported in, so I assume they've abducted him. I gambled selfishly with a man's life—all for one goddamned double agent—and I lost. Now I must quit.

"My problem was," he continued, "I just couldn't bear to bring him that sorrow. No point in sorrow." He rubbed an eye and thought aloud. "Grief and guilt are life's biggest burdens, son. I guess I traded one for the other. . . . Now I've lost. Yes, I've lost. . . ."

Daniels' wineglass slipped from his hand and shattered on the table.

Terry Stone closed his eyes. He could barely be heard. "I truly believed that Andy was the best agent for this assignment . . . that he could beat the odds. They'd tried for him before, you know. Jesus Christ, Son of God, forgive me my decision. Bless that man wherever he may be. Bless him and give him strength, for certainly now, he needs it more than ever." He sobered and looked up, staring Daniels in the eyes. "You had better change all the codes. . . ."

11:00 P.M.
The Pacific Ocean

Andy touched his nose and cringed. It hurt like a son of a bitch! His right eye wasn't tops either—swollen nearly shut and stinging from the salt water that rolled off the overhead net. Hell of a condition, he told himself. Hell of a piss-poor predicament.

He tried to guess how many were aboard, and how well armed, wondering if he was going to have to kill each of them—a thought that turned his stomach. And what then? he asked. Navigate this stinkpot back to shore in a goddamned winter storm complete with gale-force winds?

He had only seen a small crew. He guessed the minimum at a captain, an engineer, and possibly two hands. If they needed him they could enlist the services of Borikowski. That totaled five.

Knowing sailors, Andy crawled to a nearby cleat and loosened an overhead line so that it flapped violently against the hull and dragged in the sea, expecting that even in this weather an experienced crew would hear the line. And they did.

A man in a black slicker came out of the pilothouse and hurried toward the line to fasten it. "*Fuck your mother, you shithole freezing bitch,*" he cursed in Russian as he approached. Then the man turned his back to the stern, to the wind, and approached incredibly close to Andy. He bent over and grabbed the nylon line, then tied it off on a large cleat.

Andy stood, wrapped another line tightly around the unsuspecting man's neck, and pulled him quickly down, smashing the sailor's head against the deck, and feeling him go slack. He dragged him out of sight and removed the man's slicker, putting it on immediately. He bound and gagged the the man and hid him under the nets. He untied the line so that it whipped the overhead boom loudly. He hid, facing the bow, and waited.

The wind whistled across the stays. Atonal harmonies pierced the air. The clapping brought a second seaman topside. Only a man of the sea could have heard that line in all this racket, Andy thought.

This man shouted, "Ivanovich, Ivanovich!" Annoyed

by no response, he worked his way back toward Andy, tightening and checking lines, still calling out into the night. Andy reached for his gun, but felt only fabric. Gone. Lost.

The boat rocked suddenly, releasing the body of the unconscious man from the net. He slid across the deck close enough to be seen by the approaching sailor. Then, like a puck on ice, the body glided to starboard, slipped under the rail, and fell feet first into the seething waters.

Andy rushed the sailor from his blind side, but the man sensed him and ducked. Andy's swing missed. Startled, the man blocked with his left and jabbed with his right. Andy ducked and avoided the punch, managing a right of his own that caught the man's chin.

The sailor produced a gun. Andy knocked it from the man's hand. It slid along the deck and caught in the netting behind them. Then the sailor withdrew a knife and, as the ship leaned heavily to port, both men lost their balance and the knife plunged deeply into Andy's thigh. But the ship rocked steeply and only Andy was able to keep his hold; the sailor slid across the open deck, arms flailing, legs spread, and vanished over the side.

Andy removed the knife, his scream unheard. He fought for balance, and battled his way back to the snagged weapon, retrieving it. Then he clawed his way back to the pilothouse stairway. It felt like miles.

As he pulled the heavy door closed behind him, the groan of the engines replaced the deafening roar of the sea. The captain, a fat man, didn't even turn around. He struggled with the wheel, knees bent, pipe spewing scarlet sparks and gunmetal gray smoke into the air. He grunted in crude Russian, "Find Ivanovich?"

Andy answered in high Russian, "As a matter of fact, I did."

But the captain didn't recognize this voice, so he turned around. His jowled face took on a look of horror, and he released the wheel.

The trawler shifted to port.

They wrestled briefly, the captain unprepared for a fight, and Andy quickly dominated him, despite the weight difference. The man lost consciousness. Andy would need him later. Hopefully.

He used the captain's belt to tie off the wheel, hoping to steady it, but the ship pounded through the rough sea poorly. It reeled to starboard and then yawed forward, dumping Andy partway down a steep stairway. He recovered only to fall again, this time to the narrow aisle leading to several rooms—a galley off to port, a bulkhead to starboard, captain's quarters straight ahead. . . .

Stuhlberg was propped against the wall, his shirt covered with caked blood. Borikowski had given him an injection ten minutes earlier.

Stuhlberg began to awaken.

He opened his eyes first and could not believe the sensation in his nose. He looked about, groggy, trying to focus. He saw Lydia's beautiful body and thought he must be dreaming, except that she appeared terribly frightened. He spotted the briefcase across the room—the briefcase containing his bacteria.

No one had a right to that discovery but himself. No one.

Then he saw Borikowski's badly bruised face; wads of red-stained tissue paper plugged his nose.

Borikowski said, "Welcome, Doctor."

"Who are you?" Stuhlberg's voice could barely be heard.

"You knew me as Alex Corbett," Borikowski announced proudly.

"Bastard," the feeble voice hissed. Stuhlberg looked again to Lydia, and then touched his own nose. He stared at Borikowski. "We're contaminated?"

"You tell me. . . ."

Borikowski had to move closer to understand the man's

words. Stuhlberg asked, "Nosebleeds?" Borikowski nodded. "Uncontrolled bruising?" Another nod. Stuhlberg smiled, self-amused. "You see? I knew you would not succeed."

"Oh, but I have, Doctor," Borikowski said arrogantly. "We are almost home, Doctor. Our home!"

"You can't be serious? You could infect them all."

Borikowski looked over to Lydia, whose face was pained. She could not face the idea of her own death. She was bordering on silent hysteria.

Borikowski said confidently, "There is a cure, is there not, Doctor? I know there is a cure. . . ."

Before Stuhlberg answered, they heard someone, or something, fall down the stairs.

Borikowski opened the door a crack, and saw the back of one of the dark rain slickers as a man headed down a steep ladder to the engine room.

Andy changed plans. He wanted to take Borikowski one-on-one. But if he failed . . . then something would have to sink the ship. Something already put into motion.

He surprised the engine room mechanic and overpowered him, clubbing him with the other mate's gun, which Andy had retrieved from the netting. The man collapsed and fell to the oily floor.

Andy inspected the twin diesels—twins, he thought—and quickly located the governor: a small set-screw on an oily box that was mounted on the far end of the engines. Using his belt buckle, he turned the screw clockwise as far as it would go. The rpm's increased and the engines screamed. At this new rev they would blow apart in a matter of minutes.

Deafening now.

He climbed back up the steep ladder.

Voices straight ahead.

He checked his watch.

He stood by the door, listened, and then his patience ran out. He swung open the heavy door. Borikowski stood less than ten feet away. Andy lifted the gun. The Bulgarian reacted immediately, pulling Lydia in front of himself as a shield. She struggled to be free of him, the gun now aimed at her equally bruised face. "Let me go!" she protested.

"You cannot shoot, Clayton," Borikowski said, recognizing Andy immediately.

Andy shot her in the shoulder.

Borikowski was horrified. Lydia screamed and tried harder to break free. The Bulgarian shouted, "No! If you kill her, you release the bacteria." He cocked his head to the briefcase. "Then we're all—"

Andy fired again. The shot broke the thick glass port-hole behind Borikowski. Sea water slopped in.

Neither man moved. King against king, pawn against pawn.

A stalemate.

Borikowski's nose began to bleed and run into Lydia's hair.

Stuhlberg spoke to Andy. "Listen to me. Please." His voice was stronger. "I am Dr. Eric Stuhlberg. We must sink this ship. The three of us are contaminated and quite possibly contagious."

Andy had never liked the word "contaminated." He looked over at Stuhlberg, who looked more dead than alive, and then back to Borikowski, who said, "No. He is lying. He is lying!"

"No!" Stuhlberg commanded. "I'm not lying. We must sink this ship!"

Borikowski made no attempt to stop his nosebleed. He looked instead like a monster, and his eyes were wild. He knew his own chances of survival were slim, but that if he was shot or made to bleed externally, he had no chance at all. He would bleed to death.

Andy, more to himself than to the others, said, "You killed Duncan Clayton." He raised the gun again.

Desperately, Borikowski pleaded, "No. Not true. *He is alive!!* I swear to you. *He is alive.* I have spoken with him in Leningrad. I swear to you. . . ."

His conversation with Testler flew through Andy's head: ". . . a hospital used for debriefing in Leningrad . . ." He wanted to squeeze the trigger. Oh, how he wanted to squeeze the trigger.

". . . it is the truth. . . ."

"No!" Andy thundered, intentionally firing a shot that missed Borikowski's head by inches.

"Let me go!" Lydia begged Borikowski, who refused to.

"He called you 'Sport,' did he not?" Borikowski stated.

Andy fired the gun again, but this time Borikowski did not even flinch. He knew the man was not going to shoot him. He had already passed up his chance.

Andy was devastated. No one but Duncan knew that childhood nickname. He had not heard it in years and years.

"He defected, Captain Clayton. He says America is full of lies."

Andy felt his hands begin to tremble. He felt the knot in his throat. This was the truth. He knew. "I'm bringing you in," he told Borikowski. "You're under arrest."

Then, the first explosion rocked the ship. . . .

The ship heaved to port.

Andy dropped the gun.

Lydia fell and bumped her head, and lay motionless on the floor.

Both Andy and Borikowski fell and slid toward each other. Andy pulled the knife from his pocket and attempted to plunge it into Borikowski's arm, but missed.

Borikowski yelled to add confusion, taking hold of Andy's hair and butting Andy's broken nose against the metal floor.

The ship rocked again and the fallen gun slid against Andy's hand.

Eric Stuhlberg's attention had fallen to the briefcase. He had fought his way weakly across the room toward it.

His bacteria. All he cared about. Sink the bacteria.

He took hold of the handle and fled from the room, clawing his way topside as the ship lurched port to starboard. He was drained of any strength or energy, but was determined that this, his last effort in life, would be to take this bacteria away forever.

It's mine. And it's cursed.

He climbed the stairs into the wheelhouse.

Andy felt the cold metal and took hold of the handle of the gun and fired; but his world was turning dark and cloudy, and all he could feel was a sledgehammer pounding against his broken nose. He fired five wild shots and the gun was empty.

Lydia Czufin took one of the slugs in her chest, very close to her heart. Her blood spotted Andy's left hand.

Andy rose slowly—fogged, knowing nothing of hitting Lydia—but saw Borikowski heading up the stairway, chasing Stuhlberg.

Oh, you pitch-holed son of a whore! You dung-licking lizard, you nearly stabbed me, Borikowski thought as he headed up the ladder and into the wheelhouse. He saw the captain lying on the floor, saw the wheel tied off. Flames leaped at the window. She was on fire!

Andy invaded the wheelhouse, yelling and moving to confuse his adversary. He fell to the floor, dodging anything meant to intercept his entry, but he caught Borikowski in a moment of delirium and confusion: there were no weapons aimed at him, no surprises planned. Andy's face was smeared with blood from his nose. He struggled to his feet just as the stunned Borikowski knocked him back down. Stuhlberg, who was wrestling with the heavy steel door, accidentally dropped the aluminum briefcase, which flew to the steel flooring and slid away as the ship tossed again. Andy lunged across the floor toward the bacteria, as did Borikowski. They attacked each other. Borikowski's large rain slicker allowed Andy no purchase, so he resorted to pounding the man with what little strength he had left.

The ship rocked again, and the case slid further toward the wheelhouse's outer door, which, at the same instant, was opened by the frantic Stuhlberg. The briefcase hit the doctor in the shin, richocheted off and up over the raised nautical sill, and slid smoothly out and down the metal stairway. Shocked, Stuhlberg turned to try and grab it, but the ship listed again, throwing him forward and down the staircase after the bacteria. He took the fall poorly, crying out as he fell.

The second explosion spread the flames quickly.

Borikowski leveraged an elbow and managed to briefly knock the wind from Andy, but in doing so, he hit his own head violently against the deck. As he headed for the doorway, blood began to trickle from his mouth.

That is it, he thought, I am going to die now.

Andy hooked a foot and sent the man tumbling out the door. He pulled to his knees and sprang toward the black slicker. Borikowski avoided him and slid down the stairway in a painful but controlled fall.

Andy saw Borikowski reaching for Stuhlberg, who clutched the case. He ran—fell—down the staircase, and managed to land against Borikowski's back, propelling the man out of the way. The ship shifted further to port. Sinking quickly.

The briefcase began to emit a high-pitched beeping. Only Borikowski knew what this meant: Lydia was dead.

Stuhlberg fell onto the briefcase like a fullback after a fumble.

Borikowski slid across the deck. Lyditchka . . . my sweet Lyditchka . . .

Stuhlberg stood, and with both men watching him, hugged the briefcase firmly and jumped overboard. He disappeared beneath the eight-foot waves.

Underwater, he began beating on the case.

Nothing happened.

He sank deeper and deeper, his fingers forcing the latches. . . .

The beeping stopped.

Then it exploded, sending a thirty-foot plume of water into the air, along with Eric Stuhlberg's left arm.

Borikowski had pulled himself onto his knees and had crawled over to Andy, who turned and fended off an attempted blow to his head.

A steady stream of blood poured from Borikowski's mouth now. All strength was lost. He reached out, as a blind man might, fanning the air helplessly. He began coughing, unable to breathe. His pale face turned a sudden brilliant red and he collapsed to one side, clutching his throat.

A tremendous wave raked the stern.

Leonid Borikowski washed overboard.

Tuesday, December 2

Terry Stone answered the door wearing a cardigan sweater and suede slippers, his glasses perched on the tip of his nose. He looked like a living, breathing, Norman Rockwell painting. "Ah, come in, Chris."

Daniels entered uncomfortably, a ream of paper in his grasp. Stone led him into the study and the two men sat facing each other. "Well?" Stone asked.

"It doesn't seem the same without you there, sir. Here are some of the papers you asked for."

"It's only been a few days, Chris. Don't make it sound like a year."

Daniels looked at the Old Man and felt like crying. To him it felt like years.

"What about Andy?"

"Coast Guard confirms the ship went down," Daniels replied, avoiding the question. "They picked up an oil slick and some flotsam due west of Vancouver Island."

"Then they can't be certain."

"No. But as I explained over the phone, the reconnaissance flight . . ."

"Yes, yes, yes . . . but that could have been anything."

Anything? Daniels wanted to say. Not just anything burns in the Pacific Ocean. "We have the first reports from the Canadian hospitals in."

307

"And?"

"Two cases so far. Service personnel: a dishwasher and a chambermaid. Severe hemorraging . . . what we expected."

"Prognosis?"

"They're being treated by large dosages of salt and full blood transfusions. The chambermaid went critical, and she's been transferred to Quebec and is now stable. I think we're going to be all right. I doubt we'll lose them. The press knows nothing of it."

"That's a relief."

"Yes, sir."

Stone scratched a stain from his pant leg. He had spilled gravy there and had not noticed until now. Daniels's eyes roamed the carpet and studied the fleur-de-lis pattern. Stone asked, "And what about Andy? Any word?"

"None so far," Daniels said quietly, looking Stone in the eye.

"But I read that the phones were back in order."

"Yes, sir." Daniels looked away, back to the carpet.

"Oh . . . I see." He paused and then asked, "What's your opinion, Chris?"

"I don't buy Central's report that the ship was sabotaged after the transfer was made. The Navy claims the sub never surfaced."

"Typical of Central, eh? Whatever solves the problem the easiest."

Daniels noticed all the citations on the wall for the first time.

"What then?" Stone asked.

"In my opinion, sir, we must consider the possibility that Captain Clayton made it aboard that ship somehow and that he was responsible for the sabotage."

Stone looked up from his stain. "But that would

mean . . . No. That's ridiculous, Chris." He hesitated. "Have they searched. . . ?"

"The weather's been prohibitive, sir. It was only by chance that they spotted the wreckage of the ship."

Stone said sternly, "We don't *know* that that was the wreckage of the ship, eh? No. We don't know that for certain. And Andy could have jumped ship after all. Yes. He could have jumped ship . . . why, any number of things could explain this. Any number of things."

"Yes, sir," Daniels replied. "But for the moment he's listed as missing." Daniels watched as Terry Stone's face tightened.

Stone scratched at a stain that was no longer there. "Any number of things," he said, "any number of things . . ."

Epilogue

Falling into the ocean—the salt water—saved his life, though he never knew it. Lydia's blood, which had contaminated his left hand, had been washed away by the sea, the bacteria neutralized. Borikowski and Stuhlberg had passed through the contagious stage several days before.

He had no memory of climbing into the jettisoned life raft, nor of breaking the transmitter so no one could locate him, nor of wrapping himself up in a blanket; but that was how he found himself: floating in a raft off the deserted coast of northern Oregon. He had been adrift for two and a half days; his clothes were dry, his leg mending. The canopied life raft was designed to assist evaporation and hold in the heat.

If he had not been so badly beaten, so pained in every joint, so coated with blood, he might have believed it all to be a bad dream. But it wasn't. It was real. Borikowski lay at the bottom of the sea, somewhere behind him. And so did the ship. And Duncan? Andy pushed the thought from his mind and decided to deal with it later.

Now, he thought, it's time to get into shore, and if this damn wind wasn't offshore, I'd be there by now.

Mari knew it had been wrong to try this.

He had passed out again, but this time, three hours later, found himself washed ashore, still promising—to whomever it was that such things were promised—never again to go against what he knew to be right. Never look for justice where none can be had.

He closed the door of the summer house he had broken into, his sanctuary for a week of recovery. He consumed their canned goods and burnt all the wood. But he left them fifty dollars—keeping just under two hundred for himself—and felt good about the trade. He burned his wallet and all identity of Andy Clayton beyond recognition.

He did not exist.

He walked carefully for three miles, limping, eyes alert for police or any more of the overhead helicopters he had heard recently, walked until he hit a small coastal highway heading south.

I don't know if you'll have me, Mari. But here I come.

Life is too good to pass by, and so are you, Mari. I think I've finally learned, if I'm not too late. What was it you quoted me? "The serenity to accept those things I cannot change, the courage to change those things I can, the wisdom to know the difference?" Ah, wisdom.

And life. And you.